Cuban Conspiracy

COLLIN GLAVAC

First published by NIMA 2022

First edition Title: Cuban Conspiracy

Format: Paperback

This publication has been assigned: ISBN 978-1-7776578-7-1

Title: Cuban Conspiracy

Format: Electronic book

This publication has been assigned: ISBN: 978-1-7776578-5-7

Please sign up for our newsletter, watch the book trailer and stay tuned for more at:
www.collinglavac.com

For the people of Latin America.

Prologue

The invasion of Castro's Cuba was underway.

An unmarked transport plane soared through the cloud cover at thirty-five thousand feet, off the west coast of Cuba. It was a reliable 'Flying Boxcar,' a Fairchild C-119, its signature twin-boom design instantly recognizable if anyone could see through the current air conditions. But no insignia or tail numbers would be visible even if someone had been watching.

"Five minutes!" the jumpmaster called.

"Five minutes!" the team of paratroopers called back.

Nerves were tight. Night had not yet begun to give way to morning, the black sky mirrored by the dark ocean below.

The five other men in the transport stood and lined up as one.

The door of the C-119 slid open with a heavy metal grating, slamming into place as the wheels met the edge of its rails. Wind rushed past them and the sharp cold air filled the cabin.

"Check equipment!"

They began to check over each other's gear in the dim red glow of the aircraft, making sure everything was as it should be. There wouldn't be a second chance.

The C-119 dipped into a new course and banked east, curving toward the upcoming coast and closing the distance.

Seven thousand feet of altitude was lost as the transport neared the drop zone. It would be tight.

Corporal Tyler 'Zeddy' Christiansen finished checking the equipped gear of the man in front of him. Then the team turned in unison to inspect once more.

Parachute on proper. Helmet. Goggles. Rifle. Sidearm. Pack.

"ETA two minutes!" the jumpmaster called over the thumping propellers.

"Two minutes!" the team called back.

The transport continued its lazy bank before straightening out. It dipped another few thousand feet for good measure.

One of the men kissed a metal cross hanging from his neck on a silver beaded chain. The sergeant behind him slapped his shoulder for reassurance, and the jumper tucked the cross under his shirt.

A knot of turbulence interrupted the pre-jump ritual and shook the aircraft, jostling the troopers. The man behind Zeddy tripped and the corporal turned to catch him, but he regained his balance. The rest of them held fast. Another team member cracked his neck. Someone else coughed.

"Thirty seconds!"

Zeddy focused on the open night in front of them.

"Ten seconds!"

The light in the aircraft turned bright green.

"Green light!" the jumpmaster yelled. "Go! Go! Go!"

He slapped the shoulder of each paratrooper as they ran forward, nodding to each of them.

Zeddy kept his steps and pace focused as he followed his teammates, running down the aircraft's length and toward the door.

One by one they disappeared into the wind, dropping out of the aircraft and swept away by the deep black. It was as if they were plucked from the aircraft by a giant invisible hand and taken away into a void. Zeddy swallowed and followed the sergeant in front of him.

The cold wind smashed into his face as he felt the slap on his arm from the jumpmaster.

Zeddy approached the darkness with a bounding pair of steps...

He jumped.

The woosh of air pressed against him from all sides as he plunged feet first like a comet careening through space. His stomach flip-flopped as his body realized there was no more ground beneath the jump, and adrenaline spiked through his spine, invading his system with an electric current of energy that banished any possibility of distraction. Zeddy was of one mind, and one body, seized by gravity's uncaring grip.

He broke through the clouds and looked through his goggles to try and see where his team members were. They were nowhere to be found. Zeddy had the sudden feeling of being utterly alone in the darkness, falling to his doom as a solitary paratrooper, but he shook the thought out of his mind. He had trained for this. He had jumped out of a dozen planes before. This was a familiar feeling. He was descending on Cuba's Western coast. He knew the drop zone. He knew the mission. There was nothing to do but complete the task at hand.

He forced himself to breathe steadily as the ground grew before him. Then, with a well-practiced movement, he spread his arms and legs and flipped himself onto his stomach.

The winds of the Gulf of Mexico blew into his face more forcefully, and the fabric of his outfit whipped loudly like sails on a boat. Zeddy had heard rumors of R&D developing certain material that would allow a paratrooper to spread his arms and glide like a flying squirrel. That sure would be an improvement to what they had now.

He could make out the patches of different shades of darkness below now: the Gulf of Mexico, the narrow strip of land that was Cuba, the various small islands dotting the coast. As the earth grew closer, he saw whitecaps crashing on the surface of the gulf. The strip of land grew less narrow, filling his view. He mentally pictured the map they'd all painstakingly memorized in their training and briefings.

He spotted the DZ...

Zeddy reached behind his back and felt the loop attached to his release cord. He gave the thing a hard yank.

He was suddenly lifted in the air like a marionette on a string, flip-flopping haphazardly as the parachute exploded from its pack. He withheld a cry even if no one would hear him; his commitment to their covert operation was unwavering even seven thousand feet up. The pressure around his chest and groin were immense as the harness pulled hard at his body with its grip.

The parachute finished unfolding with a whipping pop, then everything seemed to succumb to silence.

Zeddy found himself gliding at last. He was finally in control. He surveyed the land in front of him, down below, and pulled at the steering cords on the 'chute to edge him past the ocean.

It wasn't until he was another couple thousand feet lower that he realized the problem.

He was way off course of the designated DZ.

Fear began to pierce through the focus of adrenaline. He re-adjusted his cords, pushing his parachute to its maximum, trying to gain more lift and cruise at a shallow angle to get past the beach and inland. But there was no changing the basic trajectory.

It wasn't his fault, he realized. The C-119 had been too far out. He had heard the jumpmaster and pilot arguing earlier about getting close enough to the coast, but the pilot said he was ordered to stay clear a certain distance. No one could know Americans were landing in Cuba.

"Shit!" Zeddy hissed as he confirmed what he already knew. He managed to spot a team member — he couldn't tell who it was at this distance and in the dark — but there was another parachuting figure falling gracefully through the early morning sky. He watched as his fellow man tried the same maneuvering Zeddy was desperately trying for, and failing just as spectacularly.

The ground was rushing up now. Zeddy heaved on the cords, grabbing one last thrust and bounce before bracing his knees for impact.

Wham!

The ground dragged at his feet as he slid through mud, and then into water, splashing and chilling his legs to the bone. Gnarled black trees thick with moist bark and moss sprang out from the surrounding water. Zeddy felt his feet being sucked by the goop as his parachute landed neatly beside him. A sudden root caught his left foot and he went careening face-first into the muck.

He'd landed in a swamp.

He coughed and picked himself up, unclipping his 'chute with grimy gloves , pulling them off when they proved too soaked to be useful.

Shit.

He wrapped up the fabric and tucked it in an ugly looking shrub trying to grow alongside the trees. He unclipped his rifle and unslung it from his pack.

Zeddy scoured through the gloom for the others.

A splash nearby alerted him instantly, and he took off in the direction of the sound.

He found Jem struggling to balance himself in the slippery mud when he turned past a pair of trees.

"Jem," Zeddy whispered as loud as he dared. He bounded over and took the man by the shoulders, looking him over to make sure his team member was alright.

Jem nodded. "Present and accounted for. Is it just you and me?"

"So far."

Jem nodded again. "Alright, I'll take point."

"Roger," Zeddy said, looking over his shoulder and scanning the swamp with his rifle before turning back to follow Jem.

They advanced in an ever-growing loop, like the spiral of a snail.

"Drop was bad," Jem said.

"Missions never go as planned," Zeddy said idly. He kept his voice low, continuing to scan the swamp. Staying alert was the core of military tactics. The real crap happened as soon as one's guard dropped.

Zeddy unzipped a uniformed sleeve and pulled out a map tucked in a waterproof pocket within. He produced a compass from a cargo-pant pocket, and followed their directions as they moved.

Twenty minutes of splashing through knee-high swamp and slippery mud brought them to the others. The dark figures of their team grew more defined as they approached and grouped up.

"Who's that?" Sergeant McIlroy asked.

"Alpha three and five," Zeddy said, trudging forward.

"Hey, I told ya they'd survive the jump," Corporal Sam 'Tickers' Toutonson said, slapping Zeddy on the shoulder.

"Any problems?" McIlroy asked, ignoring Tickers.

Jem shook his head, although it was hard to make out the gesture in the darkness. Zeddy couldn't tell anyone's expressions.

"We're fine, other than the drop zone."

"Yeah, what the fuck was that?" Tickers asked.

"We've got a bigger problem," McIlroy said. He grew quiet and they all turned to the fifth man that had landed with them.

He didn't wear the same uniform as the others. His outfit was darker and his pack smaller. He was like an eel among fish.

"The supply drop is missing," the CIA operative said. The others didn't even know his name. He didn't turn to face them as he spoke. He seemed fixated on the distant fog before them.

"Sank in the swamp," McIlroy said darkly. He spat into the mud.

Their supplies included the necessary equipment to carry out the demolitions they were specifically tasked with. Without the supplies the entire mission was botched.

"Get on the radio," the CIA operative said. His voice had an airy quality to it, like he was talking in a dream. "Get in touch with the brigade and get a SITREP."

Tickers shrugged off his pack and pulled out the radio, handing the phone piece to the sergeant.

"*Blindado, Blindado,* this is Alpha Team. SITREP request, over."

He waited, but no one replied. He began to repeat the message. "*Blindado, Blindado*, this is Alpha —"

"Radio's busted," Tickers interrupted. He gave the radio a shake, then dropped it on the ground, slumping next to it.

"Shit," McIlroy said.

The CIA operative pursed his lips. "Did it get wet?"

Tickers stood up and took two mean steps toward the operative. "Of course it got wet, look where we landed man!"

The CIA operative didn't reply. He unholstered his pistol with a smooth and practiced motion and Tickers flinched. But the operative simply held it low, finally turning to the others. "The mission has changed." He snapped his fingers at the map Zeddy still held in his hands.

"No shit Sherlock..." Tickers grumbled. Sergeant McIlroy slapped the man over the head and he shut up.

Zeddy passed over the map but the operative didn't take it. He simply scanned it with pursed lips.

"We'll head around the coast and raise hell where we can."

"Raise hell where we can? We don't have the C-4 for the anti-aircraft guns!" Tickers said.

This time the sergeant didn't rebuke him.

The CIA operative blinked. "We don't need to take out the guns. We just need to create a distraction."

"Hold on a minute," McIlroy said, and everyone but the CIA operative whipped their heads around at that. "We have orders for Bahia Honda. We've got to scout the landing for the boys. I don't envy us for having to hump it all the way there but we've got no choice."

The CIA operative pursed his lips again. "We don't have to scout for a landing. There is no landing."

Jem took a step forward. "The fuck?"

"We're leading an invasion, man," Zeddy said.

The CIA operative spoke as if he were explaining something to a young child. "The invasion is happening elsewhere. We're the diversion."

"That's just great!" Tickers said, turning around in a circle and kicking up swamp water.

"And they couldn't think to tell us that?" McIlroy asked.

The CIA operative began moving forward, seemingly unperturbed by this change of events and reaction from the team. "Need-to-know basis."

"As if the Cubans don't already know we're coming..." Jem muttered.

Zeddy couldn't help but agree.

"*¿Hola? ¿Quién está ahí?*" Hello? Who's there?

Everyone snapped their weapons up immediately, trained on the distance in front of them. They backed into a semi-circle, staying silent, moving weapons back and forth, eyes darting outward into the fog.

"*¿Hola?*" came the voice again. It was soft, but nearby.

McIlroy tapped Tickers and Jem on the head and pointed them forward. The two crept ahead. Zeddy turned around to watch their rear, occasionally darting his head over his shoulder to see if the others had spotted their enemy.

"Civilians," Jem called.

McIlroy and the CIA operative moved quickly to meet the others, while Zeddy slowly backed his way through the swamp and onto a patch of land to meet them.

When he turned around, he saw a small fishing boat with a man and woman spreading out nets into the swamp water. Their eyes were wide at the sight of troops in this isolated area. Their hands were raised, and the woman was shaking. Tears were beginning to run down her face.

"Civilians," Jem said again softly.

"Damn," McIlroy said. "Alright we'll —"

Two hollow blasts of gunfire broke the air with their mighty cracks. The team began to duck for cover and set up defensive positions before they quickly realized the CIA operative had fired the shots.

The man in the boat fell straight backward, flipping head over heels over the keel and into the water. The woman crumpled into an unnatural squat then fell over onto her side. Blood stained her shirt and pooled in the curve of the boat's hull.

"Shit!" Jem said.

"What the fuck did you do that for?" Tickers cried.

McIlroy dashed over and lowered the operative's firearm with a hand, giving the man a glare as he did so.

"Nothing personal," the operative said calmly. "We don't know what they overheard."

"We don't kill civilians," McIlroy said.

"You kill whoever the mission demands you kill," the operative said.

The two stared each other down for a long moment. The body of the man in the swamp water bobbed up and down.

"Let's get moving," McIlroy finally said.

The team was more alert now than it ever had been, and made sure rifles and senses were at the ready.

"Nothing personal..." Zeddy whispered to himself, scanning the gnarled trees at their six and then turning and falling into the column.

They didn't bother to search the boat further. If they had, they would have found a young girl and boy hiding under the damp tarp at the stern, bundled under a seat. The girl held the boy tight, hand over his mouth, hardly breathing for fear of alerting the men.

For her, it was personal.

Chapter 1

Shit had officially hit the fan.

Linda Kim, the head of the Special Operations Group had called for an early morning meeting. And when Linda called a meeting, her subordinates fixed figurative bayonets and prepared to leave the comfortable trenches of their offices.

Meetings with Linda could go one of two ways. Someone was either getting one of her famous 'talks,' in which Linda took on the role of a medieval inquisitor and forced her subject to understand the error of their ways, or shit had hit the fan.

Barker figured it was the latter, because Linda had mentioned someone else would be joining them, and her lambasting talks were always one-on-one.

Barker had gotten the call at six in the morning. It was a particularly bad time to get a call — he'd been in the middle of crushing an online opponent in his latest real-time strategy gaming obsession. But, alas, work called. And when the CIA called, its officers answered.

When Linda called, her officers ran.

Seven a.m. was early for most people. In fact, it was borderline ludicrous for most people to be having a work meeting at that time. Linda called meetings when she was free, and when she wanted them, and seven a.m. was the time Barker was given.

It was well enough for Barker. Not that he was an early bird. His sleep schedule was such a mess he hardly knew what time it was at any given moment. He was unaware of the last time he'd slept, or the last time he'd eaten for that matter. His mind simply buzzed with whatever was happening at the time, and a meticulous memory and efficient categorizing brain allowed him to show up at the places he was needed.

In this case, it was a Starbucks.

Most people didn't know about the Starbucks at Langley. Most wouldn't think there was a Starbucks at Langley. But even spooks needed their coffee. It was known as 'Store Number One,' and its presence at Langley solidified their legacy of opening up anywhere.

Barker walked up to the counter. Behind, employees were bustling around, grinding beans and getting the store ready for the day. They weren't unused to customers coming in this early — one or two had already popped in — but they were rare enough.

A young girl with pigtails spotted Barker and was about to ask his order but stopped before she opened her mouth. Barker blinked his beady eyes and the girl nodded, then got to work on his order.

The Starbucks at Langley didn't take names. Employees weren't allowed to ask for them, and had to undergo extensive background checks. But they didn't need Barker's name, or even to ask his order. He was a regular.

"Venti salted caramel mocha Frap, extra whip!" the girl called.

Barker frowned. "With —"

"...a pump of caramel sauce, a pump of mocha, and double blended, yes sir," the girl passed over the drink.

Barker beamed as he reached out to take it. "Perfect, thank you." Barker's system ran mostly on sugar. It was one of the secrets to his success, and somehow didn't affect his snake-like frame.

The girl flinched at the lanky man's intense gaze and sporadic eye twitch and quickly returned to grinding beans.

Barker found the only table with anyone sitting at it.

Linda was a thin Korean woman who could almost seem frail at first glance. But anyone who spent a single moment in her presence would be proven sorely wrong by her sharp mind and perfectionist competence. She also managed to rule with an even hand of respect and fear, which gave Barker the willies.

The other woman sitting at the table was unknown to him, she was a little older than middle-aged, with dark hair and slightly tanned complexion; she was attractive by conventional standards and seemed to have an air of friendliness mixed with business. She gave Barker a weak smile when he approached the table.

Barker stood there for a moment in front of the two women sitting at the table, holding his Frappuccino between both his hands and slurping as much of the sugary drink as he could in one go.

"I have to drink as much as I can to balance out the whip ratio," he explained unprompted, and Linda nudged a chair forward with her foot as the other woman continued her small smile.

Barker fell into the seat offered, straw dangling from his mouth, ready to get on with things.

"I thought it would be good for you two to meet," Linda said without preamble. "Lauren, this is Barker. He helps run one of our Latin American task forces for SOG and the desk."

She stood and reached out a hand to shake Barker's own. He stared at it for a moment, looked her in the eye — dark brown, intelligent — then took it in both of his own and gave it a little shake.

"Barker?" she asked. "Do you have a first — or last name?"

"Just Barker," he replied quickly. "People call me Barker."

Barker knew he was socially awkward. He knew he saw the world differently and strangely than others. Barker preferred things and analysis and problem-solving to people. He didn't really understand other people's emotions and wasn't great at empathizing. He had no love-life, and hardly desired one. Social cues were largely lost on him. He fixated on irregularities and ignored most trivial (normal) things. These didn't negatively impact his work — they were largely a boon, if anyone cared to notice — but they severely impacted his ability to connect and work effectively with others in many cases. Barker was aware of these things and had tried desperately long ago to change and be 'normal.' But his efforts had failed remarkably and he had instead focused on his work.

Barker's eccentricities were largely ignored or accepted by the high-caliber work places that eventually sought out to hire him. He was a brilliant young man with an insatiable appetite for performing tasks properly and to the best of anyone's ability, and was usefully equipped with a desire to please his superiors — assuming he liked them, which wasn't always the case. After a slew of successful Silicon Valley tech projects in his high school years, Barker found himself being recruited by various three-letter government agencies looking for talented programmers and computer wizards. It wasn't long before the CIA came knocking. While the money was nice, they gave Barker the things he craved: competent superiors, near-unsolvable challenges with high stakes, and, secretly, acceptance.

Barker had lost the anxiety that came with meeting a new person and worrying about what they might make of him. And it was a good thing he was good at what he did, or someone like Linda would never be able to put up with him.

"I haven't heard anything about you up until now," Lauren said, sitting down once again.

"That's generally how it goes," Barker replied coolly. He didn't like this woman. For absolutely no rational reason whatsoever. It mostly had to do with the single hair that had fallen on her shoulder and lingered like a slug climbing her arm. He tried not to stare at it. But he did.

Linda interrupted his scrutiny. "Barker, Lauren Lopez is our new head of desk for Latin American Affairs. Our replacement for Locklee. She's sometimes your boss, sometimes not — you know how this goes by now. She's a PAG transfer, so be nice."

Barker puffed up his cheeks with air and nodded. Lauren furrowed her eyebrows but didn't say anything. At least he knew why he didn't like her anymore. The Political Action Group had been messing around in CIA affairs in questionable ways for quite some time.

"You two can do the small talk thing with each other another time. We have to talk about a situation," Linda began.

Barker sat up straighter and slowly lowered the straw poking out of the Frappuccino from his mouth. Lauren hadn't touched her coffee and didn't bother now. They were both at attention.

"Our meeting today is on a sensitive topic. What I'm about to tell you is classified within SOG only." She paused letting that sink in for them. "Chief Operations Officer Mike Morrandon is the head of a covert operation known within Latin American Affairs as Blackthorne. Blackthorne is our resource for black ops in the Latin American sphere, after regular options have been exercised or are not viable. Assets of highly trained, highly independent caliber are scattered across the countries comprising that region. This would've been in your briefing," Linda nodded to Lauren, and she nodded back.

"As of oh-nine-hundred yesterday, Morrandon has seemingly abandoned his position. I received a call from him saying he would be coming to Langley to make a report. Instead, he decided to disappear. This is after meeting with Russian elements and losing a civilian asset to the Russians in a questionable manner. So, we may be looking at a turncoat situation.

"Huh," Barker said. "Does this have anything to do with the gunshots reported at his house?"

Linda scowled. "Those details are classified."

"CIA must've missed scrubbing those police reports," Barker said idly, staring at a corner of the building. One of the lights was out, and it irritated him. He frowned, not realizing Linda was glaring back at him.

"We're keeping this very close to the chest. I don't need our PAG friends to be noting a chink in our armor — no offense Lauren — let alone the brass at SAD. We're going to keep this in-house and clean up our mess on our own, like the happy little family we are. And if the neighbors peek in through the windows, I'm to be notified personally and immediately for damage control. Understood?"

"Yes ma'am," they both responded in near-perfect unison.

"Good. I want to hear options."

"We should comb through surveillance in DC first and branch out from there," Lauren put in, stating the obvious but most surefire opening move. "Traffic cams, establishments, run it all through facial recognition — if a single camera snagged him, we'll have him right away, he's embedded in our systems."

Linda nodded. "Naturally."

"Cut off all CIA resources that we can. Block accounts, change passwords, track anything that gets tapped. Alert all faculties for any SOG requests and have them report any suspicious activity."

Linda took a sip of coffee. "We've already begun. But it will take time and we can't catch everything."

"Contact friends, family, and coworkers," Lauren continued. "Find out if they know anything...if Morrandon said something in passing, even."

An awkward silence fell on the table. Barker sipped loudly at his drink as the two women avoided eye contact with him. He wasn't particularly good at reading body language (even if he was trained in it), but then considered Lauren's statement.

"Ah," he said. "What do you want to know?"

"Did Mike contact you before he abandoned his post?" Linda asked.

"You already know the answer to that. You would've tracked the call."

Linda bit the inside of her cheek, and asked her next question with exaggerated diction. "What did Mike say to you?"

"Ah," Barker wiggled his lips. A smattering of whipped cream coated some unkempt facial hairs below his nose. "Guess we didn't talk long enough for that. Ah well. Just that he was set up."

"Just that he was set up?" Linda repeated, incredulously.

"Yeah. Seems to make sense. I helped him with the Russian meets. We were following a lead and got screwed over at the end. But funny enough...I think that was part of his plan. You know, to stop the PAG from getting to that Barry guy."

"He *wanted* an American civilian to be captured by the Russians?" Lauren asked, also incredulous now. "And he allowed it to happen?"

"Well, when you put it that way..." Barker sighed.

"Where do you think he's gone?" Linda asked.

"What a great question," Barker said sincerely, and Linda suppressed a frown. "That depends most on what he's trying to achieve."

"He didn't say anything?"

"He wanted to keep me out of it," Barker said softly.

"I want a report — a damn *full* report — of the interactions with Russian elements and any other interactions between you and Morrandon during the Nicaragua operation." Barker was about to open his mouth but Linda added, "*Relevant* interactions, Barker." He closed his mouth and didn't say anything. "What else?" Linda continued, mostly referring the question to Lauren.

"Then...move onto purchases — credit or debit for planes or trains, that sort of thing," she said, as if Barker hadn't said a word.

Barker used his straw to start digging out whipped cream from his Frappuccino. "He'll pay in cash."

"Some services won't allow that," Lauren countered.

"Then he won't use those services," Barker shrugged.

"The point is," Lauren continued quickly, irritated, "we track everything and run it through the system. See what turns up."

Linda looked to Barker expectantly.

"I mean, sure. You're just not going to find anything."

Lauren huffed.

Linda nodded at Lauren. "Barker, people can't just go invisible. Not in this day and age, and definitely not a CIA officer who has their entire identity coded into our network."

Barker raised his eyebrows, surprised at the naivete in Linda's statement. "I don't think either of you seem to understand who you're trying to track. You're right. This isn't a civilian. This is a CIA officer. But more than that, Mike realizes the stakes here. He's out on a mission. There's no room for failure. He's been cultivating resources and assets his entire career. He'll pull all the stops."

"He's not used to being in the field," Linda said flatly.

"Did pretty good with the Russian," Barker countered. He didn't realize that he really needed to stop talking.

"Do you have any better ideas?" Linda asked, her expression growing dark. "Please, share with us."

Barker rubbed the back of his head. "Nope. Just that this might be a waste of time."

"Careful, Barker. Careful."

Barker gulped. He hadn't realized he'd done anything wrong. He tried to repair things. "All I'm wondering is what if we can't bring him back in?"

"You already know the answer to that," Linda said, as calm as the water on a summer pond.

A heavy silence hung over the table. Barker resorted to slurping at his drink for some strange form of comfort. Lauren cleared her throat. Linda leaned back and delicately placed her hands on the edge of the table.

"Barker, you're acting head of Blackthorne now," Linda said. Her mouth curved in a wry smile, and her tone spat the words out like she found an intense private irony in them. Barker got the impression she wasn't exactly happy granting him that acting power but there wasn't much he could do about that.

"Alrighty," he shrugged.

Lauren's eyebrows went up and she exchanged a glance with Linda before hiding a smile — the kind bullies make to their friends. Barker looked from her to Linda in confusion, then realized that he'd just been put in charge of one of the most powerful clandestine forces in Special Operations.

"I won't let you down, ma'am!" he said a little too loudly. The Starbucks employee with the pigtails glanced up from shuffling some receipts around and then quickly ducked her head, pretending like she hadn't heard a thing.

Linda pursed her lips. "Thank you, Barker." She turned to Lauren. "Lopez. Back to work. Keep me in the loop."

Linda took her time finishing her coffee, then stood and exited the café.

Barker sat up straight in his chair and sipped long and hard on his drink until it burned the back of his throat and the freeze crept up into his head.

"Ah!"

Lauren blinked, then held out her hand. "Nice meeting you Barker. Looking forward to working together."

Yeah, right... Barker thought, knowing this woman thought nothing of the sort. But he put down his drink and took her hand in between the two clammy palms of his own and gave it a rapid shake. "Likewise," he said.

She stood, gave him a sharp nod, and departed. He watched her go while he sipped at the bottom of his Frappuccino. She wiped her hand on her pants discreetly as she reached the door.

"Hm..."

Barker looked back up at the dark spot on the ceiling, near the corner where the light was burnt out.

"Hm..."

He crossed his arms and frowned.

He thought about his current predicament. His boss, and the most trustworthy individual he knew, had just skipped out on his job as head of one of the most high-profile task forces in the entire SOG. That left Barker filling shoes until they found a more suitable replacement. Barker wasn't ambitious really — he was happy to be a second-in-command, as long as he worked under someone competent and tolerable, and although he had the proper rap sheet to run Blackthorne he wasn't leadership material.

Linda was after Mike. Preferably alive, but if he resisted, she'd put a hit on his head without hesitation. CIA officers didn't desert. They died.

That meant that Barker needed to find Mike first, and try to uncover just what he was up to. It would be a race against Linda and the rest of the resources of the SOG. It would normally be no contest. But Barker had just been put in charge of an entire black ops taskforce.

He grinned to himself, stood, and tossed his drink container in the trash.

And of course, he'd failed to mention that he'd bought Mike a plane ticket to Miami — off the books — the night previous.

Barker's brain was overactive. It must've slipped his mind.

Chapter 2

The hotel they'd booked was classier than John would've liked. Anyone who knew to blend in meant to stay away from things like luxury — anything that could stand out from the hum-drum of daily life, anything far or above average, anything that could be remembered. The second best spies were the ones who could get seen and then forgotten. The best spies were never noticed. But they'd needed something fast and it was the first hotel they'd spotted. John liked the location — plenty of exit points and central enough in Miami's downtown that they could blend in with the crowd. Between Mike's slight limp and John's hunched frame from his bullet wound, their party looked like an infirmary.

So they'd booked the place for an undetermined stay for an extortionist's price. Marcela swept the room looking for bugs out of habit, while John unholstered his gun and lay it on a small eating table. Mike watched the other man's movements warily as he slumped into a chair, frame creaking slightly under his weight. The big man sighed and rubbed his leg.

John leaned against the marble countertop and took a deep breath, feeling the pull of his stitches against his flesh. He was healing, but he needed rest. John knew this, but he wasn't particularly happy about it.

Finally deciding the room was clean, Marcela found a kettle and began to boil water.

John raised an eyebrow in a question for her.

"Tea," she said without a second glance.

John grunted and began to stretch, flinching when he reached the edge of his wounded mobility.

"What happened to you?" Mike asked, breaking his silence since John and Marcela had ordered him to follow them through Miami's streets. He hadn't refused, but he wasn't happy about having a gun trained on him either.

"AK round," John said, lifting his shirt and checking his bandages.

"Hit anything important?" Mike asked.

"Obviously not," Marcela snapped. "And you? What's wrong with your leg? You've been limping like a flamingo since we met you."

"A flamingo?" Mike asked. John reciprocated the confusion with his expression.

Marcela blew air at her bangs in exasperation. "Flamingos stand on one leg." She pointed to Mike. "What happened."

"Ballpoint pen."

"Ouchie," Marcela said. "That's why you don't fight with women."

Mike furrowed his brows. "I didn't say it was a woman."

"Was it a woman?" Marcela asked.

Mike didn't respond.

"What I thought," Marcela said.

John turned over his shoulder and whispered for only Marcela to hear. "How did you know that?"

"Fifty percent chance," she said with a wink, then growing serious, "and we're vicious."

She turned back to the stove and began rummaging through cupboards until she found a mug and teabag. She put a mug out on the counter for John, but he shook his head. He didn't want tea. He didn't feel much like anything at the moment.

Mike began to shuffle from his chair and Marcela put the kettle down hard after pouring, whirling around and gave Mike a dark look.

Mike raised his hands to his waist. "Can I get up from this chair? Am I allowed to stand?"

"No one's keeping you down." Marcela said. "You're not tied up."

"This is just starting to feel like an interrogation. You know, offer a cup of tea, gun on the table and all."

"I didn't offer you tea."

"Washroom..." Mike mumbled.

John motioned with his head for Mike to get up.

He crossed the room and entered the washroom, locking it behind him.

Marcela rolled her eyes. "Wonder if he's grabbing a ballpoint pen..."

"No," John said. "He'll play ball, unless we're completely unreasonable."

Marcela hid her grin with a loud long sip from her mug.

"No," John repeated.

"Alright," Marcela said, turning off some of her playfulness and considering the business at hand. "How do you want to do this? *¿Policía bueno, policía malo?*" she laughed. "I can't believe I just suggested that."

26

"We need to call him out for all the crap he's put us through," John said. "And then we need information. In that order."

"Alright. I will keep my torture tools ready just in case."

"He's CIA."

Marcela nodded, as if that explained everything.

The door to the bathroom unlocked and Mike returned to his chair. "Want to pat me down? There's a pair of big nail clippers in there."

"Shut the fuck up," Marcela said. "Sit down."

Mike collapsed back into his chair. "I'm sitting."

"Good! You've been a *malo* man and we're not happy with you!"

Mike blinked. "Um, okay."

Marcela slammed her mug on the counter and tea sloshed out over the lip. John was surprised the thing didn't break.

"You fucked us over! The mission in Guatemala —"

"I killed American operatives for you," John said darkly. "To protect a drug lord."

Mike winced and scratched at his forehead. "That was a mess. But I can explain —"

Marcela interrupted him before he could go on. "And Puentes — Sandor — John says he was working for the CIA? *¿Qué mierda?" What the fuck?*

"Yeah, that's a good place to start actually —"

"You sent Brian in to kill a CIA asset," John continued, his tone level. "Maybe he wasn't doing what you wanted. I don't know. It doesn't matter. The Firm changed their tune and betrayed him. Brian gets killed —"

Mike sat up straighter in his chair and his eyebrows raised. "Now wait a minute, the Firm didn't —"

"Or the intel leaked somehow, but Brian was sent in to die. You killed him."

"Then we're sent in to clean up Pablo's inheritance..." Marcela picked up her tea and wiped the mug with a paper towel. She gestured to John as she sipped.

"And it turns out Pablo wasn't playing ball either. He's Sandor all over again. But this time he has leverage over the CIA. Pablo was trying to shut down the trafficking op. You wanted it kept open."

"Sick bastard," Marcela muttered into her mug.

Mike pursed his lips, not even trying to interject this time.

John felt a warm flush of anger prick at his ears. He tried to project calm as he continued. "So we eliminate the new Puentes head —"

"Only for Juan to take over," Marcela murmured again.

"...and stopped the world from knowing that the CIA was sponsoring international human trafficking with American tax dollars. I have a feeling Juan kept that ball rolling."

"Oh, he did," Marcela said, downing the remainder of her drink. The spoon clattered as she tossed it on the counter. "He was communicating with the CIA. It was business as usual."

"And you had me record those details instead of sending them to you via email, so there was nothing to be tracked." John finished. He allowed himself a pause, then: "Fast forward a month. Nicaragua."

"You blew my cover!" Marcela pointed at Mike.

Mike shifted uncomfortably in his seat. "We needed to save the asset, and John."

John almost laughed at that. He knew this man didn't give a shit about him. "We escort a civilian through the country only to get tangled up with Cuban intelligence..."

"*¿Cubanos*? What the hell?" Marcela pulled her hand through her hair as she stared Mike down.

"And then at the end of it all, we get outplayed by the Russians, who steal our asset, but you reassure us that that's all part of the plan."

"And now that John is dying, you ask to meet us in Miami and expect us to work with you on a new mission?"

"The only thing I don't understand is why you'd break your cover and meet us in person," John said, tapping his chin with a finger, talking more to himself than the others. "That's the part I don't get."

"Alright, alright, enough," Mike growled. "Do you want me to explain or do you want to keep complaining about your jobs?"

Marcela looked as though she was about to say something particularly rude, but thought better of it. She huffed and muttered something in Spanish under her breath neither man could make out.

"A cup of coffee *would* be nice," Mike said, offering an olive branch.

Marcela glared at him, looked to John, and John gave a short nod. Marcela huffed again, then went on rummaging through cupboards again for coffee grinds.

John crossed the room and approached the window. Thick and clean white curtains covered the view. He pulled them open and allowed sunlight to invade the room. The window was broad, nearly covering the wall, and shined with the afternoon Miami sun.

John smelled the coffee maker beginning to brew in the background as he stared out across the buildings that made the Miami skyline. The buildings weren't particularly tall, but he was used to Latin America. Everything was bigger in the United States. It was strange to be back. It didn't feel like home, even though it was supposed to be.

Outside, people were milling about on the street. John felt a simultaneous bout of disdain and then envy. They were either oblivious to the political wheels spinning around them, or they just didn't care. For most of his life he followed orders at face-value. It had made life simple.

Now though...

Unloading all his thoughts at Esteban...at *Mike* had been cathartic. And he hadn't exactly broken any rules. Mike was the one that reached out to them, after all. But Marcela and John weren't being professional...or hospitable. A part of him was wondering what Mike would have to say. But the other part...well, the other part didn't want to hear a word. It would be CIA bureaucratese. Expect a soldier to follow orders. Not dig too deep into the consequences. Into the information. The real heart of the matter...

Spook shit, an old SEAL friend used to say.

"Thanks," Mike said, struggling to half stand from his chair and slumping back down once Marcela had handed him the coffee. "No sugar?"

John turned away from the window and let the curtain fall slightly, casting a shadow against him. Marcela tossed a sugar packet at the CIA official.

"Now talk," she said.

Mike mixed sugar into his mug, drank deeply, then, satisfied, looked down into his mug.

"I'm sorry," he said.

Silence. John stared at Mike.

"The shit you two have been through...I'm sorry for it. There's a lot happening behind the scenes. And I'm not asking you two to sympathize with me about it. But unfortunately, you've been caught up in a much bigger conspiracy than you know. I'd like to think we're still on the same side."

Marcela snorted, but John was listening. He hadn't expected an apology.

"I'm going to lay everything out on the table, and I'm hoping you'll do the same with me. No secrets," Mike chuckled, taking another drink of coffee. "That sounds stupid between CIA assets, huh? But I mean it. I'll tell you two everything, because truth be told, I need allies I can trust right now."

Marcela exchanged a glance with John. Neither of them said anything.

"Are either of you familiar with the PAG?" Mike asked.

"Should we be?" Marcela asked quietly.

"Political Action Group," John guessed. It could be any number of things but that was the only CIA-related thing he could think of at the moment.

"Right, right. Political Action Group," Mike looked around. "Okay, either of you have a sheet of paper? A pen?"

Marcela grinned as she found a pen and made a stabbing motion as she passed it to Mike. They found a hotel pad on a nearby side table. Mike began writing words and drawing lines between them, like a family tree or similar.

"Okay so up here we've got the CIA. But as you both know, that's pretty nebulous. The CIA is huge and made up of multiple departments that hardly communicate with one another, because there's just so much bureaucracy happening, and so much to manage. Sometimes they even have different goals..." Under the CIA he wrote *SAD*.

"Special Activities Division," Marcela said, looking across from the counter.

"Yep, the arms-length part of the CIA that gives us a little flexibility from the public and such. And under them we have..." he wrote SOG and PAG, both with links under SAD. "Special Operations Group, and Political Action Group. Among others. SOG is tactical black ops, PAG is aggressive strategic politics." He drew another line and wrote the word *the Firm*.

John narrowed his eyes from across the room at the pad of paper.

"This is me totally breaking protocol," Mike said. Then, next to *the Firm* he wrote *Blackthorne*. "When I say everything on the table, I really mean everything. This is the name of the taskforce you two are part of. For agents, it's known as the Firm. In reality this is known as Blackthorne. Most officers even in the SOG wouldn't know it exists. It's need-to-know, and it only deals with Latin American Affairs."

Marcela raised her eyebrows at John but John didn't look up from what Mike was writing.

"Alright. Under both the SOG and PAG there are a series of regional desks, right? Russian, Oceania...Latin American. Blackthorne operates in tandem with the Latin American Desk in the SOG, but it's still an independent project. Lots of wiggle room."

"Alright," Marcela said. She seemed to be debating if she was impressed.

"I'm the head of Blackthorne," Mike said simply.

John and Marcela were both taken aback. This time John answered her glance with a surprised one of his own, and they both turned back to Mike who was drinking his coffee.

"Why are you telling us this?" Marcela asked.

"As I said, trust. And..." Mike put down his mug again. "You might need to know this stuff. For what's coming."

John wanted to ask what that meant — and he could tell Marcela did too, but both of them held back so they could let the man continue.

"Alright, basically what you need to know is that there's a rivalry between the SOG and PAG. Which is fine. These things happen in the CIA. But the PAG pressured SOG's Latin American desk to task us with the Guatemalan op. Turns out it was PAG trying to clean up a mess, which you so aptly described, John. They were using us, and it's bullshit."

John nodded, and Mike nodded back.

"The problem is this isn't just a story about rival departments stepping on each other like I had originally thought. The SOG Latin American Desk guy — name was Paul Locklee — ends up committing suicide after telling me about corruption with PAG."

Marcela poured herself a second cup of tea and pulled up a chair, stirring rapidly with a spoon. She looked like she was watching the latest *telenovela* and things were heating up.

"Well, I didn't think it was suicide. So I started investigating things. Found out what you concluded, John, that the PAG was working Sandor Puentes and things went sour. Not sure if he stopped playing ball or if he wanted more — he was aiming to become an *oligarcas familias* and Locklee at the time said that could've been a problem for the PAG, or it could've let them have a man in there but the *Familias* might have rejected a known dealer and trafficker."

"*Dinero viejo, dinero nuevo*," John said. *Old money, new money.*

"Exactly. So PAG decides to kill him off. The problem is they still want their operations flowing. Including the trafficking. I do a lot of bad shit, but that...that's not what I'm about to support."

"*Bastardos*," Marcela spat, although she seemed more enthralled than angry.

"Yeah, there's a lot of that going around. So the PAG pressures the desk by providing Pablo with Locklee's info so it'll look like he's the one in bed with Puentes. Locklee can't cry wolf, PAG gets rid of Pablo, and now, as you're assuming, they probably have Juan."

"Because if they didn't, he'd be dead by now," Marcela said. "Like the other Puentes."

Mike nodded. John's expression was growing increasingly dark. Mike averted his gaze as he continued.

"Hope that explains that. The real question is, why was the PAG so determined to have a trafficking operation in Latin America? This is the question I'm still working on, although I have my theories. It really depends on if they're as dirty as I think they are."

"Talk about Nicaragua," John said.

Mike sighed. "Right, well, that's an interesting one too, because it involves the PAG just as much as the Puentes thing. Because guess who requested we pull an American billionaire vacationer from the beach? Barry Bridges has that app, oh what's-it-called..."

"*Anono*," John said.

Mike grunted. "...*Anono*, right, and it turns out a lot of powerful Americans — senators, judges, I don't know — a bunch of them are on that app. PAG wanted to turn Barry into an asset by circumventing the oversight committee to approve the app's security rating."

John narrowed his eyes again. "I don't follow."

"Right. This might come as a surprise to you two, but I don't have all the answers either. Again, one of the reasons we need to work together."

"How did you find out about the PAG wanting Barry?" John asked.

"Worked a PAG officer. Found out lots I wasn't supposed to."

"It was a woman, wasn't it?" Marcela asked. She pulled a lollipop from her pocket and unraveled its wrapping.

"Uh, yeah, but it doesn't matter who she was," Mike replied quickly.

"And they were sleeping together," Marcela said to John, then smiled sweetly back at Mike.

"What? What do you...why do you say that?" Mike asked, a soft blush creeping up his neck and hitting his ears and cheeks.

Marcela grinned wickedly and tapped her nose. "We're trained to interrogate and observe Mr. Morrandon. We are very good at it. That leg wound makes a lot more sense now. Feisty."

Marcela turned to John again to share in the mischief, twirling her lollipop in her hand. But John wasn't interested in Mike's sex life.

"Barry was the Cuban's asset though, not the PAG's. Involved with a guy named Antonio Romero," John said. "Who we did some digging on."

"Who *I* did some digging on, while John was lounging," Marcela stuck her tongue out the side of her mouth and raised her hands like she was a beached fish. "He is a very interesting character."

"Good work," Mike said, "that's what we need to do next. Profile him."

"Don't get ahead of yourself," Marcela snapped.

"Talk about the Russian connection," John said.

Mike sighed. "I'm going to have to go to the bathroom again..." he picked up his mug, found it empty, then gave it a little wag at Marcela with sympathetic eyes. She rolled her own but took the mug and proceeded to top him off, tossing another bag of sugar his way. "Thanks, yeah, so the

PAG thing is bad enough, but I *really* fucked up when I met with an SVR officer. Long story short: he provided possible proof that the Cubans had an infiltration program from the Cold War that never got shut down. I was skeptical, but then we uncovered — *you* uncovered G2 agents running around in Nicaragua —"

John was piecing everything together now. "And running Bridges."

Mike tapped his mug. "Correct."

"You let the Russian play you..." Marcela realized, tasting her lollipop thoughtfully.

"...and allowed a double cross to let them snatch up our American Civilian — who is actually a Cuban asset *and* a potential PAG asset..." John said nodding.

"But it led to a confrontation — yes Marcela," Mike said before she could interrupt, "with a very attractive woman I may or may not have been involved with — ending with a dead PAG officer and my ass on an anonymous ticket to Miami to meet with the only two Blackthorne agents who could corroborate my story."

Another silence fell on the hotel room. Marcela and John were acutely aware that Mike had killed a CIA officer now, and was on the run. Neither of them had seen that coming.

"So...what?" Marcela asked, cracking her lollipop in her mouth and tossing the stick in the trash. "You want us to tell your bossman that you're okay so you can go back to working *nueve a cinco*?" *Nine to five?*

"No," Mike sneered at her. "I don't give a fuck about my job. I want to finish the mission."

"What do you mean?" John asked. "What mission?"

Mike closed his eyes and seemed to say a silent prayer to himself for patience. "We have a clandestine United States intelligence department pulling strings in our own governance and offing anyone who gets in their way. Their assets include one of the largest sex and drug trafficking *dons* in Latin America, an American billionaire app developer who is now in fucking Russian custody, and God knows who else in or out of the largest and most powerful intelligence agency in the world. And the PAG are running a show that's *actually* an elaborate web woven by Cuban intelligence, because the Cubans want the same damn thing the PAG wants."

"Control," Marcela and John answered at the same time.

Mike closed his eyes again, but this time he seemed pleased with their answer. "That's what it's always been about. I don't know how much deeper this shit goes but we've established some of their main assets. We need to seek and destroy, and prove the whole thing to an intelligence agency that might be in the enemy's pocket already. This is a clusterfuck of monumental proportions. And we're the only ones who can really do anything about it."

The only sound was the crunching of candy in Marcela's mouth. John and Mike looked at her.

"*Lo siento*," she whispered. *Sorry*.

"So, do I have my Blackthorne agents with me?" Mike asked. He broke eye contact, focusing on drinking his second cup of coffee.

John and Marcela looked at one another. Marcela rocked her head back and forth, but wasn't about to say anything.

She was waiting for John. John opened the curtain again and looked out the window. He let the hot sun fall on his face. Cleared his mind. Thought about everything Mike had just told them...

"If you two need to talk things over..." Mike started.

"I need a shower," John said suddenly. He was quiet, but his words startled the others.

"A...shower?" Marcela asked.

John left the window and crossed the room and rummaged through his bag, eventually pulling out a pack of gauze and a bandage pad. He'd need it for his bullet wound. Then he opened the bathroom door, replying with a simple, "yes."

This time Mike and Marcela exchanged glances, but neither of them said another word as the *click* of the lock slid home.

Chapter 3

John removed his shirt slowly, careful not to graze his side too badly as he stripped. With his shirt off, he examined his wound.

Marcela had disinfected and wrapped a bandage in the back of a bouncing truck in Nicaragua — all things considered she'd done a remarkable job. But the U.S. medic aboard the submarine they'd occupied re-examined the work and replaced the bandage. He unclipped the pin holding things in place and slowly unraveled it.

The sensation was a strange mix of relieved tension from the wrap releasing, but prickles of pain joined the feeling as John moved to peel back the pad. He hissed through clenched teeth as he took a look.

The bullet hole had largely scabbed over. It had gone clean in and out and the medic had confirmed that it hadn't hit any organs on its way. In other words, he was damn lucky.

He gave it a sniff out of habit. He'd smelled another's wound gone bad before. No other smell in the world could compare. He'd never forget it, or the man who'd died from sepsis.

John stripped the rest of his clothes, turned on the water and adjusted the temperature and got in the shower.

The water felt good on his skin, but he still winced as it ran over his bullet wound. The hospital corpsman who'd treated him on the submarine had okayed showering, but with care. He focused on the pain until it became part of him, and faded away, just another irritant he had to deal with. That was the way with things. Life was never perfect. He moved on anyway. Stopping was what caused problems. Stopping gave you time to think.

Now though...

He had never brooded more than in the last couple months. Ever since his best friend Brian had been killed. He'd found out who'd done it. That man was dead. But there was still unfinished business. Brian hadn't been avenged yet.

John idly turned the shower knob, turning the water to a low sear.

You've been caught up in a conspiracy that threatens everything. I'd like to think we're still on the same side, Mike had said.

John didn't question his orders. Sometimes he didn't like them; sometimes they were poor orders, but he didn't disobey them. That's not how that worked. He had killed targets without question. Waiting for days. Pulling the trigger. Leaving without a trace. That was his job. Orders were orders; "right and wrong" was never the question. But if the orders were coming from the wrong side...

I'm the head of Blackthorne.

His handler was here, in person, meeting for the first time, spilling secrets. Marcela and John knew his name now. He was no longer Esteban. He was Mike Morrandon. And John knew the unassuming man was dangerous as hell.

John turned up the heat. Steam began to rise around him.

I want to finish the mission.

There was still work to do. If what Mike said was true. If he could be trusted. The Political Action Group wouldn't stop. The *Dirección de Inteligencia* of Cuba wouldn't stop. They threatened everything.

He wanted to think of other things. Tutoring English and interacting with Latin American locals, and his Navy days. The pretty sailor stationed on his cruiser when he was twenty-two. Her dark skin. Eyes shining like the sun. Lips that seemed to dare him to make a move...

Thoughts that still made him feel human.

Something snapped in his mind. There was a time to dwell, and a time to move. He was done brooding.

John turned off the shower, retrieving a too-clean hotel towel and dried himself off, careful around the wound. He delicately placed the clean pad over the scab and wrapped gauze tightly around his waist. He re-dressed and exited the bathroom, finding Mike looking out the window. Marcela was rummaging through cupboards again.

"I want something to eat," she said, stopping short as she was caught by the intensity of John's expression. Mike turned around as Marcela grew silent.

"Promise me one thing." John said to Mike. Mike stepped away from the curtain and waited for John to finish. "Whoever killed Brian, they're mine."

"We know who killed Brian," Marcela said. "Sandor — Pablo's brother —"

"No. They pulled the trigger. But they weren't responsible for the gun. He's not the reason Brian's dead. There's someone higher up." John turned to Mike and gave a snarl. "You're going to tell me who it is. And then I'm going to kill them."

Mike opened his mouth but thought carefully about what to say before the words came out. "Alright."

John nodded. "Then I'm in."

Mike looked up at Marcela, and John turned his head to look for her response a moment later.

Marcela rolled her eyes. "Well fuck, I can't say no, I'll look like an ass."

Mike and John nodded to one another.

"That leaves one question that's been bugging me," Mike said. "What do you two know that I don't?"

"Oooh yes," Marcela said. "John, shall we tell him?"

"Coffee," John said to Marcela.

"What, do I look like a *sirvienta*?" she asked sourly, but complied anyway.

"Thank you," John said, accepting the steaming mug black and pulling up a chair. "The first thing you should know is that I have the interrogation with Pablo recorded and uploaded to the cloud," John said. "I was keeping it as insurance. And proof that the CIA was using him." *Proof that Brian was right*, he thought.

To John's surprise, Mike smiled. "That's good. I don't have my own copy. That's one piece of the puzzle we can use."

"We have a 'wig with Isabella Puentes' hard drive downloaded," Marcela said.

"And now it has Barry's app program too — the backdoor stuff he was forced to pull up," John added. "I snagged it when we were held by the Cubans."

"Excellent," Mike said. "You said the Cubans had mentioned someone named Romero?"

"Antonio Romero," Marcela said.

"He seems to be who Barry was answering to," John continued. "Barry made it seem like they were business partners, but it seemed a pretty lop-sided relationship."

"Kind of like you and I," Marcela winked at John.

"The Cubans were interested in a place called *Isla de Anticipación*. While I was out cold on the sub, Marcela took the time to do some digging." John drank deeply from his coffee and gave Marcela a pair of raised eyes, expectant for her to take over.

"Right," she said. "So this Romero guy is actually a pretty high profile man. Almost like a celebrity."

"I haven't heard of him," Mike grunted.

"Most people haven't — if you're not in that circle," John said.

"What circle?"

Marcela swatted her hand at the air. "Who's doing the talking here?"

Mike pursed his lips and John went back to his coffee.

"Celebrities, rich people, politicians — those sorts. He's friends with plenty of presidents."

"The types on Barry's app that the PAG would love to have in their pocket..." Mike said. He chewed his cheek thoughtfully.

"*Sí*, things are coming together now, aren't they? This Romero guy also has a private island."

"Off the coast of Cuba," John said.

"Romero's Cuban?" Mike asked.

"*Sí*," Marcela sighed, resigning her ability to lead the briefing alone.

"What's on the island?" Mike asked.

"That's what we don't know," John said.

"But we do know where it is," Marcela said, rooting through her bag. She pulled out a map she had picked up from one of the tourist stores and made a shooing motion at the table. John and Mike removed mugs and other clutter that had accumulated as Marcela unfurled the folded paper and spread it over the table. "While waiting around for you, I started looking for the island." Marcela poked Mike in the chest. Mike blinked but didn't bother to swat her hand away. He apparently knew what Marcela was like.

"Alright, what have we got?"

Marcela pointed to a very small island off the north coast of Cuba. "Here it is. Private little Romero."

"Alright. Then that's where we need to go," Mike said.

John narrowed his eyes.

The room began to take on the quality they were all intimately familiar with: briefing.

John didn't actually know how many briefings he'd been a part of. He didn't know how many missions he'd been on. But all of them were the same in a way. Learn the objective. Develop how to accomplish the objective. Identify obstacles. Clarify plan. Extraction.

It was easier when all you had to do was sit and have a CO tell you what you needed to know. This was active planning. They had to figure out the mission as they went and brief themselves.

"It's across the water. That means we need transportation," Mike said.

Marcela snapped her fingers. "Plane? Helicopter?"

"No. Too easy to mark us — Cuban *and* CIA radar."

"Boat," John said.

Mike nodded. "We don't need anything fancy, but we can't exactly go down to the docks with a couple g's and buy a junker off someone."

"Why not?" John asked.

"We'd be hard-pressed to find something quickly — I don't exactly want to be spending the next few days haggling for a deal on Craigslist. It's also conspicuous, but more importantly, too unreliable. We don't know what kind of boat we'd be sailing at the edge of the Gulf. Getting stranded because of engine failure or something stupid isn't an option."

Marcela pulled another lollipop from her pocket and unwrapped it, popping it into her mouth.

"Which means requisition," John said. His expression grew dark.

"Right. With all the regular channels being monitored, they'd catch that kind of request real quick."

"Okay, so, we're screwed," Marcela said, removing the lollipop from her mouth and examining it. "Unless we do it anyway and just move really really *rapido*."

Mike gave a wry grin. "That's an option. But I can do you one better."

Marcela raised her eyebrows. John's expression stayed neutral, but he looked up from the map.

"I may or may not have been storing PAG codes ever since our little 'incident.'"

"*Mierda*," Marcela said, impressed.

John narrowed his eyes. "Meaning —"

Mike's grin grew. "I can make a requisition on *their* books. While the SOG is trying to track requests and seeing if I'll slip up, I'll be on a completely different channel. It's also nice that it hits the PAG budget instead of ours, ah but anyway..." Mike chuckled to himself. He suddenly looked sad for a moment but then returned to his mischievous smile. "That includes gear. We won't have anything as slick as we have in SOG but weapons, ammo, tools...make a wishlist kids. Then I'll place the order."

Marcela's eyes grew wide and she gave John a giddy look.

"How long does this sort of thing take?" John asked.

"Assuming we're not getting anything too complicated, eighteen hours wouldn't be unreasonable."

Marcela gave a low whistle. "Wish the CIA delivered other online goods, eh John?" she gave him a playful nudge.

John rubbed his chin, not acknowledging Marcela. He was doing mental calculations. Thinking about all the things they'd need. Sorting out every contingency. They didn't want to be too overburdened but they'd want to make sure they could tackle any surprises thrown their way...

"John?" Mike asked.

John didn't say anything for a long moment. Then he spoke.

"I'll start making that list."

Marcela's phone chimed.

John's body automatically responded. That chime was the sound that meant a message had been sent from the Firm — Blackthorne — on his issued non-descript flip phone used to contact assets. Marcela fished out her phone from her bag. John wondered if he'd be getting the same message if he hadn't destroyed his device before getting captured and taken in by the Cubans in Nicaragua.

"Oh. Ooooooh," Marcela said. Her face was a mix of excitement and horror. John recognized it as schadenfreude.

"What is it?" Mike asked, getting up to stretch.

Marcela held out the phone for John to see and Mike sidled over.

Target: Mike Morrandon

Target may attempt to make contact. Capture immediately and bring to nearest safe house. Contact handler.

John's eyes went wide. Mike let out an ugly bark of a laugh.

"There it is," Marcela said, "and we've already captured him."

Mike scowled at her. "Now hold a minute. I thought you two said you were in."

John frowned. If they didn't turn Mike in, it was directly disobeying an order. From the organization that they worked for; from their superiors. This was the Rubicon.

John looked at Marcela. She shrugged and gave him a tight smile back.

"No going back now," John said.

Marcela snapped the phone shut and turned back to the map. "Where were we?"

Chapter 4

Evening crept up on the group like a snake in the grass. John handed off a list of things for their mission and Mike surveyed the paper. It was all fairly reasonable. He made the call to the acquisition depot under the guise of a PAG officer, giving a code he'd been storing up for the last little while. Lucky too, because it would change out at the end of the week. Two days later and he would've been shit out of luck.

A boat, weapons, and gear, were all being prepped for them. Twelve more hours and they'd be good to go. Come morning they'd hit the Gulf.

John looked at Mike with that perpetually stoic expression of his, a darkness behind his eyes. It gave Mike the heebie-jeebies. He pulled his gaze away. Marcela hummed as she tinkered on a laptop she'd produced from her bag. She hummed sweetly as she sifted through data on the 'wig.

As much as Mike had to stay wary of John and Marcela, they were good agents. He was glad they let him explain himself.

He was also glad he was still alive.

John and Marcela were smart and reasonable, but they were also dangerous. All the more so now. The CIA didn't need to fear its enemies. It needed to fear its officers and assets questioning their orders. Mike had a feeling John and Marcela had been growing wary of their orders for a while, but he hadn't thought he could turn them so quickly. Then again, if he were lying, or if they suspected foul play on his part, they'd turn him in. Or kill him.

Trust was a hot commodity and he wasn't about to give it freely. But a part of him also liked them, he had been their handler for years, and felt like he knew them a little. They could get down to business, they could take orders, and they were highly competent. They were able to communicate and plan without getting bogged down. Able to criticize when necessary and take it without crying.

Besides them being lethal killers, Mike found himself concerned with one other thing.

Had John and Marcela developed feelings for one another?

Besides being unprofessional and unsustainable in their line of work, Mike was concerned it could jeopardize the mission. There was a reason he avoided most personal relationships.

Hell, I killed my last partner...

"Okay. Sleeping arrangements," Mike said, refusing to put off the uncomfortable question any longer. "There are two beds, three of us. How do you want to do this?" He looked back and forth between John and Marcela.

"Oh. Oooooh," Marcela grinned mischievously and reciprocated, dramatically looking back and forth between Mike and John.

"We can book another room," John said.

Mike shook his head. "I'd rather us stay together."

John thought for a moment, then nodded.

"John, are you going to share a bed with me?" Marcela asked, sidling up to him and batting her eyes. "I have been waiting for this day since we first —"

"I'll take the floor," John said. It seemed to make little difference to him.

Marcela frowned, then threw herself onto the hotel bed, like an Olympic diver. "*Qué puto caballero de mierda*," she grumbled. *What a fucking gentleman.*

Mike's face screwed up with a strange look of bewilderment.

What a weird relationship...

"I'm going to get a snack," he muttered.

They'd splurged for room service a few hours ago and Mike kept reminding himself he was on a diet, but it had been a rough couple of days.

He pulled his hood over his head and slipped on his aviator sunglasses as he limped out of the room. He wasn't sure if his leg was getting better or worse, but he probably shouldn't be walking much.

Elevator it is...

He turned his head aside as naturally as possible and veered to the edges of the security camera's field of vision.

He rode the elevator down with an attractive woman also wearing shades and expensive clothes. He stood slightly behind her, keeping his face down, knowing the elevator would have a camera as well. She was also going to the lobby.

She reached into her handbag...

Mike tensed, ready for the woman to pull a gun. The first move he'd have to make was for the gun-arm, then push her up against the elevator wall. He knew he could overpower her, but disarming her would have to be the initial move...

The woman pulled out a small cylinder of ChapStick and applied it to her lips. She turned her head slightly to glance at Mike out of the corner of her eye, unsure what he was up to.

Mike tried to relax, feeling sheepish.

The doors chimed and opened and he entered the lobby. The woman walked off, oblivious to what was happening in the mind of the man behind her. Oblivious that he was a wanted fugitive.

He was on edge. He knew he was on edge. But he had no choice. Relaxing would get him killed. The CIA was actively hunting him down, and although he knew that would be the case as soon as he fled DC, Marcela receiving orders to turn him over had shaken him.

At least they're not trying to kill me...

Mike made his way past the front desk — the lobby wasn't busy at this time of evening — and he made his way down a short hall where a set of vending machines were. He eyed the different sugary treats hungrily and licked his lips. The whole thing got him thinking of a last meal, and what a sad one this would be.

A man wearing a long black peacoat was walking toward Mike. Mike tensed again and glanced at the man without turning his head, then reminded himself to act natural and not consider everything a threat.

The man stumbled and fell, careening into Mike. Mike turned, surprised, but spread his arms wide to catch the man by the shoulders.

The man cried out as Mike caught him. Although he set his good leg back to catch the weight, the man pressed down hard on the wound in his thigh.

Mike grunted with pain and collapsed, the man doing a half somersault off his chest and to the side. But as all this happened, Mike's training kicked in and he recognized the proximity of a hand that had slipped inside his coat.

A quick pat confirmed his wallet had been swiped.

The man sprung up to stand and bent down to offer Mike a hand.

"Hey, my bad. I —"

Mike windmilled his good leg and struck the man's shin. The man cried out in pain and surprise equally, and Mike moved to sit. This put him squarely at waist-length on the man who reached down to catch the pain in his shin.

Mike punched the guy hard in the sack.

"Ah!"

This time the man buckled over and grabbed at his crotch, wheezing.

"Give me my wallet, asshole," Mike hissed, struggling to stand again. His leg was throbbing. He could feel it moisten. As he stood and tested his balance with a practice step, he knew his limp had grown worse.

The man looked up and might have tried to defend himself but Mike already had a fist ready to clock the man in the nose, and he grabbed the man's cuff and pushed him up against the vending machine.

The man weakly held up Mike's wallet, and Mike dropped him.

The man staggered off. Mike would've preferred to turn the guy in, but he couldn't exactly go to the authorities right now. It wouldn't accomplish much anyway.

A soft thump sounded as a chocolate bar fell from the clutches of the vending machine, and into the depository below. Mike grinned and retrieved the treat, turning to bare his teeth at the jerk who had decided to tag a CIA officer as his quarry.

But instead of seeing the man in the peacoat, Mike's eyes were drawn to the heavily armed SWAT team that was crossing the lobby. They all wore full-dress tactical gear: helmet and goggles, flak vests, flashbangs and the like on their belts and MP5s locked and loaded. SWAT identification markings were printed clearly on their uniforms. Four of them approached the elevator, while another four hit the stairs. One heavily armed man opened the door and held it for the others as they silently crept by, assault weapons at the ready.

They can only be here for one reason...shit.

He hobbled into action. He turned tail in the hallway and limped away from the vending machines, forced to pocket his precious chocolate bar for now. He pulled out his phone and dialed Marcela. She picked up after the first ring.

"*Hola, señor,* do you have a happy tummy —"

"Don't open the windows, they'll have a sniper," Mike said automatically. He risked a glance over his shoulder. Two of the four SWAT team members entered the elevator as it chimed open. The other two took up positions on either side of it.

"What's happened?" Marcela asked. She began to say something indistinguishable to John. Probably informing him as Mike gave the info.

"SWAT team," Mike said, continuing his painful limp to the end of the hall. "I've got to disappear. I'll call you as soon as I find a secure location."

"How did they find us?"

Mike was wondering the same thing. Departments didn't report that kind of activity to one another, not that quickly, and certainly not rival ones. It'd have to be someone who was actively looking for him, but was also monitoring PAG activity. He shook his head. A problem for later. "Don't know. But must've tracked my call somehow..." he glanced again behind his shoulder. One of the men at the elevators was staring at him. Then he pointed and held up a flat palm.

You. Stop.

"Hell..." Mike hung up not wanting to stay on the phone too long and risk analytics picking him up again. His previous call for the boat and goods from storage would have given the CIA ample time to find him. They could pinpoint within a few feet of the phone's location. Which meant SWAT was heading straight for John and Marcela.

The SWAT team member started making his way down the hall toward Mike, still giving him hand directions.

Mike turned back around, limping away until he reached an emergency exit. He opened it, and the building alarm fired off as he hobbled into the Miami night as fast as his leg would allow.

Chapter 5

John and Marcela both automatically checked over their handguns and stuffed them into waistbands.

"Stay or go?" John asked.

"Do they know we're with him?" Marcela asked.

John was about to reply but there was a pounding on the door.

"Miami police, open up!" came the bark of a SWAT sergeant.

John opened the door and backed up as four men charged in, MP5s raised and sweeping. John raised his hands and Marcela followed. One man pointed his gun at John and another at Marcela. The sergeant moved to the washroom and the last SWAT team member finished watching the hallway at the rear and moved in to sweep the kitchenette and beds.

"Clear!" the sergeant barked.

The other SWAT member began checking under beds.

"Who are you two?" the sergeant asked harshly.

John kept his hands up and eyes level with the sergeant. "CIA. We're here for Mike Morrandon."

The sergeant wavered for a heartbeat, then narrowed his eyes. "ID's?"

"We're off the book," Marcela said, jumping in with John's plan. "But you can call it in."

"Alright," the sergeant lowered his weapon and walked a few steps away, pulling out a cell phone.

They waited in tense silence, except for the mumbling that came from the sergeant's call in the bathroom. He came out a moment later, still on the phone.

"Names?"

"John Carpenter," John said. "And Marcela..." he stopped short, realizing he didn't know Marcela's last name.

"Ortiz," she said, giving John a wink.

"The sergeant repeated the names, then nodded a moment later. "They're clear," he said.

The SWAT members lowered their weapons.

"We got the call less than an hour ago," the sergeant said, giving a hand signal to his team to exit the room. They led the way and the sergeant walked fast with John and Marcela following close behind. "Large black male, possibly armed and dangerous. Not many more details than that. How'd you two get here so fast?"

"Plenty of cardio," Marcela said, diffusing the question with humor.

"We're here to take him in once your team makes the arrest," John said. Rules for the CIA were restrictive when operating on U.S. soil. The CIA couldn't actually operate unless it conducted itself alongside another detachment such as the FBI, or a civilian aid.

"Let's see if we still can't get him," the sergeant said, following the other SWAT members down the hallway.

A shrill alarm sounded from the hotel ceiling. Sleepy and annoyed guests poked out from their doors, some of them jumping back and ducking back inside their rooms when they saw the SWAT team moving quickly down the hall

The sergeant suddenly twitched his head and held up a finger to his earpiece. He listened to something for a moment, then said, "understood. En route." The sergeant turned to the other two. "Sounds like they caught a fish downstairs. Let's move!"

Chapter 6

Mike made it outside and was immediately spotted by SWAT team members who had set up a perimeter. Of course they made sure to cover the emergency exits.

Mike grunted in frustration and the growing pain in his leg and continued to limp away. Someone began to yell at him and he ignored them, continuing down the sidewalk like he hadn't heard anything.

The SWAT team member that had spotted him from inside the hall burst through the emergency door, swinging it open again and letting the high-pitched wailing of the fire alarm ring out onto the street. Mike continued to limp for no other reason than to keep doing something, but SWAT moved on him. The one running out of the emergency exit made to pounce like a cat and tackle Mike down. Mike tried to time things as best he could, swerving out of the way and sidestepping the dive. His arm got tagged anyway, and he was dragged down to the ground.

The SWAT member bent down to try and get on top of him and Mike forgot about trying to stand up and opted for a blow instead. He aimed his sucker punch for the man's throat instead of the nose, avoiding the tactical goggles.

The hit bounced off the man's shoulder as the SWAT member flipped him over. He mumbled something under his breath and grabbed Mike's head in his gloved hands like a vice gripping soft wood.

Another SWAT member jumped on Mike's back and grabbed his hands, pinning them together and squeezing his shoulders tightly and with pain.

"Search him! Search him!" one of them yelled, he couldn't tell who.

They patted him down and took his wallet, pulling his hood back and removing his sunglasses while they were at it.

"That's him," one of them said.

More bootsteps were on the ground. Mike managed to crane his neck around against the pavement to see the rest of the team that had gone upstairs run over to him, followed by John and Marcela.

What the...

He had expected them to tuck tail and take off. Which was probably the smart thing. He wasn't sure what they were doing...

John and Marcela both had their guns out and pointed down, as if ready for Mike to be hostile.

He didn't struggle. He was also careful not to say anything, waiting to see how this would play out.

"That's him?" one of the SWAT guys was saying.

"Yes," John replied, tucking his gun away and examining Mike's wallet. Marcela followed suit. "We'll take it from here."

John bent down and gripped Mike under the armpit along with the other SWAT member, hoisting him up. Mike hissed against the pain in his leg, not to mention the general roughhousing. He couldn't tell if John was acting.

Which got him thinking...

Shit, did these guys plan the whole thing from the beginning?

Mike looked at John coldly. John ignored him.

It made sense. SWAT getting called in right on their position. Them holding him stationary for the day, and bringing his guard down.

Marcela moved next to him and replaced the SWAT member that had him by the arm so her and John were handling him.

"Car's around the corner," she said.

John nodded. He looked to the SWAT team. "Thanks. Good work."

The sergeant nodded back and turned to his team, giving them orders to depart.

John and Marcela dragged Mike to their rental car in the hotel parking lot.

"Clever plan," Mike spat.

"I thought so too," Marcela said.

"Where are we going?" John asked Mike.

Mike stared at him. "What do you mean?"

"We could stay at another hotel, but I'd prefer to get out of here in case they figure it out."

"I thought you two were taking me in," Mike said.

Marcela laughed. John gave him one of his stern looks.

"We said we're with you," John said.

Mike breathed a sigh of relief. They made their way to the parking lot and loaded into his rental car, Mike in the backseat with John driving and Marcela riding shotgun.

"The gear won't be ready until tomorrow," Mike said as John backed out of the lot.

"What if we...oh *mierda*..."

As John drove toward the end of the lot, a SWAT BearCat pulled out in front of them, blocking the way.

The sergeant got out of the passenger side and waved a hand at them.

John rolled down a window to hear him out.

"Drive," Mike said.

"...just got a call!" the sergeant was saying. "We're supposed to take the target —"

"We have our orders!" John called back. "We're taking him to a drop site!"

"So do we! Langley says you're compromised!"

John didn't respond to that.

"*Mierda, mierda!*"

The sergeant signaled to his team and they began to pile out the back of the truck.

"Drive," Mike said again.

John wouldn't be able to push past the truck even if he wanted to. Which meant he'd have to go another way...

SWAT members began to fan out and raise their weapons at the car, moving to surround it.

"Hold on," John said.

He put the car into reverse and slammed on the gas pedal.

Chapter 7

The parking lot only had one true exit. The rest of the lot was surrounded by raised curbs and decorative shrubbery leading down onto the sidewalks around the hotel.

John gritted his teeth as the car lurched backward and the sound of squealing tires and burnt rubber overtook them.

"Down!" Mike roared.

John and Marcela ducked low as they responded to the all-too-familiar command. The SWAT team opened fire.

John glanced back out the front windshield, staying low in his seat. Muzzles flashed in the darkness as ten-millimeter bullets tore through the night and ripped into the car like a metal rain. John could feel the whizzing of rounds in the air inches above his head as the car retreated. He refused to peek above the wheel to see how close they were to the edge of the parking lot, instead estimating the distance.

"Brace," he called calmly.

The others held on to whatever they could as they hit the tall rear curb.

The car bobbed up and down violently as metal met concrete, an ugly screech followed as the car scraped over the barrier. The car collided with another object, then tore a hole through the scraggly shrubbery that surrounds the property. Dry twigs clawed against the windows, as if they could halt the speeding vehicle.

But their car continued with a second harsh bump and the popping of MP5 rounds slowed to a stop. John hoped there hadn't been anyone on the sidewalk. But there wasn't much sense worrying about that now.

John pulled the handbrake and spun the wheel hard to the right. The car spun like a door swinging open wildly, and he pulled himself up in his seat with the momentum.

"Go!" Mike yelled, struggling to right himself.

In the rear-view mirror, the SWAT truck and two police cruisers tore around the corner. Lights and sirens blaring with anticipation. John shifted the stick into drive, righted the wheel, and hit the gas.

Mike and Marcela craned their necks to watch their pursuers from behind. John glanced in the rearview mirror to see them closing. They had had more time to gain speed and the truck could easily ram them into submission.

"They're gaining on us," Marcela said, voice tense and knuckles going white as she gripped a safety handle above her door.

John didn't reply. He knew they needed more space to maneuver and build up speed. Luckily, the hotel was a block away from Brickell Ave, which was practically a highway.

He swung a wide right through an intersection, narrowly missing a Cadillac, horn honking at him. John worked to pick up speed again, weaving his way through the evening traffic and ignoring the bullet holes in the windshield that distorted his view. He placed a large truck between their rental and the inbound police.

"There they are," Mike said.

John glanced into his side mirror. Sure enough, their pursuers were just behind them. The highway traffic had hindered their pursuit momentarily, but they had already started closing distance again. With their sirens they'd be able to push through traffic easier too.

They flew past deluxe high rises, clubs and bars, and chic restaurants. Brickell Ave was known for its nightlife. People were out partying in the warm nighttime air, enjoying the electric pulse of the city. In some ways it reminded John of Latin America. That thought was pushed aside by Marcela interjecting.

"John," Marcela said, slapping his arm and pointing ahead.

John nodded. Traffic had begun to slow as the traffic lights turned yellow. Everyone tensed. They couldn't afford to stop. SWAT would be on them in a heartbeat.

John swerved halfway onto the hedge-covered median, squeezing past traffic and into the intersection. Once clear, he again pulled the handbrake and turned the wheel. The opposing light turned green as John slid through the intersection on two wheels. A jeep advanced through the green light against them...

John slid their car in front of the coming jeep, receiving more angry honking and the frantic squealing of tires as other cars narrowly stopped for John. He just barely managed to see the shocked expression of a woman in the jeep staring at him and slam her hand on her horn.

"They don't like you much," Marcela said.

"Don't blame them," John mumbled.

He completed the U-turn and sped back down the other side of Brickell Ave.

More frantic honking followed as they surged forward again, this time moving south. They passed their pursuers on the other side of Brickell, and John could swear he could feel their frustration. Traffic clumsily made way for the SWAT vehicle and cruisers to get through the intersection, buying time for the three agents to create some distance in their bullet laden rental.

"Where are we going?" Marcela asked.

"Mike?" John asked, as John pushed past the slower cars on either side of him. He weaved his way like a snake between the cars, pulling onto the left lane and increasing speed.

"Original plan was to pick up at the U.S. Coast Guard base between Dodge Island and South of Fifth," Mike said, more to himself than John.

"Map," John said to Marcela. "Need a map."

She pulled out her smartphone and was about to open an app when she froze, swore under her breath and tucked the phone away. There was too much risk for tracking, especially after how quickly they'd found them with Mike.

Marcela cracked the glove compartment and rooted through until she found a map. She unfurled it and began folding it to fit their current location off the Miami south channel.

John heard the sirens grow in volume before he saw the flashing lights. A quick glance in the rearview told him they hadn't lost their pursuers yet, and they were running out of options.

"Coast Guard base is north of us," Marcela said, struggling in her seat as John swerved around a slower car in lane. John could hear bullets rattling around the chassis as he swung between lanes.

"I have to turn around again?" John asked.

"If they tracked us through my request, they would've canceled my requisition," Mike replied, staring out the back window. "We're going to need a new location."

John's brain moved into autopilot driving the car as he began to sift through the information they had. "What's our objective?"

"Get away from the *policia!*" Marcela cried.

"Still need to infiltrate the island," Mike said.

"Still need a boat," John replied.

"Don't suppose we could break into the Coast Guard base..." Marcela thought out loud. The sirens grew louder as they continued to lose ground.

One of the police cars wound its way around a series of cars, closing in on John, Marcela, and Mike. In the distance the SWAT BearCat could be seen doing the same.

Marcela spotted it first in the side-mirror. "They're gaining on us!"

"I see it," John said, pushing the car further. Their rental wasn't about to compete with a Ford Interceptor that was meant to go fast and end chases. They had to think of something quick.

Marcela pulled out her gun.

"We can't shoot at them, they're cops," Mike said.

"Oh, we're going to let them capture us?" Marcela asked.

"No...but if we start gunning down cops that's not going to help our case."

John swerved around a pickup truck with a violent pull of the wheel as he forced another car next to him in the middle lane out of the way. The car honked at him and the pickup truck driver rolled down his window, giving John the finger. He ignored both distractions and pulled ahead of the truck, revealing more room in front of them.

On the one hand that was good — he didn't have to keep weaving around cars to speed up the left lane. On the other hand...

One of the police cars finally made its way past a tractor-trailer holding up the middle lane. The pickup truck and car that John had passed began to pull over, allowing the cop to move through. They were both in the open now.

"Shit..." Mike said.

The police car tore through what remained of their lead in seconds and smoothly transitioned into pacing them in the right lane.

John's face was becoming increasingly stern and focused. He thought of all the possibilities and outcomes that could happen in the next half-minute. This part of driving was always tricky, and he'd only been in this position twice before. If they didn't end in a crash, car chases usually ended with the lead car disappearing into the mass of cars and city in front of them, or pulling over and accepting defeat. But in the case of a chased car's refusal to give up, it forced the pursuer to drive their quarry off the road.

"Brace!" Mike called.

Everyone held on as soon as the command was given, and the police car attempted a PIT maneuver. John slammed on the brake throwing off the officer's aim; there was a thump as the cruiser collided with the rear passenger door. John kept the car on the road through the bump, preventing them from spinning out. He could give more gas but that would put them at risk of another attempted PIT. The officer was already repositioning to try again. Eventually they would be pushed off the road or he would lose control anyway.

The sound of whipping wind suddenly invaded the car as Marcela rolled down her window. Her hair flew wildly and they could only barely hear what she was saying.

"...aim for the tires!" she cried.

She unclipped her seatbelt and shuffled sideways in her seat, throwing her legs up and over onto the seat, edging out of the passenger window.

John instinctually wanted to help but couldn't take his hands off the steering wheel. He didn't dare drive with one hand at these speeds.

"Grab her legs," he told Mike.

Mike nodded and grabbed hold of Marcela's ankles with both of his hands.

"Always with the legs..." John thought he heard Marcela say.

She continued to edge out until half her body was out the window, sitting on the car door, hair billowing like smoke.

She had her gun out.

The police car rammed them again.

John's hand stuttered as he struggled to right the car again. They entered a dangerously tight swerve but he got the car under control. Mike bounced in the back seat, holding onto Marcela's ankles with desperation.

"*Mierda!*"

Marcela pulled herself back into the car.

"Lost the gun."

"You what?" Mike asked.

"We swerved, I..." Marcela turned to John. "Where's your gun?"

John frowned and shifted uncomfortably in his seat, eyes frozen straight ahead, spotting a sign for a bridge and some other exits in his peripherals.

"Ah okay just hold tight *amigo*, you know I don't bite...often," Marcela chuckled and reached behind John's back and into his waistband for his gun.

"Going to be making a turn soon," he said.

Marcela nodded and hoisted herself back out the window.

The police car moved to ram them a third time.

Marcela fired liberally, and before the police car could ram them again, John saw it make a sharp jarring turn to the left. The entire car spun out like a pinwheel. Seconds later, as it shrunk from sight, he saw the pickup truck smash into its side, t-boning the car with a mighty crash.

"Good," Mike grunted.

John grimaced. "Get inside."

Marcela tucked herself gracefully back into the car and rolled up the window, bringing an eerie almost-silence to them, the steady hum of fast tires on pavement the only thing in their ears once more now.

"Hold on," John said.

He slowed the car as they came upon a highway intersection. John drove below an underpass then approached the red light.

"We don't have time to stop," Mike said.

John gritted his teeth as he forced the car to a stop. Mike was right, but cars were speeding by.

"Here they come again — the others," Marcela said, craning her neck to look out the rear window with Mike.

John watched in the rearview as the SWAT truck and the other police car began to catch up to them. He was hoping the police car they'd evaded would slow them down a bit, but their pursuers were making good time.

"Green light!" Marcela yelled.

John slammed on the gas and made a hard turn. Marcela flew out of her seat and nearly ended up in his lap. He pushed her off gently.

"Okay, that one wasn't on purpose..." Marcela muttered, struggling off John and back into her seat, doing up her seatbelt.

"John, go straight," Mike groaned as John completed the left turn. "This is going to eventually lead to a dead end."

John was on the Rickenbacker Causeway now, coming up on a toll booth.

Mike shook his hand with a metal rattle. "Change for the booth," he said.

John ignored him. He continued to increase speed as they dipped under the booth. A heavy wooden snap sounded out as he crashed through the gate and pressed on.

Mike grunted. "Yeah okay," he muttered.

They sped along the bridge and onto an island, but this time the SWAT truck came on them fast. He could barely make it out, but John thought he saw something peeking out of the passenger side window...

"Gun!" Mike called.

Marcela and John ducked instinctually but Mike shook his head.

"Too many civilian cars, plus a moving target...I hope that's enough to stop them."

"Don't count on it," John said.

Marcela snatched the map up from Mike's grasp, finding where they were with the trace of her finger.

"Mike is right John, this bridge leads to roads that go nowhere," Marcela said, straining to contain her anxiety.

"We're going to make a move," John said. "Brace again."

He saw Marcela and Mike exchange glances. They didn't like the ominous tone of his voice.

The sirens grew loudly as they left the island and fell back on the Rickenbacker Causeway Bridge. John turned his head periodically to look out over the water. The SWAT truck continued to edge closer to them, filling the rearview mirror. The second police car was right behind, cars moving aside to let them forward as John honked the horn and struggled through the traffic.

"They're going to catch us," Marcela said. "There's no —"

John swerved the car hard to the right — toward the edge of the bridge and into the bay.

Chapter 8

"John! What are you —"

Marcela's cry was interrupted by the screeching of rubber on asphalt as John jerked the wheel. The three of them felt their seatbelts lock as they rocked in their seats.

The car smashed through the thick metal railing.

The grating sound and short squeal of metal-on-metal ground in their ears as the crash hit the front and the railing edges scraped against the sides of the car. The airbags in the driver and passenger side seats exploded from their compartments, filling John and Marcela's spaces with white balloons and powder.

The sound of police sirens whirred by above and behind them as the SWAT truck and police car streamed on by, completely taken by surprise by John's turn.

"Holy —"

John didn't hear the rest of what Mike was saying. He let his hands off the wheel.

The car launched into the dark air.

They flew through nothing, and the surreal feeling of the earth dropping away as their bodies became briefly weightless. They were where no human was meant to be, and gravity was taking control.

"Brace," John called.

John had hoped for a simple nosedive, but their car had been going too fast, or had gotten caught on some edge of twisted metal as they were sent flying, because their car was slowly turning in the air, flipping upside-down...

John grabbed the bottom of his seat and tucked his head, hoping the other two were doing the same. Gravity pulled the three of them toward the hood, then the top of the car as the water rushed up to meet them.

They smashed into the bay with a mighty crash — at this speed the water might as well have been a wall. They flew up in their seats, bashing heads and shoulders against the roof of the car.

John took a moment to reorient his internal compass. Water was already beginning to pool up above.

Up is down, down is up.

He fumbled for a knife strapped to his ankle and pulled it out slowly, turning to check on the others.

"Injuries?"

"Fine," Mike called.

"You stupid *mierda*, of course I'm not fine!" Marcela spat.

John grunted. "We've got about a minute. First thing, seatbelts off."

"Stay calm, watch your movements," Mike said.

John nodded to himself. Being trapped underwater was dangerous. Most people panicked in these sorts of situations. Especially without proper gear or proper training. Not only was swimming twice as hard with clothing, a loose sleeve could get caught on a hook and drag someone down. The front airbags had deflated and the side curtain airbags began to wilt moments later. He cut through the cushion's fabric and shoved it aside, exposing the window. He handed the knife to Marcela to do the same.

The car was beginning to sink. The murky water of the bay covered the windshield already, creating an uncomfortable sudden darkness in the car as the last of it was swallowed up by liquid.

"Mike, you're going out the left side," John said.

They were falling fast now, the water swallowing them up and covering the other windows. Darkness enveloped them.

"What's the plan?" Marcela asked, passing back the knife. "I mean, once we surface?"

John grimaced. "I'm counting on a good Samaritan. Ready on three..."

They counted down together, steady, hands on door handles once they were situated and ready to take the plunge.

"One...two...three!"

Using the hard tip of his knife John shattered the driver side window. Water streamed inside as if the bay wanted to invade the car. The swirling green-brown bay water filled the bottom of the car and rose quickly, gobbling up their feet and legs and reaching waist height. John steadied his breathing as his body protested the chill. John looked Mike in the eyes.

"Remember, the whole time you are rising, you need to be exhaling."

"What?"

"If you don't exhale as you rise, the air in your lungs will expand and your lungs could rupture."

Mike looked like he was going to vomit.

"Just scream the whole time and you will be fine."

As the water climbed past his shoulders, John took one last look around at the others. Marcela, hunched in the footwell of the passenger's side of the car, flashed him a smile that didn't quite make it to her eyes. She was scared. John could hear Mike cursing to himself under the seat of the car, but was cut off from the rest of them by water now.

He took a deep breath, braced himself against the center console and slid through the shattered window.

Water took him over. He was in the deep. No air, limited vision, slow movements.

John felt at home.

He was a SEAL first and foremost. Nothing could erase his training. The missions he'd been on. The experiences he'd had with his fellow team. The water was an old friend. His instincts kicked in, making his muscles move in ways he hardly thought about.

He moved to Mike's door first, pivoting in the water, making sure his directional sense was still intact. Mike had gotten the door half open but was struggling.

John grabbed the handle and pulled it open, then watched Mike take a breath before pulling him out by the arm. Mike gave a few good kicks before he flew toward the surface, a constant stream of bubbles following as he screamed his way.

Onto Marcela.

Marcela hadn't gotten her door open. John swam over the bottom of the car, moving down with it as it slowly sank through the deep. He grabbed hold of the chassis and pulled himself over, upside down in the water so he could see Marcela right-side up.

She had a look of panic on her face, long hair floating around her like a phantom. But at the sight of John she gave him a mock kiss and pointed to the door handle.

John grabbed hold of the handle, dragged deeper under the water as the car pulled him down. He used the movement to leverage the door open, stopping his movement and letting gravity do the work.

Marcela swam out as the door opened. She began to float upward, mouth open and bubbles flowing until suddenly she stopped rising and started to sink again...

Her eyes scrunched in confusion, then widened in concern.

John didn't see the problem at first. He held onto the open door and allowed himself to be dragged further downward, poking his head around to see what the issue was.

Marcela kept tugging her feet, but kept getting pulled downwards. Something was caught and she couldn't break free.

John made a mental note of how much air he had left and how much Marcela would need. Then he swept down and faced her, tapping her on the forehead to get her attention. Making eye contact, he held up a single finger.

Hold on. Stay calm.

She nodded, but it was hard not to panic in a situation like this. Panic made things difficult. Panic could get you killed.

John pushed past her and squeezed into the upside-down passenger side seat. He grabbed her legs and gave them a tug, looking to see what was caught. If she could talk, he knew she'd probably say something flirtatious about this.

A soft pounding sound came from the back end of the vehicle. A squishy sensation hit his legs next. They'd hit the bay floor.

Which meant they were as deep as they could go. John knew how long he could hold his breath. But he was concerned for Marcela, she had lost a lot of air in those first moments of free ascension...

He found the problem at her left ankle. The seatbelt had found its way around, twisting itself into a half-knot. It seemed like a silly and improbable mistake, but Marcela had probably become disoriented with being upside down. He made quick work of the seatbelt with his knife. Cutting her free had only taken moments but in those moments they had spent air.

She looked back at him with wide eyes. He pulled the seatbelt free and patted her calf, letting her know he was done. But before letting her go, he tapped his lips and then hers, moving close.

It wasn't a kiss. He wanted to give her some air. He knew he could spare it.

John felt something stir within him when their mouths met, but suppressed the feeling. He was professional, and he'd done this before. It shouldn't feel any different.

When they parted, Marcela had a strange look in her eyes. Then her eyebrows rose and she gave John a wink. John gave an awkward thumbs up, then Marcela nodded, steeled herself, and kicked off the seat and began towards the surface.

John took a moment to make sure he wasn't entangled anywhere himself, then pulled himself out of the car with a series of hand-tucks. He found himself standing on the bottom of the bay. They were lucky the bay was so shallow.

The water was cloudy. He could see tufts of plants waving in the water as if they were moving with a wind on a spring night. Bits of garbage — pop cans and bottles, wrappers, and what looked like a monkey wrench sat complacent in their habitat. Mud sucked at his feet as clumps rose and evaporated into a collection of dirty particles, torn apart and joining the murk around him. Up above, the surface glittered like stained glass, moving randomly as various veins of moonlight played far away and out of reach like a series of silver fish.

It felt good to be in the water again. It had been a long time.

He felt a bit naked without his gear, and he kept wanting to breathe because he was so used to having his equipment. But he was running out of air time and he had to reach the others. He hoped the plan would work. If not, well...

He bent his knees slowly, and gave a mighty push, kicking his legs quickly to build momentum. His ears began to pop again as he rose. His lungs burned as he ascended, pushing through the water, breaststroke and frog kick, sweeping as much liquid around and past his body as he possibly could. The surface filled more of his vision. The murk grew clearer, lighter, like a spectrum of color from dark green to light brown.

His lungs continued to burn until that last possible second of...

Release.

He made sure his head was fully above water, and waited a second for it to rush down his face. Too many inexperienced swimmers would choke on their first inhale because of greedy lungs and lack of control. But once that passed, he finally gasped for air, realizing now that he'd pushed himself farther than he should've. He was out of practice. His lungs worked, drinking in air as sweet as honey, and the sounds of the city returned to him. The rush of traffic from the bridge thumped above him as the water sloshed around his body, seagulls crying far up in the air.

"Thought you weren't joining us for a minute there," Mike called.

John spotted Mike and began to swim over to the man who had drifted away from their position.

"Okay, what is this brilliant plan?" Marcela asked, following John's lead to group up. She didn't say anything about him sharing air with her, and he was thankful for it.

The sound of a motor made John turn around, as they watched a pure white, 50ft yacht creep toward them, lights beaming in the dark.

"Do you still have my gun?" John asked Marcela.

She furrowed her brows, then tucked a hand under the water, pulling up his Glock. "Funny how those instincts don't quit..." she muttered.

He treaded water in her direction and took the gun. "Follow my lead," he said to the two of them. They both nodded back, sensing now what he planned to do.

The boat continued to push through the water toward them, slowing to a crawl when it reached thirty or so feet away.

"Oi!" a man called from the boat. He was at the side railing, waving his hands. "Are you okay?"

"Do we look okay?" Mike muttered.

"We could use a lift!" Marcela called back.

The man disappeared for a moment, then came back holding a large orange lifesaver attached to a bit of rope.

"We'll get you outta there!" the man cried in his thick British accent.

He tossed the lifesaver and undershot. He drew it back in to try again.

John looked up at the bridge, and saw dozens of cars pulled over and people crowding the ledge. He didn't spot the police car, but the SWAT truck had pulled over. SWAT team members began to pile out.

"Better hurry this up..." Mike said quietly to John as he realized Mike was looking in the same direction.

The lifesaver flew over their heads and splashed in the water. Marcela swam past them to grab hold and brought it closer to the other two.

The man began to haul the lifesaver in with Marcela attached, while John and Mike swam closer to the boat. John turned as he swam into a backstroke, watching the SWAT team begin to push past the crowd and move them out of their way.

They reached the boat and Marcela found purchase on a series of metal rungs on the side. John and Mike lined up behind her, ready to board.

A woman in white joined the British man, scowling and looking the three of them up and down as they pulled themselves up the ladder and onto the deck, wet clothes dumping dirty water on the pristine white of the ship.

"Are you lot okay?" the man asked again. "We saw your car go over and —"

John pulled out his gun and pointed it at the man. "Off the boat." He jerked his head to the side.

The woman's reaction was faster than the man's. She dropped a martini glass she'd been holding and it shattered on the deck as she gave a squeal of fright.

The man slowly raised his hands, a look of utter confusion plastered across his face.

"I don't...but..."

"Off the boat," John repeated. "Now." He backed away from the side of the boat, opening the way up for the two to approach the bay.

The woman looked at the man then took off at a run, holding her sunhat as she flew over the side and into the water. She emerged a moment later, gasping for air and spluttering.

The man was about to say something else but Mike stepped in. "You heard the man," Mike said. He took the man by the shoulders and steered him over the side. The man looked back and Mike rolled his eyes, then gave the guy a shove. He flipped head over heels into the water.

"Maybe toss them a lifejacket?' Marcela asked, evidently feeling bad for them.

John tucked his gun away and dug through a bin, finding a life saver without a line attached to it. He approached the side and tossed it over. It landed precisely between the two in the water.

"We've got to go," Mike said.

Marcela gave the two a dainty apologetic wave as John moved to the ship's wheel.

"Bloody Americans!" the man cried as John opened the throttle. He spun the boat around to point south, away from Miami, and deeper into Biscayne Bay.

Chapter 9

Antonio Romero was a man of routine.

The sound of his alarm woke up him as it always did. Six in the morning. He opened his eyes immediately and turned off his alarm. He didn't hit the snooze button like so many others. He enjoyed being awake too much. It gave him more time.

Antonio took off his sleep apnea machine mask and swung his feet out of bed and into his monogrammed slippers. He stood and retrieved his matching monogrammed silk robe hanging on a peg beside his door. Both were pure white except for the baby blue monogram. It always gave him pleasure to see the *AR* sewed onto his featured clothing.

He walked to the kitchen and embraced the bright sun rays shining into his villa. His lavish estate was at the top of a long walkway up a hill, overlooking West Palm Beach. He looked out of the window with a smile, marveling at the water lapping calmly against the sand below his dwelling. Nature was beautiful. Constant. He was happy to be a part of it.

He had a chef to cook him meals, but breakfast was the most important meal of the day, and he preferred to prepare it himself. His chef could take care of lunch and dinner.

Not that breakfast was a lavish affair. Antonio poached two eggs, plated them, sprinkled salt and pepper, and added some fresh cut chives. After he ate, he went for his run.

CUBAN CONSPIRACY

Antonio was a fit man. He was average height and build for a Cuban, but his lifestyle kept his face youthful and fresh. He looked to be enjoying his middle age instead of a man pushing through his sixties. He smiled at the remembered compliments he received.

After his run, he stripped in the washroom, turned the shower on hot, and proceeded to clean his muscular body. His libido always worked up after he went for his run, and he masturbated, embracing the control and power that came with the rush of orgasm induced by himself.

After his long shower and getting dressed to prepare for the rest of the day, Maxine stopped by.

Maxine was a tall, attractive woman in her forties, Czech roots and a cute-as-a-button accent to match. Her dark hair was short and crisp, and she always had a lingering smile, like she knew the answer to a joke she was about to tell but wouldn't give the punchline away.

Antonio liked Maxine. They spoke the same language. That was something he once thought impossible. But since meeting Maxine at a European art showing, he had learned how many things could be possible.

"Ackerman is on your eight o'clock," Maxine said, checking her phone and scrolling through emails. "Oh, and final touches for the party. I'm going to the island tomorrow if that works well for you."

She was leaning on the kitchen counter, allowing a particularly generous view of her breasts. Antonio sauntered on over behind her and grabbed her by the hips, pulling her close. She gave a mock gasp of surprise.

"I have work to do," Antonio said.

"As do I," Maxine said, still scrolling aimlessly through her phone.

Antonio reached under Maxine's loose shirt and felt her bra. The cups were smooth and firm...a texture he adored, because it reminded him so much of the female body. "I know what you are trying to do," he whispered in her ear. "Leaning over the counter like that."

"I don't know what you're talking about," she said back with a chuckle.

Antonio tugged at her skirt. She turned around. Her eyes filled him with an electric shock of pleasure. She always had the ability to do that to him. It never failed.

He spun her back around, and she dropped her phone.

"You have work to do..." she said, her words becoming a moan.

"I do."

It was an old game they played. It always ended the same.

When Congressman Gerard Ackerman came to visit Antonio at his home office, Antonio was beyond prepared. He knew how men liked to be treated. After all, he was one himself.

"This is excellent scotch," Ackerman was saying. He seated himself comfortably in one of Antonio's handcrafted designer chairs, sipping from a tumbler clinking with ice.

Antonio wanted his office to be less of a place of work and more of a place of play. It resembled something of an ivy league university office or common room; dark wood colors, burgundy upholstered furniture, tall bookshelves laden with books. Antonio loved how it had come together after years of designers fussing and failing to deliver his vision. But now he could reap the benefits — and how could he not share them?

Antonio waved the compliment off. "I don't pretend to know much about Scotch," he said.

"Well, I can tell you I'm doing it wrong," Ackerman laughed, shaking his glass to make the ice cubes shake.

"Ah." Antonio replied, not particularly interested in the etiquette. "But this..." he picked up a small wooden box from his desk. "This I know plenty about."

He grinned as he revealed the contents of the box, flourishing as if he were about to propose with a ring.

Ackerman grinned at the Cuban cigars. His greedy eyes drank in the sight before reaching out to take one.

"Ah!" Antonio shut the box, nearly snapping the man's fingers.

Ackerman pulled his hand back, looking at Antonio inquisitively.

Antonio laughed. "Allow me."

He opened the box and removed two cigars, rifled through his desk for a cigar cutter and pack of matches, then gave the cutter a habitual couple presses.

"Congressman —"

"Gerard, please," Ackerman said with a honey-coated smile.

"Ah, alright, *señor* Gerard," Antonio replied, and both laughed at that. "I am wondering how things are in Washington." Antonio slipped the cigar into the cutter but didn't make the cut. He looked to Ackerman with curious eyes.

"In Washington? Uh well..." Ackerman looked from the cigar to Antonio, then back to the cigar.

"Oh please," Antonio said. "When we are at the island it is all pleasure. But here, unfortunately..."

He snipped the cigar. He thought he could hear Ackerman swallow nervously.

"...it is *negocio*," Antonio finished. *Business.*

"Business...of course. And what do you —"

"Congressman, I understand you were going to vote with the tech bill last week."

Ackerman furrowed his brow and gave Antonio a quizzical look. "Well, yes of course. That's no secret...my constituents expect me to —"

Antonio laid down the uncut cigar and struck a match to light the one he had cut. He puffed a few times as he did so, and curls of sweet smoke rose into the air before them.

"I don't suppose I could convince you otherwise," Antonio said, suddenly looking up from his cigar.

"Well one has a duty to one's constituents," Ackerman said tightly, staring into his glass.

"Constituents, yes," Antonio said. He laid the cigar down on an ashtray he had been gifted by an Italian real estate mogul he'd befriended years ago. It was Murano glass, in the shape of a whale. He was fond of the thing. "I'm sure a congressman has many different constituents. You have to represent all kinds of different people."

"That's true," Ackerman said. He took a sip from his tumbler, almost defiant in his motion.

Antonio chuckled as he sniffed the second cigar. "Come now, Congressman. You must have understood that our friendship would come with certain expectations. I'm simply...a new constituent."

Ackerman slammed his glass down on the side table next to him. "You bastard. You targeted me."

Antonio raised his hands in a placating gesture. "Peace, Congressman, peace. You're not *that* special. I am a constituent of many of your colleagues. They seem to understand I'm simply a friend."

"Friend? You're blackmailing me."

Antonio raised the cigar he was holding. "So cursed are we, men of pleasure and excess." He gave the cigar a little wag. Then he inserted it slowly into the cigar cutter. "But always we must return to reality." He snipped the tip of the cigar, and the piece fell onto his desk. He locked eyes with Ackerman, deadly serious for a moment, then smiled. "You are welcome to come back to the island anytime. In fact, I've sent you an invite for our upcoming party. It'll be the largest event I've held in a long time. I would hate for you to miss it."

Ackerman grimaced. Antonio handed the man the cigar. Ackerman hesitated, then took it. It was like forbidden fruit. In the end, everyone wanted a bite.

Antonio lit a second match and held it to the tip of the cigar, allowing Ackerman to puff the flames into motion. Antonio waved out the match and deposited it on his ashtray, while Ackerman fell back into his chair, defeated.

Antonio gave a mock frown as he picked up his own cigar. He almost felt bad for the man. But pleasure always had a price. Antonio was simply selling his wares.

Late in the evening, long after Ackerman had come and gone, Antonio's phone received an incoming call.

It didn't ring out loud. In fact, it didn't exactly ring at all. But he received a ping on a notification app on his phone that someone was calling. The app was innocently-seeming enough. The notification would disappear in a minute, revealing that no messages had come in at all. A Silicon Valley entrepreneur named Barry Bridges had designed the thing, along with the other incredibly useful *Anono* app. But Antonio hadn't heard from the man in the last little while as he'd expected.

He walked through his estate and to the basement, locking the door behind him. The first part of his basement was like the rest of the building — white, pristine, bright — but also like most others, Antonio's basement had a dark side. He hunched over and moved through a crawlspace where pipes led to the boiler room, which jutted off the rest of the space in a little nook. He shuffled inside the room and closed the door, locking it, and noticed the air around him taking on a hauntingly isolating quality.

The room was insulated for noise, just in case.

A hidden panel behind a small table revealed an old style rotary telephone. He pulled this out and placed it on the table, sitting on a small stool as he did so.

He fingered a number, allowing the rotary to circle the phone fully before picking up the receiver.

"Clear," he said. His tone was uncharacteristically serious, and the word came out crisp and businesslike.

A woman's voice came over the other line, creeping through static. "How did it go with Ackerman?" She too had a hard voice, all-business like Antonio's.

There was only one woman in the world Antonio truly loved. He adored Maxine and her partnership. But only this woman could hold his heart.

Antonio smiled, wolfish. "He'll fold. Once he saw how the game was played..." Antonio left his statement at that. He thought he could hear the other woman through the phone smile. He liked to make her smile when he could. In their business...real smiles were rare.

"And the party?"

Antonio nodded to himself. "Arrangements have been made. I am still getting some last-minute guests with the app, but it looks like it'll be quite a crowd."

"How are you using the app without Bridges?" the woman asked, a note of concern poking through her usual confidence.

Antonio scratched an eyebrow. "I can still use it, I just...can't track everything like Bridges could. It still functions as the app," he said, realizing how weak he sounded.

There was a pause on the other end of the line. He considered apologizing, but then the woman spoke. "The Russians have him."

"The Russians?" Antonio took a long moment to blink, then composed himself. "What are the Russians doing with him?"

"Hell if I know," she said. "I've got a player on our side who didn't want us to have him."

Antonio narrowed his eyes. "Where does that leave the tech bill?"

"Dead in the water."

"That's a good thing then, right? We won't have to worry about them digging into the app. It's still ours to control."

"For now, yes." The woman sighed. "For now."

Antonio thought to himself. "And this dissenting player?" He wished he didn't have to ask. He thought he could feel the woman wince at the question.

"Working on it."

There was a lengthy pause this time. Not for the first time, Antonio wished he could ask the woman how she was doing. Have a normal conversation with her. But this was their job. This was their life.

His app pinged. Antonio checked his phone. It was Maxine, with his final appointment of the day.

"Anything else?" Antonio asked.

"No, that's it. Keep me updated. And good luck with this party. This one's a biggie."

"I know. Take care."

That was the extent of kindness he could offer with such clandestine affairs. A simple statement that would helpfully urge her on.

He tucked the phone back in its hidden panel, pushed the stool in under the short table, exited the boiler room, and hunched back through the crawlspace.

Once he got up out of the basement, Maxine was in the kitchen waiting for him.

She knew not to go into the basement. She had no idea what he did in there, but knew when it was locked he was not to be disturbed under any circumstance. It was one of the reasons he could work with her. Because she could be trusted with his odd little curiosities.

Speaking of little curiosities...

The girl was petite, but still had the telltale signs of one who'd gone through puberty. And she didn't seem shy to show it. Her midriff showed through a tight tank top and a ripped pair of jeans revealed more skin. Her hair was done up in pigtails and she blew a gum bubble as she twirled one, looking up at Antonio with...fascination? Fear? He couldn't tell.

"This is Aurora," Maxine said, taking her friend by the hand. "She's ready for you."

Antonio smiled. This was his favorite part of his day. His favorite part of his routine.

"Come," he said, gesturing to the stairs. "I want to show you something."

Maxine smiled proudly as the girl followed Antonio without question. Everyone knew their role. Everyone played their part. It made the game work. And the game was the most important thing.

He never asked how old they were. That would ruin the game.

Antonio sighed with satisfaction. He'd done a lot of work today. But like those he brought to his island, he always made sure there was pleasure. It was important to play, just as he had as a child.

Tomorrow, things might be a bit different. But not too different.

Antonio Romero was a man of routine.

Tomorrow he would wake and do it all again.

Chapter 10

"That was a really dumb idea," Mike said as John steered them out of Biscayne Bay.

The water was cleaner as they left the bay, shining under the moonlight, and reflecting shimmering mirror-like spears that danced on the waves. The water was a deep green, almost black instead of the murky brown they had swum through, the ocean air blew cool across the water...

Behind them the lights of the city twinkled in the distance, but John didn't take his eyes off the horizon. He stood at the helm of the ship, steering silently, occasionally checking something on the instruments surrounding him. He grunted something non-committal.

Mike didn't know much about boats, but he knew this one cost a pretty penny. John seemed satisfied with the controls and nothing had gone wrong with it this far. Still, it always made professionals like Mike nervous when they weren't using their own equipment — let alone equipment they didn't know anything about. He was happy to have John's expertise.

"I didn't say it was the wrong idea, or even a bad idea. Just really dumb," Mike said. He shivered, his clothing still damp from their sunken car. The wind was cold on his clothes and body, and everything stuck to him uncomfortably. "Glad it worked."

John simply nodded.

A man of few words," Mike thought. He wasn't normally one to prattle on with nervous conversation, but damn, he wished the man would talk a bit.

"They'll be sending air support. And the Coast Guard soon."

That was apparently good enough to get John talking. "I want to get outside of United States waters as soon as possible," he said.

Mike nodded. "Well, it's nice weather and at least we get to enjoy ourselves —"

"Best to get situated below soon."

Mike blinked. "Why?"

"There's going to be a storm."

Mike looked around at the sky. It wasn't completely clear, but to a land layman it didn't look as if a storm was coming. Not that he supposed that meant anything out at sea.

"How can you tell?"

John turned to look at Mike with his gray eyes, piercing the air between them. As if that was an explanation.

The sound of Marcela's feet on the stairs interrupted his thoughts. "Storm coming!" she cried, wagging her phone.

Mike found himself following Marcela back down the steps belowdecks, grumbling about navy boys and their supernatural weather senses at sea.

"My phone works!" Marcela said, shaking it in Mike's face as if he couldn't see it if it wasn't under his nose.

"Great," Mike said, pushing her arm away.

"And look!" She opened a little chest freezer at the far end of the cabin and pulled out a fancy looking bottle.

"Champagne!" She gave the bottle a twist then moved her hands to pop it open while Mike shielded himself with his hands.

The bottle burst open as the cork went wild, and foam dripped down the bottle and over her hands and onto the cabin floor.

I can't believe I'm in the field with these two lunatics, Mike thought to himself.

Still, champagne was champagne, and he accepted a glass as Marcela handed it to him. He wasn't a sommelier in any sense of the word, but even he could realize it was good stuff.

"I've set our course for now," John said once he'd descended the steps to join the others. He had that same grim stoic expression on his face that gave Mike the willies. "We're out of the bay, and I've got us pointed for the *Isla de Anticipación.* Pretty much straight on, depending how bad the storm is. If we're blown off course, we'll right it."

Marcela handed John a glass of champagne and he looked at it, bewildered before he realized he'd taken it. He gave it a sniff and sip as Mike downed his own.

"Change of plans," Mike said.

"What do you mean 'change of plans," Marcela said. "We hardly have a plan."

"Exactly," Mike continued, becoming more and more used to Marcela's quips. "I have a contact who has information we could use. Badly."

"You know a guy," Marcela asked, arching an eyebrow and looking at Mike like he just suggested they drive off another bridge. "Yeah, I know a guy," Mike replied.

"What kind of a contact?" Marcela asked, pouring herself a second — or third? — glass of champagne. John placed his own barely touched glass carefully on the table as the boat sloshed over a particularly large wave.

Mike's stomach lurched and he cleared his throat. "Ex-pat out of Mexico. Used to be a reporter...well he might still be one, I don't know what he's up to these days really. Anyway, worked for one of the big rags before falling off."

"And he has intel?" John asked, folding his arms.

Mike nodded. "Yeah. Covered tough scoops — you know, one of those guys who'd risk it all to expose the truth, yadayada. He's got info on the island, not to mention equipment we'll need." The other two didn't look convinced.

"Oh my God," Marcela said rolling her eyes. "Mike wants us to meet up with a conspiracy theorist."

"No! And look, I'm not exactly making a suggestion here."

A tense silence followed.

Oh boy. Play nice with the boys and girls Mike. Play nice.

"You're taking point." John said. Not a question. But the way the man said it...was there a challenge there?

Marcela sipped at her champagne loudly, looking back and forth between the two men excitedly, as if she were waiting for a cage match to begin.

"You said you were in," Mike frowned.

Please no tough guy crap...I don't need that high school alpha male bullshit.

"Yeah, but you're no longer our handler," Marcela shrugged.

That struck a chord with Mike for some reason. He fought his anger down. "Well, the orders are still coming from me."

"We're still not too sure about you," Marcela snapped at him. She turned to John and cocked her head. They exchanged a silent expression with one another.

Mike sighed. "Look. We need someone in charge. Someone to call the shots. I'm the most equipped at this, I have the most experience, and I'm the most in-the-know. I'm not pretending to be a field officer here. You two take that spot. But I'm still the operations expert."

There was a long tense silence. Marcela finished her champagne. John kept his arms folded, eyes focused like a bird of prey on a tasty morsel of meat. Mike bit the inside of his cheek.

"Fine," John said.

"Fine?" Marcela asked, surprised.

"Fine," John repeated.

Mike sighed with relief. "Alright. Now that that's sorted, I'm calling my guy. Going to see if he can island hop somewhere nearby for us."

"He'll be willing to do that?" John asked.

Mike smiled. "Yeah. I'm going to bait him hard."

John didn't smile back. Marcela walked over to him and gestured with her hands. "Let me see."

John didn't move for a moment, then slowly lifted his shirt. Marcela examined his bandage.

"How bad?" Mike asked.

Marcela looked over her shoulder, glancing at Mike as if she hadn't realized he was there. "Not great. We'll change them again."

"I can still operate," John said. "Just nothing fancy."

"We don't need fancy," Mike said. He pulled down his pants to examine his own leg wound. He didn't feel the urge to be shy in front of these two. Marcela didn't even make a sleazy comment, which was saying something.

"I'll stitch it up," she said. "Should've back at the hotel."

"Should've done a lot of things," Mike shrugged. "Now, let's figure out sleeping arrangements..."

This time Marcela grinned, mischievous as ever.

Chapter 11

The storm had been small enough that John didn't seem worried, but was large enough that Mike was glad to have an actual sailor aboard driving them on through. Mike had heaved over the side twice before his contact had gotten back to him. Mike had lost his phone to the Miami water, but that wasn't too much of a travesty considering he could hardly use it without being tracked. Thirty second phone calls wouldn't get him far, and they had Marcela's phone still working. Their bigger issue was coming down to cash, which was only what they carried in their wallets at this point. The hoard Mike had brought along from his personal safe in Washington would've been long confiscated by whatever authorities were cleaning up the hotel where his duffel had been woefully left behind. Change of clothes, cash, gun...God, he didn't even have a toothbrush anymore.

His contact had managed an immediate flight to Nassau, which was as good as anything was going to get in the luck department for Mike and the others. They hit the main port and tied off at a sleepy looking dock and left John to deal with any customs agents that grew suspicious. They had enough cash for bribes at least. Mike and Marcela picked up a couple of burner phones and toiletries in the time it took for Mike's ex-pat pal to travel.

Nassau was a popular place for cruises, and for good reason. The weather was hot but chipper, the streets held a diversity of shops and oozed with local culture, and pleasant pastel buildings lined the path for Mike and Marcela as they picked their way to the meet.

"Wish we could go snorkeling," Marcela said. "Wouldn't that be fun?"

Mike grunted in response.

The meet was set at a local restaurant. The kind that spilled out onto the street and boasted tables with plenty of room from one another. In other words...

Typical spy shit, thought Mike.

At least his contact wasn't a spook. No, this guy should be a piece of cake.

"Anything I need to know?" Marcela asked as she prepared to fall into a spotting position. Mike didn't care if she was in earshot or not, but needed her to be ready to spring into action if shit hit the fan. He didn't expect anything, but he also hadn't expected to be involved in a police chase through Miami either.

"Just...be calm."

"Calm?" Marcela asked.

"You know, just don't..." Mike gave a vague gesture to Marcela that wasn't helpful in the least and seemed to insult her. "Hang back, hang tight. Standard stuff. I'll indicate if I need you."

"Yes sir," Marcela said. Mike expected her to give a mock salute, but she simply moved off to buy a scratch ticket from a convenience stand. The thing even had a thatched roof for tourists to ogle at.

Mike was glad he didn't have to sit and wait for his contact. The guy must've been eager.

CUBAN CONSPIRACY

Edward Robbie, known to most as 'Ted' or 'Teddy' was a plump middle-aged man who looked to be struggling with, well, everything. His sandy-blonde hair was a mess of grease plastered across his forehead and scalp in a pathetic attempt at a combover. His button-up shirt was rumpled and was an off-white on what should've been an otherwise pleasant island shirt. His patchy facial hair put his five-o'-clock shadow closer to eight, and his beady eyes swiveled nervously as his hands played invisible drums on his lap.

Oh boy, Mike thought to himself. Hopefully this wasn't a mistake. Mike didn't actually know how far off the deep end this guy was. It's not as if they were old friends or anything...

Teddy looked over his shoulder just in time to see Mike approaching. At first the guy didn't seem to notice Mike, but then he did a double-take. His eyes grew wide.

"You! I know you!" he was shaking his head, either in disbelief or trying to remember where he'd seen Mike before.

"You know, I don't get that often," Mike murmured, squeezing into the chair across from Teddy. "Hey Ted."

"Shit! Are you kidding me?" Teddy was standing up and raising his voice.

Because that's just what a subtle meeting needed.

"Oh, sit down and shut up Teddy."

Teddy gave Mike a sour look, then looked around, as if trying to figure out where he'd run to. He eventually sighed and slowly sat back down, his face clouded with disgust.

"You bastard," Teddy said. "You lied to me."

"Yeah I might've said I was someone else so you'd actually come out here. I didn't think you'd come if you knew it was me."

"You got that right." Teddy took a swig from a tumbler on the table, which had a couple of ice cubes and some sloshing clear liquid.

Edward Robbie had had quite the career. A reporter working for some of the biggest print and television news media around, he was known for going the extra mile and finding the truth on sticky subjects, especially ones involving 'American imperialism.'

He'd become infamous in Latin American coverage. Unfortunately, Mike's post at the time had been a counter-intelligence position under the Latin American desk. It wasn't long before Mike had picked up on Edward Robbie and followed his movements. And it wasn't long before Edward Robbie made a mistake. After a leak revealed some particularly sensitive documents regarding American interference in Nicaraguan elections, Edward pounced on the opportunity, loudly denouncing CIA interference in foreign affairs and spreading the documents far and wide. While the CIA played damage control, Mike was promptly tasked with destroying the reporter's career as the only appropriate response.

Mike wasn't proud of the information he'd used after digging deep to discredit Edward, but really, who picked an information fight with the CIA?

"What do you want? You here to arrest me again? Make my life a living hell? Don't have much left for you to destroy I'm afraid."

"Calm down Teddy, I don't want any of that. That's not why I'm here."

"Doubtful."

Mike resisted the urge to roll his eyes. "Right, well here's the thing. I need anything you've got on *Isla de Anticipación.*"

Teddy's eyebrows rose for a moment but he was quick to return to neutral, as if the words hadn't piqued his interest. "And why would I be interested in helping you with anything?"

Mike narrowed his eyes.

Teddy laughed and took another swig from his glass before flagging the waiter. "I'm all washed up. You made sure of that."

Mike nodded. "I did. I'm good at my job. But this isn't a threat, Ted. This is an opportunity."

Teddy snorted. "Opportunity? My ass." He downed his drink and stood up to go.

Mike resisted the urge to grab the man by the shoulders and pull him back into his seat. Instead, he used the one thing Teddy couldn't resist.

"We're going after Antonio Romero."

Teddy turned around, eyes widening. He hovered over the table, idly picking up a toothpick from a little dish in the center. He stuck the piece in his mouth and chewed thoughtfully.

"You're not going to pin Romero," he said finally.

"I said what I said."

"No, I know that's what you're saying," Teddy said, finally swinging back into his seat and leaning in to speak. "I'm saying you won't be able to get the guy."

"And why's that?" asked Mike, resisting the urge to grin. He knew Teddy would rise to the bait.

"Because...because the guy has fucking everything! He's rich out the wazoo with properties in Latin America, Caribbean, and Stateside. He's got some of the most powerful friends in the world — we're talking ex-presidents and the like, billionaires, socialites...he's pals with a member of the British royal family for Christ's sake! And hell, that makes him impossible to touch."

"Uh huh, I've heard all that before."

"Then you should understand why you can't touch him."

"You tried to take him down before," Mike said. It had been in Teddy's rap sheet when Mike had worked against the man.

"Yeah. Didn't go well. The man's goons nearly washed me up before you did. One of my accounts was frozen and a car parked outside my place for two weeks. Oh wait," Teddy rubbed a temple for dramatic effect. "That was you people. Hard to keep track these days. We done here?"

Mike grimaced. "I'm serious Teddy. The guy's as good as dead."

"And why's that? Did you guys have a falling out?"

"What's that supposed to mean?"

Teddy gave a smirk. "I've thought that guy was a CIA spy for years. He's not?"

Mike wavered for a moment. Teddy wasn't a friend, and he wasn't about to treat him like one. But he was an asset. An asset who would resist. It'd take a little give and take to get what Mike needed. He knew that. Mike wasn't so sure he should be sharing any of his intel with the guy. Then again, so what if he did? He'd already gone rogue, and Mike didn't give two shits if the scandal in the CIA went public

106

at this point. And who'd believe it from someone like Teddy nowadays anyway?

"Not that I know of," Mike said truthfully. "We've got some indicators that say he's Cuban intelligence."

"Cuban intelligence?" Teddy asked, interest finally piqued again, his eyebrows shooting up in wonder.

Mike raised his hands as if to calm the man. "Or at least working for them, yeah."

"And the spooks want a shooting war with G2?"

Mike recognized the slang for Cuban intelligence. He was impressed — Teddy knew his stuff. "Not exactly official."

"Oh," Teddy said simply. He was losing track of the conversation.

Mike wanted to keep him teetering. "Just so happened he pissed off the wrong guy."

"That you?"

Mike's eyes grew cold. "Someone worse."

"Jesus," Teddy said. Then he laughed. "And you thought it best to talk about your little clandestine operation with a loud mouth reporter? You want this off-the-record? Ha!"

"No," Mike said. "I have something better in mind."

Teddy cocked his head as Mike stared him down. He still wasn't sure if this was the best idea.

"Well? I'm waiting." Teddy rolled his eyes.

Mike ignored him. "The stuff we have is enough to redeem your reputation twofold. We already have evidence the CIA would go nuts for."

"You want a fall guy."

"You're a journalist. You're already a fall guy."

Teddy snorted at that.

Mike continued. "If you give me what I need, I'll give it back to you on a silver platter. You can break the scoop of what we find. Do whatever you want with the info, I don't care."

Teddy blinked. Then his eyes went wide with realization. "You're giving me an all-access pass."

Mike grinned, wolfish. "*If* you give me what I want."

"Holy shit," Teddy said, eyes still threatening to bulge out their sockets. "I can't tell if you're trying to screw me, but for that it might even be worth the chance."

"Did you bring what I asked for?"

Teddy nodded slowly, bending down to reach into a bag. Mike looked over to see Marcela drift closer. Someone reaching down into a bag was usually a concerning move. Mike shook his head subtly, letting her know he was fine.

Teddy pulled out a file folder and handed it over. Mike opened it up and pulled out the first item — a folded sheet of paper, which he expanded and flattened against the table. There was an aerial photograph paperclipped to another sheet of paper, and then a thin stapled document, making a neat stack at the bottom of the folder.

"Map of the island," Teddy said, tapping the first page Mike had unfolded. "You wouldn't be able to find this anywhere, trust me on that."

"Thought the island was private."

Teddy grinned mischievously.

"Nice work Teddy," Mike said, examining the map. "Now tell me what I'm looking at."

"I've marked it up as best I can. But you can compare everything with that photo. Aerial drone picture I managed to get. With security as tight as it is around that bastard, trust me, it was a feat."

Mike grunted, eyeing the map and photograph. "This looks like a landing strip."

"It is. Private jets from around the world. Mostly U.S. though."

Mike grunted again. "I see two properties...what the fuck is this?" He pointed to a strange little building with a domed roof.

Teddy nodded. "Yeah, no one on my end is sure either. Some sort of temple? There are a lot of conspiracy theories surrounding that one. But this is the main property."

"And this?" Mike tapped the other large building.

"Secondary building. I'm assuming that's where he puts up guests or something? Kind of like a private hotel."

"Weird."

"Oh, everything's weird with this guy. You know he's a pedophile, right?"

"What?" Mike asked, a little louder than he meant to.

"Yeah. The guy's fucked."

"Convicted?"

"As if that means anything. Like I said, powerful friends, lots of money. Lawyers shut a lot of people up."

"Looking forward to bagging this sad sack of shit. What else is here?"

Teddy pulled out the next paper, beaming with pride. "Floor plan. I know, I know, it's only the one building. But it's something."

Mike wiped his hand across his stubbled chin in frustration. He realized he hadn't shaved in a while. He needed a shower too. "Alright, fine. And this?" Mike gave the stack of papers a riffle with his finger.

"The crown jewel of the lot," Teddy said, a genuine smile touching his face. He looked like he was about to cry. "Flight manifests."

"Flight manifests?"

"Everyone who's visited the island in the last seven years. I tried to go further back, but you take a look at the names on here and you'll get a good picture. If the guy's really a spy for the Cubans, he's connected to people you really wouldn't want the Cubans cozying up to."

"And, what? The guy just flatters them? Pays for campaigns? General schmoozing?"

"As far as anyone knows. But listen — the island has disgusting security. We're talking armed guards. Patrol boats. People are patted down when they arrive. This isn't just some rich boy's fantasy island, it's a fortress."

Mike frowned. He wondered what level of security they were talking in CIA terms. Civilians thought a couple of bodyguards was security.

"Can you give me accurate numbers on that?"

"Nope."

"Nice."

Mike closed the file folder. He'd go through it again with a fine-toothed comb and make sure the others had all the intel as well. He wanted to make sure everyone was on the same page.

"Equipment?"

Teddy passed over a plastic grocery bag and Mike counted out some bills from his wallet.

"Laptop's cheap but it works," Teddy said. "The listening stuff isn't fancy but it's served me well. I'd like it back."

"We done here?" Mike asked. He couldn't say he was disappointed, but he wasn't sure if this was enough. It didn't matter. It'd have to be.

Teddy nodded, and Mike stood, pushing in his seat.

"I'll give you what I can. Take care Teddy."

Teddy nodded, giving Mike a dark look. "You too, asshole."

Mike grunted, tucked the folder into the plastic bag and put his shades back on. Marcela would fall in behind him discreetly, moments later.

They had an opportunity to blow the whole thing wide open. They'd been running for the last little while but now...

Now they'd strike back.

Chapter 12

Isla de Anticipación, or *Anticipation Island* was a place shrouded in secrecy. It helped that it was tucked away in the Sabana-Camagüey Archipelago off the north-central coast of Cuba. When people thought of Cuba, they thought of the main big island in the Caribbean — that long curved strip off of Florida. The island responsible for the Cuban Missile Crisis and a last bastion for communism in the world.

But few considered that Cuba was actually made up of *hundreds* of islands and cays, many situated in archipelagos in different regions of the main island. *Isla de Anticipación* was one of such islands, and Antonio Romero enjoyed the anonymity.

His island — because the entire island belonged to him — was his refuge. His escape. His *home.* It was where he could get away from America and be reminded of his native culture. And when he was alone on the island and he had it all to himself, he could forget about business and meetings and even money. He could come here, and be himself. And he loved himself, just as he loved his island.

It was a protected environmental sanctuary as much as it sported his buildings. With much untouched nature, he'd been able to garner money and support from various environmental initiatives. There were gorgeous white-sand beaches and precious coral reefs surrounding its jungles. Palm trees grew freely, in and out of the more developed areas, while mangroves dotted the swamps and edges of the island, their tendrils wandering into the water like a series of tentacles guarding the border. The only problem with untamed nature, of course, were its pests. Mosquitos and 'no-see-ums,' or sandflies, named for being pesky unseen creatures that snuck up on their prey, still prowled through the air, especially in the damp evenings, thirsty for blood.

When Antonio had first purchased the island and began his designs, he had set out to dominate the island. It was virgin territory, and he intended to claim it wholly as his own. His endeavor quickly became a struggle with clearing jungle and flattening rock and shipping in supplies; he nearly gave up on the entire project. But through his frustrations he learned not to move against the island, seeing it as an enemy, but instead working with the island.

Antonio sipped his *mojito* as he walked leisurely past his hotel and around the main building, through its arches and onto the walkway. In many ways the island and its property was reminiscent of the *Isla de Rosario*, where Pablo Escobar had built his own villa. Located off the coast of Colombia , Escobar had built an expensive getaway villa, and the island was still full of mystery so many years after his death. While Antonio Romero didn't move drugs, he was very *very* rich, fairly famous, and needed his privacy, and in those ways he could relate to the man.

Pablo Escobar's villa had been an architectural marvel — it still was, although now in decay. And Antonio had made sure to meticulously design his own buildings with his own architects and builders to be an alluring escape for himself, and from wherever his visitors might be coming from.

The only way onto the island was by sea and of course, by air, and Antonio had a pair of speedboats patrolling the waters around the island to make sure tourists or nosy reporters were chased off. Even if they made it to the island, he had plenty of armed security to deal with anything short of an invasion. Not that there would be an attack on his island. The security was more for posturing.

Mostly.

He remembered the police raid that had occurred at his Florida estate. They had come in with a warrant they'd been working to acquire for years, and even Antonio had to admit it was only a matter of time. His taste in young women — too young, according to arbitrary laws that seemed distant reminders more than anything else — had finally garnered enough attention that he was arrested and charged.

Not that the charges had lasted. Money had a way of making problems go away.

Antonio's lawyers had done well. He had been held in a Florida prison while the courts figured out what to do with him. And being 'imprisoned,' in that particular instance turned out to be pretty cushy. He was in a private wing with proper bed and television, although the latter didn't matter because he wouldn't be watching much TV. Antonio was required to check in the prison at eight p.m. and was required to stay there for twelve hours, until temporary release each day at eight a.m.. During daytime hours, Antonio was on work release. Prison staff had even ended up on his payroll for all the trouble.

That had been the extent of things.

CUBAN CONSPIRACY

It was the event that first brought him into the news. A blunder by any understanding of the incident, and the Intelligence Directorate had reamed him out, threatening to terminate his contract. It had been a rough patch. But that was behind him now.

He walked past a mural of Che Guevara. Not the famous image that had become so commercialized on the shirts of capitalists all over the globe, but a unique and sentimental painting commissioned by a private artist, who had similar tastes to Antonio. He took a moment to stand there, considering the mural, its blood red and pitch-black paint a stark contrast to the light pastels and creamy whites of most of the rest of the villa. He always found something new in a piece of art every time he examined it. If not something physical in the piece itself, then a new feeling evoked within himself. That was the beauty of art after all, and what it was made for.

He didn't know what he felt this time. Pride for the Argentine Marxist, doctor and a major figure in the Cuban revolution? Despair? For a failed effort from nothing but a butcher's hand? He couldn't decide. He never could. It wasn't about making a firm decision, it was about the experience. He didn't have a mural of Che Guevara because he loved the man. He had it as a reminder. To remind him of the past, and a different time.

His historical musings subsided and he settled on their mixture, reminding himself that people are hypocritical by nature, and that hypocrisy was to be embraced instead of shunned.

Antonio smiled. He could relate to that.

He enjoyed being able to relate to so many that came before him. He was sure those in the future would relate to him as well. That was why he threw such lavish parties. Those who could relate, came.

It was all about consolidation. Of people. Of power. Of pleasure.

Anticipation. It was the greatest part of any climax — sexual or otherwise. That beautiful tension of waiting, lusting, salivating for that final enticing moment and then...ah, perfection, cathartic release, beautiful satisfaction.

Just as he'd learned to work with his island, he had done the same with his lusts. They weren't something to fight against. They were something to embrace. To expand upon, even. And he carried the same philosophy into his business. Certainly, there would be resistance with individuals like Congressman Ackerman, as there always had been. But more and more, the Americans were learning to see things his way. Why not embrace such pleasures that Antonio could provide? They were too much for one man to hoard after all.

Antonio sighed as he wound his way through some of his jungle and began to reach the edge of a swampy patch of ground. The swamp was ugly, and his mind thought of the social dance he'd have to perform at this party.

He eyed that water and the corners of his mouth twitched and his lips peeled into a self-assured smile. A pair of bubbles rose and popped from the murky depths below, as if on cue.

He didn't have to worry about any nasty surprises from others.

CUBAN CONSPIRACY

He was the one that had nasty surprises for them.

Chapter 13

When Marcela and Mike had returned to the boat, John was waiting for them, eyeing them with an intensity Mike would normally have taken as cold fury but was now beginning to understand as John's resting face. He was getting used to it.

The boat was gassed up, and at Mike's questioning John shortly replied that he'd 'acquired' fuel. Mike decided it wasn't worth asking questions about that sort of thing.

They pulled out of Nassau without hassle from the authorities, somewhat to Mike's surprise, and were soon back on the tropical sea. John had opted to head south and dip around the cape of the Bahamas instead of looping around the north, and Mike and Marcela had agreed wordlessly. Keeping out of range of American boat patrols from Miami searching for them was in everyone's best interest.

John set their course while Mike flopped down in a chair and flipped through the papers Teddy had given him. He examined them with a furrowed brow, eventually blowing out air and tossing them on the galley table. He looked up to see Marcela similarly focused on the laptop which they'd managed to hook up to the boat's satellite internet. She looked up, noticing him staring at her and shrugged.

"Barry's *Anono* app." Her tone was smug as she shook her phone, and for some reason it irked Mike. "It's fun."

Mike looked out the porthole and watched the waves rise and fall in rhythm to the boat. He regretted it immediately and looked away. He was restless.

"What was Cuban intelligence grilling Bridges about?"

"What do you mean?'

"What did they want from him?"

"Oh I —"

"They probably planned to kill me," John said, interrupting the conversation as he stepped down into the galley to join the others. "They let a few things slip because of that." He leaned against a wall and looked thoughtfully at Mike. "It sounded like a control issue. Romero wanted to cut Barry out. Maybe keep him on as a techie to continue developing or fixing things, but Romero wanted full access."

Mike folded his arms and rocked back on his chair. "Okay, what does that mean?"

"It means I have things like the full attendance list, and I can even manipulate that," Marcela said, not looking up from the laptop, apparently doing just that. "We have full access, but I don't want to mess around too much or they might get wind that someone else is digging around."

"They can kick you out?"

Marcela nodded.

"What else do we get?"

Marcela grinned, a vicious venom lying subtly behind her exposed teeth. "I can see everything. I have a complete list of all the usernames using the app, their credit card information, addresses, *todo eso*." *All of it*.

"Can you tell who Romero is working with?"

This time, she frowned. "It's an app, Michael. It doesn't tell me who the bad guys are."

Mike scowled. "Mike."

Marcela blinked like she hadn't heard him.

"We have the identities of the people using the app and all their information," John said, thinking aloud. "We need to comb the chat feature."

"That's what I've been doing," Marcela said.

"I thought the chat makes people anonymous," Mike said.

John and Marcela both began to explain, but John deferred to Marcela. "With behind-the-scenes access, I can see past the anonymity feature."

"Ah," Mike said, leaning back in his chair. "That's what Romero wanted."

"Insurance," John said. "Or blackmail."

"What are the chats saying?" Mike asked. Then he clutched his stomach as a wave of nausea hit him. The boat swayed and Marcela took a moment to wait before answering as she and Mike struggled to right themselves. John continued to lean against the kitchenette counter, unperturbed.

"I have plenty of messages with Romero asking different individuals to meet, whether on or off the island. But most of the content is just that — setting up meets or that sort of thing. He doesn't talk much *negocio* through the app." *Business.* "Well..." she looked up as if she were considering something on the edge of her thoughts. "Let me read you a recent chat."

Mike and John waited as she scrolled through the app's data.

"Yes, okay here we go. This is a chat between Antonio Romero and Congressman Ackerman."

"Ackerman..." Mike mused, thinking to himself.

Marcela waved her hand at him. "Shush. Okay, Romero says '*Congressman, looking forward to our meeting.*' Previously he had set up a meeting with the Congressman Ackerman, and Ackerman says he's looking forward to it too. Hours later, a new chat says '*you bastard. I'll have your head for this.*'" Marcela looked to the others, grinning as if she'd just divulged the greatest gossip of the century.

"The tech bill," Mike said. "Ackerman was voting on it."

"Romero bought his vote," John said.

"He threatened his vote," Mike corrected.

John nodded.

She drooped when neither Mike or John reacted, but sighed, continuing. "The next big thing is this party Romero is hosting on the island. He's sent out invites and people seem really excited about it."

"When is it?" Mike asked.

"Tonight," Marcela said.

Mike scoffed. "Just our luck. We'll have to wait until everything calms down before we can perform our reconnaissance."

"No," John said.

Marcela and Mike both turned to him. "It'll be easier to take a look around while all his security is focused on one location."

Mike raised an eyebrow. The man had a point. "And do you think it'll be easier to gather information while everyone is having a good time too?"

John didn't say anything.

"Actually," Marcela said, but she didn't finish her statement. She left the galley, moving into the adjacent bedroom while John and Mike exchanged confused glances with one another. When she came back, she was holding a sparkling white outfit. She draped it on her chair and looked at it lovingly. "While I was snooping around earlier I found just the thing for this sort of occasion."

Mike coughed. "You mean —"

"I can put myself into the system," Marcela said, gazing at the laptop and drumming her fingers on the keys with her nails. "And attend the grand ball."

Chapter 14

The anger within Juan Puentes burned like a fire.

He was *don* Juan, head of the Puentes cartel, one of the largest and most powerful drug empires in Latin America, raking in cash by sending cocaine to Miami and trafficking persons to whoever had the money. He had earned his position, first enduring the murder of his father Sandor — the mastermind behind the cartel's formation — at the hands of his uncle, Pablo. Then he had reclaimed his birthright from Pablo in a brutal firefight that pitted their loyal soldiers against one another. After the dust settled, only Juan remained, orphaned by both his parents. Two more of the dead alongside his uncle and half of his men. He was left to rebuild an empire in his own image, even as the previous one continued to churn onward.

He adjusted his seat and lifted the window shade. He stared out to see white mist streaking by on his private plane's wing. He was on edge. He didn't particularly like flying; he'd recently had a traumatic experience involving air travel, and didn't care to relive any part of it.

Even so, his mind kept replaying the dramatic events that had shaken him a few days ago.

The ocean had roiled close below the helicopter as he attempted to gun down his enemies off the coast of Nicaragua. A missile had erupted from the water without warning and sped towards him, certain death approaching in an inevitable explosion of fiery doom.

His pilot had panicked, but to his credit, he hadn't frozen as Juan had, though he was ashamed to admit it. The pilot's immediate reaction tore a new path away from the missile, the abrupt change of course nearly throwing Juan from the open window as he grabbed hold of a handle and held on for dear life.

Juan watched the missile disappear into the darkness of the storm like a star slowly fading into the vastness of space. He had stood wide-eyed like an idiot child, breathing hard and sharp, almost painfully, when suddenly the world outside of the helicopter began to spin around them. The pilot slumped awkwardly in his seat, either shot or unconscious. Juan forced himself to relinquish his white-knuckled grasp of the handle he'd been painfully gripping. As the helicopter continued to spiral through the storm Juan clambered to the front of the rapidly plummeting aircraft, sliding awkwardly into the co-pilot's seat,

He hardly knew how to fly a helicopter, let alone one caught in the middle of a hurricane. He pulled the limp pilot from the controls and grabbed the cyclic stick. He fought with the controls, trying to remember what little training he had in the pressure of the moment. The voice of his father had come to him then, reminding him that wonders like diamonds needed pressure in order to be formed. Juan steeled himself and drove through the blinding rain and sweeping winds.

The landing had been hard.

He had been aiming for the nearby airport. He lowered the chopper to try and identify where the ground was, but once he lowered, it was suddenly before him, hundreds of feet closer than he'd expected. Panicking, and coming down too fast and too soon, he had swooped over a canopy of trees and circled back to the ocean, hoping to break his landing in the water. But he had second-guessed yet again, realizing the chance of drowning was as likely as dangerous as solid ground would be for coming down.

He had ended up splashing into the water's edge, sand flying and cushioning some of the impact. The helicopter had protested with shrieking metal, twisting and snapping as the machine bounced and somersaulted through the air before coming down hard again.

His foot had gotten twisted in the bungled landing. A sharp pain drove into his foot and ankle after his foot had slipped under the pedals. He felt a snap and saw stars as the helicopter bounced across the beach. He pulled himself out of the chopper and collapsed on the sand, water washing over his body and filling his lungs a second later. Blood soaked his shirt and was dripping into his eyes, and he eventually found a head wound he wasn't entirely sure how he'd gotten or when.

The pilot, whether alive or dead before the landing, had been crushed to a pulp where broken machinery crunched in on itself, as if a too-small metal carapace had cocooned its victim, squeezing shut in finality.

The villagers from *El Gigante* had swarmed him shortly after his crash. They had thought he was military, and it took some frantic yelling to talk them down and explain he was a Guatemalan businessman. His accent might have been the thing that saved him.

They treated his wounds warily, but with generous hospitality. He made a phone call to his people and broke bread with his hosts. A tension was in the air, and everywhere he looked villagers were shouldering AK-47s. He knew Nicaragua was embroiled in student protests, but this had the look of civil war. He wanted to get out of the country as soon as he was able, and when he requested a ride to Costa Esmeralda International Airport, the villagers had been all too eager to agree.

They had warned him no flights were going in or out of the airport but Juan assured them his private plane would have no trouble.

He limped into the airport and waited there, giving anyone a dark look if they gave him a second glance. He had no security with him. No money. No weapon. It was the first time since he could remember that he had to rely on his own resourcefulness. And he knew his greatest asset was his ability to create fear. He embraced that as he had never before, and when his private plane arrived at the airport, no one dared question what had happened as he limped across the tarmac.

His doctor was nearly shaking with fear when he told Juan that the limp would likely be permanent. He had allowed them to bind his ankle but cursed at the man when he wanted to get him a cast. A *don* struggling around on a pair of crutches? There was no way in hell he'd display such weakness.

He imagined what the previous men of the Puentes cartel would do in his place.

If his father Sandor had been injured like he had, he would make his men put rocks in one of their shoes so they were similarly uncomfortable until he healed. His uncle Pablo would have made his men carry him around in a palanquin and laughed it off.

But if Juan did either of those things...it would be seen as childish or silly. Unlike his father and uncle, he wasn't immune to the scrutiny of his men.

He felt he was constantly living in their shadows. Constantly trying to claw his way out of a pit they'd dug and dumped him into. He may be *don*, but most days he felt like a puppet, dancing to the strings pulled by the ghosts of the past patriarchs. He yearned for the day he was truly in control. Truly able to claim his place. Taste that elusive confidence of power that his father and uncle had...

"*Perdóname, señor.*"

Juan snapped his head around with a start, being pulled from his deep-seated thoughts like a weed ripped from the ground. His young assistant nearly jumped with fright, but quickly composed herself.

Lula was attractive; he knew she was from Mexico, and had failed to find the modeling work she had initially set out for. That hadn't meant she lacked the looks, it only meant she didn't know the right people.

Juan's people had pounced.

He hadn't hired her. Someone else had. He had people to take care of such matters.

He would normally flirt with her. Tell her what he wanted. Get what he wanted. What he deserved as *don*. She would comply.

But he found himself irritated and ashamed that he would consider shrugging off his anger with simple lusts.

"Champagne, *don*?" Lula asked, batting her big brown eyes.

He stared at her a moment, and she attempted a weak smile to match the stern scowl he so often wore. He thought of the last time he had been happy and struggled to reach a memory that might answer that question. The image of Marcela floated over his mind and his frown deepened as he shook away the thought.

"No," Juan answered sharply, trying to ground his flimsy thoughts in more forceful words. "*Un café exprés.*" Espresso.

He was unbelievably tired but didn't want to sleep. He felt like brooding, even if he wouldn't admit it to himself. He didn't want to be groggy when they landed.

Lula gave him a nod and a smile that seemed to suggest she was hiding a secret. Which, he supposed, she was.

He idly stared at her behind as she moved down the aisle in front of him, pausing to turn to a small group of girls sitting in seats on the right side of the plane. He listened to her speak to the girls. They were mostly Mayan, young enough to be in their teens, and pretty.

"Now when we get to *Isla de Anticipación* you are all going to be on your best manners," Lula said sweetly in a sing-song voice that was meant to sooth the girls.

Juan turned his head and saw them all nodding, various looks among them. Some looked nervous or even frightful, but others were simply looking tired. One or two had a flash of excitement in their eyes.

"What do we do when we get there?" Lula continued, asking a question that clearly had obvious answers they had rehearsed well in advance.

"Do what we're told," one of the girls yawned.

"Don't tell anyone what we do or hear or see," one of the nervous looking girls said.

Lula nodded, but wasn't quite satisfied. "And...?" she asked as a question.

Two of the excited looking girls sitting side by side, perhaps friends before they had boarded, grinned mischievously. "Don't tell anyone our age," they said in near unison. They giggled at each other as Lula nodded and handed out candy. One of the girls saw Juan watching and Juan glanced away.

He didn't want anything to do with them. He wouldn't normally fly out with them, but in this case, he was also expected to make an appearance on the island. Antonio Romero was having a party and everyone was invited. And when you were invited, you were expected to show up.

Juan was uncomfortable with the idea of a power rivaling his own. But at least Antonio was a business partner. He was an elusive man, and secretive, but charismatic and welcoming — at least he had been with Juan the few times he'd met the man. Juan made a lot of money with Antonio. And Juan knew that Antonio was swimming in cash as well. The man owned an *island* after all.

Juan shifted in his seat and a spike of pain shot up from his leg. He grimaced, cursing the events that had caused him such pain and embarrassment. He thought about limping around Antonio's island, about how it would impact the respect he commanded — no, *demanded* from those around him. But it wasn't truly the leg that he cared about. And to make it worse, it wasn't chance that had led him to such a fate. It had been an insidious deception from the *hijos de puta* that had been destroying his life piece by wretched piece the last while. *Motherfuckers.*

John Carpenter had been nothing but his uncle Pablo's tutor, a *gringo* hired on against Juan's better judgment. He had *known* something was wrong with the man. But Pablo hadn't listened, and it had been his downfall. The man had mysteriously disappeared after the conflict that brought Juan to power over his uncle, with conflicting reports from his men saying where the man had slunk off to. At the time it hadn't mattered; Juan had to consolidate his power, and a lowly tutor was none of his concern.

But later Juan had received an anonymous tip from a so-called DEA agent, claiming John had been DEA all along. Juan could buy the story, and flew to Nicaragua to handle the man personally.

All hell had broken loose.

Juan had been confronted by a strange Cuban man and his muscle, instead of being handed John. A vicious three-way firefight had ensued, and Juan had fought for his life, dodging bullets and returning fire down a hallway after killing the Cuban and retreating from an armed John Carpenter. But more than that, his own lover had betrayed him.

Juan's heart leapt from his chest in pain and he slammed the window shutter closed. One of the girls cried out at the sound and a few of the girls turned their heads to stare at

Juan. Juan gave a dangerous glare back until Lula snapped her fingers at them.

Marcela was the most beautiful woman Juan had ever known. He had known a few women in his life but none had been like Marcela. She had been sexy, and funny and...she was like a sparkler in the night. Always challenging him with her feisty way of talking and flirting and fucking him like her life depended on it. He had never truly loved a woman until he had met Marcela. Before her, women had never been much more than playthings. But with Marcela, he found himself listening to her, hanging onto every word she spoke, and he *cared* about what she had to say. And she listened to him too. He found himself spilling his feelings out to her like he had never before.

She had broken his heart.

More than that, she had enraged him. In a confusing turn of events, Marcela had joined John and turned her guns on Juan — she had weapons and training and seemed to know John, and as Juan had chased the bitch down in his helicopter he slowly came to realize that she had been undercover all the while. Everything had been a lie. Every word she spoke, all the time they had spent together, every kiss from her...all part of a complex sinister deceit.

He had yearned for her death...and had been thwarted in the storm.

But his return to Antigua and now the flight out to *Isla de la Anticipación* had cleared his mind like never before. He replayed these events that had pivoted his life so dramatically.

An explosion had gone off where Pablo's body had been found, the burnt husk pumped full of bullet holes in professional execution style. His mother's body had also been found there, apparently killed by the mysterious explosion that had been rigged to an apartment stove.

The rumor that John had been with Pablo at the time of his death seemed to check out. John and Marcela were behind the explosion. They were behind everything.

Including his mother's death.

"Is there anything else I can get for you, *don* Juan?" Lula asked. She spoke with a careful politeness and a smile that barely hid her fear.

There was something he wanted more than anything else. He knew it would be the only thing to satiate his boiling blood.

Revenge.

To find John and Marcela and kill them both with his bare hands.

Juan locked eyes with the attendant and felt his rage ready to burst as the sound of blood rushed in his ears. He channeled the anger into his hand and crushed the paper coffee cup he was holding. He hadn't finished drinking the espresso. Hot liquid burned his hand as he flexed his fingers.

He snarled at the woman and she bit her lip.

"*No de ti.*" *Not from you.*

Chapter 15

Marcela finished a shower and changed into the dress the British woman had left behind as they approached the *Isla de Anticipación*. It was silky smooth on her skin, with a stylish cut, leaving much of her back exposed. A thin cord swung across the shoulders and the back of her neck to support the fabric as it draped and pooled on her lower back. The front was tight, and it was a bit shorter than it was probably meant to be on Marcela because she was a fairly tall woman, *and* it wouldn't exactly be her first choice of dress but it had been in the wardrobe seemingly fated for their purposes.

After adjusting a bit, Marcela moved on to her hair and makeup, which she raided the woman's supplies for in the bedroom. The room would have been a decent size in a house let alone a yacht, and there was a helpful seat and mirror set up for her purposes. She straightened her curls and set to work on a slightly complex updo — of course it didn't look that way, and she had to start over a few times to make it look deceptively simple, but finally she had a stylish pile of hair leaning forward on her head, curling up from the back, and she let her bangs fall to either side of her face and over her ears. The makeup she kept simple, applying foundation darkened with bronzer, liner, doing her lashes, and with a wrinkled nose, applied the only apparent color of lipstick the woman had carried: blood red.

She tossed some perfume on before exiting the bedroom, hopping and skipping as she attempted to slip on some heels that didn't fit quite right. She knew she'd regret wearing them but couldn't find a better option.

She revealed herself to the men, Mike pouring over the plans Teddy had given him, and John cleaning his gun. They both looked up at the same time.

"That'll work," Mike said, looking her up and down and giving an approving nod. Marcela suppressed a shudder. Mike could give her the creeps.

She turned to John with a raised eyebrow and caught him staring at her, but she was uncertain what he was thinking. She could never be sure. He always looked stern and cold.

"You look nice," he said neutrally.

"Thank you, John," Marcela said, not wanting to make some joke out of what seemed to be a rare and genuine compliment coming from the man.

"Does it fit?" Mike asked.

Marcela snapped her head around at the man. "Excuse me?"

"Uh..."

"What's that supposed to mean?"

Mike looked to John but John was leafing through the papers from Teddy on the table in front of them.

"Er...okay. We just have to see if this works," Mike said, awkwardly, ducking his head and joining John in taking a look at their equipment on the table.

John nodded but Marcela gave Mike a sour face. It was her idea and it was a good one. Of course it would work.

Wouldn't it?

"Try this on," Mike said, holding a small device in between his fingers out for Marcela.

Marcela carefully took the device from him, holding a cupped hand underneath to catch it in case it fell, and examined it for a brief moment. It was about the size of a peanut and shaped like a mushroom. She inserted it head first, deep enough in her ear canal that it wouldn't be seen, even if someone were looking at her ear directly.

Mike passed over a pen. That would be a microphone, and Marcela looked at it dubiously.

"What?" Mike asked.

It was Cold War era technology. Microphones hidden in pens and tucked away in rival offices in both the United States and the Soviet Union had been used to some effect. The earpiece was good tech, but this...

"Where am I going to hide a pen, hm?"

"In your bra?" Mike suggested.

Marcela scoffed, taking the pen. "Even spy gadgets are sexist, expecting agents to be wearing a suit instead of a dress." Nonetheless, she shoved the thing in the middle of her bra strap, clipping it in place. "This will be uncomfortable," she said with a huff.

Mike had a small radio on the table, and tested the transceiver.

"Can you hear me?"

Mike's voice echoed loudly in Marcela's ear, duplicated in the cabin.

"Yes I can hear you, now shut up!"

Mike blinked as Marcela's voice came through the radio. They were silent a moment, eyeing the plans on the table and unnecessarily adjusting equipment.

Remember your training, Marcela thought to herself. *You've done this before. This time is no different. Why does it feel different?*

She shook the unbidden thought away. John was staring at her again.

"Ready to bring us in, John?" Mike asked, peering out a porthole window.

John wordlessly moved up the stairs and to the captain's wheel, and Marcela could feel the boat shift as he steered them towards the mysterious island.

Marcela and Mike moved to the upper deck a moment later. Marcela shielded her hair from the wind at first, but John was slowing the boat down to move ahead slowly, and the weather was calm. The sun beat down from a clear sky, and the weather would be hot if the cool air wasn't washing over them from the ocean. The air was moist, as it always was on the ocean, and Marcela felt an eagerness building in her chest.

"Where do we enter?" Marcela asked. The island was large enough that you couldn't just pull up somewhere and simply walk to the villa. It was also lush with jungle, and was mostly undeveloped, judging from their satellite pictures.

"Teddy's notes point at the south-central side of the island," Mike said, shielding his eyes from the sun.

An island in the distance grew as if emerging from the horizon, growing in size as a smear of shapes and color on the ocean.

John dipped their boat to the left, and he pointed to another landmass growing on the horizon, this one longer and larger.

"Cuba," John said.

They slipped in alongside Cuba's coast, John informing them they were entering the *Archipiélago de Sabana-Camagüey,* specifically the Sabana segment of the archipelago, where Antonio's island lay hidden amongst other private and public islands of various sizes.

Indeed, the island that Marcela had first spotted was not their destination, as it grew into view and they began to pass it, John leaving it behind. More islands arose and dotted the horizon, some dipping back out of view just as soon as Marcela had noticed them. It was some time before John pointed ahead for her to see what they had come for.

"There," he said.

The island crept into view ahead. It formed on the horizon like a dark blob of color squeezing through a sieve, the veil of ocean and sky slowly revealing a clearer picture of jungle foliage and beach as they moved forward.

John curled the boat to the right this time, in a shallow arc that cut through the water neatly and brought them to put the large island of Cuba at their backs, and the *Isla de Anticipación* straight ahead, approaching it on its south side.

"I hope I'm not late," Marcela said, fumbling with her phone and examining details on the app.

"I hope they accept you in," Mike grunted.

Marcela ignored him and adjusted her dress and moved a loose hair from between her eyes.

"Are you armed?" Mike asked.

"Of course," Marcela said. She lifted her dress and patted her inner thigh, her hand meeting the handle of the gun she had strapped to her leg. It was the only gun between the three of them.

Mike held out a hand. "Hand it over."

"¡Nunca lo haría!" Like hell I will!

Mike kept his hand out. "Teddy said they pat you down when you get there."

"You trust Teddy?" Marcela snapped.

The big man shrugged. "If you end up having to use your pistol, things will have gone sideways anyway. We'll be more concerned with getting you out than having you shoot people."

"And what about the pen in between my *tetas* hm?"

"They won't be feeling you up, but if they find that it's a pen, not a gun."

Marcela wrinkled her nose but eventually gave in to Mike's call. She unstrapped the holster and gun she had around her thigh and handed it to Mike.

"Sorry," he mumbled.

If they don't pat me down I'll be pissed, she thought to herself.

The water grew shallower and bluer and Marcela moved to the side of the boat, leaning over the railing and peering down below. She could see the bottom, coral, and tropical fish swam away from the rumble of the boat's motor.

"Beautiful," she said to herself.

"Dock's coming up," John said, and she turned back around to focus on the island.

They were drawing nearer, and a series of white shapes had come into view as they came around a bend of mangroves, their tangle of roots seeping into the ground like thirsty worms.

Looks like I'm not the only one here. Maybe I am late, Marcela thought.

A dozen yachts were floating in a small cove of shallow water and beach, while a rustic-looking dock jutted out from the sand. It was nothing more than a thin series of wooden planks stretching out into the water, offering passengers a way onto the island without beaching their boats. One of the yachts had pulled up next to it and Marcela could see a couple disembarking from their vessel, a man helping his female partner onto the dock. The man wore a light blue button up and cream shorts, while his partner wore a white dress and sunhat that nearly blew off her head. They laughed as they began to walk up the dock and to the beach where a pair of stern-looking security guards waited for them.

Marcela idly considered she might have dressed incorrectly, but she eyed a bag the couple carried with them, probably with their formal wear they'd change into once they were inside the villa.

"You ready?" John asked.

Marcela felt a pang of nerves, but she fought down the feeling in her belly. This was reconnaissance. She'd done this a hundred times. It was what she was trained for. Blend in, gather some info, enjoy the party.

"Of course I'm ready."

John carefully steered their boat up to the dock, sidling up next to the strip of planks and parking across from the ship the couple had just disembarked from. Their stolen yacht looked paltry in comparison to some of the other vessels docked near the beach. The one across from them was easily twice their ship's size, and Marcela couldn't imagine how much some of the others must cost.

"These people are rich alright," Mike muttered, voicing Marcela's thoughts.

She moved to the edge of the boat as the engine began to putter, and removed her heels before she carefully stepped onto the series of metal rungs jutting out from the side of their boat, serving as a ladder. She landed on the dock with a little hop, and opted to keep her heels off. She was beginning to regret wearing them altogether.

Although they have been useful before, she thought to herself, remembering killing one of Juan's guards with a stiletto heel.

She felt naked without a gun and turned back to the boat where Mike and John stood on the deck, eyeing the island. John looked to her. She gave a nervous smile back and opted for a little wave.

She huffed when he didn't wave back and began to walk down the dock towards the two armed security guards standing at the end. They wore tight gray t-shirts and cargo pants; both had pistols clipped to their waists and Marcela imagined there were more surprises to be found in the other pockets on their belt and pants.

Alright señor Antonio Romero, she grinned to herself. *Let us see what you are hiding.*

Chapter 16

Antonio looked over the ballroom, beaming with pride. Chandeliers dotted the ceiling which stretched far above his head, lighting the massive room. Corinthian pillars jutted out from the walls, providing a lavish but functional decoration, while also giving a sense of mystery as private conversations drifted between the columns. Long white-clothed tables ran in its center, piled lavishly with food.

A pig had been brought to the island and set on a spit roast, and the chefs had gotten to work. There was plenty of chicken as well, and seafood — full Cuban lobsters sat piled high on a massive platter near the center of the hall. Antonio had splurged for the Wagyu beef and imported a hundred pounds of the marbled meat, as well as *Dom Pérignon* champagne. But Antonio didn't ever want to lose his roots, so made sure there was good Cuban fare as well. The expected *sándwiches cubanos* made the rounds; the hard bread crusted ham, roast pork, and cheese, with mustard oozing out and pickle poking through the edges. *Tamales cubanos* and fried bananas followed on server's plates as they danced around the hall, generously offering their fare to guests. A different rice dish sat on each table, including *arroz y frijoles negros, arroz moros y cristianos,* and *picadillo a la habanera.* He had argued with the chefs about providing *arroz con huevo frito,* a simple rice and egg dish that he had survived on when his poor grandparents had first taken him and his sister in, but appearances had to be kept up, and

Antonio had relented. He watched as some guests sniffed their noses up when they saw *ropa vieja* or 'old clothes,' a fantastic meat dish that looked unappetizing to some, but Antonio knew those who would reach past their culinary prejudices would be richly rewarded. He flagged a server walking by with his favorite — *chicharrones* — and placed them on a plate and ate them with his fingers.

"Happy?" Maxine asked, slipping an arm between his own and giving him a wry smile.

"Almost."

But even as his eyes drifted over all of this bounty and his taste buds enveloped with flavor from the pork fat, his eyes landed on the greatest feast of all.

A gorgeous Mayan woman in a white dress was nibbling off a small plate held in her delicate hands. He had never seen her before. And Antonio could *feel* her fingers in his mouth as he licked grease off the tips of his own.

"Ah," Maxine said, eyes raised. She was impressed too.

He grinned to himself. He would have her.

But he forced himself to wait. Even as he watched the woman with hungry eyes, and even as she reciprocated by giving him furtive glances, Antonio wanted the hunt to last. Besides, he had as much business as pleasure to attend to, discussing future machinations with politicians, schmoozing with PAG officers that thought they were the ones playing him, and delicate situations like Ackerman needed to be coaxed into submission. He made his rounds, played the host, and made sure everyone was satisfied. And each time he grinned at this enchanting woman, and each time, her eyes darted away with a smile or a pout.

CUBAN CONSPIRACY

Night fell upon the party swiftly, but the warmth of Caribbean dusk just encouraged the merrymakers. Cuban cigars and rum were brought out by impeccably dressed staff, and once everyone seemed satisfied, Antonio clapped his hands and quieted the crowd.

"And now for something very special, for those who would like to participate," Antonio's honeyed voice carried through the warm night air to his expansive room of guests. There were just over a hundred of them. "Follow me."

Those who had been to Antonio's parties before knew what to expect. Many did not. Antonio grinned in anticipation.

***

Juan's plane touched down on the runway next to a series of other private planes. He exited once the door had been opened and ladder extended, fixing his suit jacket and adjusting his belt. His pistol sat tight and hidden in the back of his waistband, a constant comfort and assurance. He didn't like being on someone else's territory. But he understood the importance of connections and making appearances, just as his father Sandor had. Juan wasn't supposed to be armed; Antonio's island was notorious for its security and promise of safety to others, but Juan found that there were some rules that needed blatant breaking in order to assert dominance. Otherwise one would always be cowed before his partners and rivals.

You are a don, he thought he could hear his father say to him. *Do not forget that. And do not let others forget that either.*

So when he got off the plane and Antonio's guards patted him down, and they found the gun he was harboring, Juan stuck his chin out and glared at the men.

"If there is a problem, Antonio can deal with it himself, like a man."

The guards frowned.

"Let's go girls," Lula said, herding the girls off the plane and onto the runway. "We're going with *don* Juan now."

Juan looked over the girls. Some were yawning or wiping away confused tears, but most looked around in awe at the island. It was incredible, he had to admit. The lights were lit amidst the palm trees as they swayed in the calm tropical breeze, their warm glow granting the island a sense of mystery. Strong pillars held up white archways and red clay-tiled roofs, while modern-tiled pathways speckled the island's manicured grounds, before fading away into the dark primal jungles that surrounded them.

The one guard looked as if he were about to say something, but moved away instead and pulled out his cell phone.

"What are you doing?" the other guard asked, stepping away and trying to get out of earshot of Juan. Juan could still hear them anyway.

"He has a gun."

"He's a drug lord, of course he has a gun."

"Antonio says no guns."

"Antonio is a little fucking busy to be taking phone calls right now." The guard with the phone put it away but almost looked to be pouting. "Look I'll talk to him about it but without this guy Antonio doesn't get his girls, and what do you think he'll be more pissed about?"

The guard nodded then gestured to Juan.

"Welcome to *Isla de Anticipación, señor.*"

"It's *don*," Juan said. He pushed past the guards and walked up the entryway, palm trees and tiki torches lining the left and right of his stride, their light suddenly ominous in his presence.

***

The crowd of guests carried their drinks and cigars with them as they made their way down the long walkway leaving the main hall and property. The conversations and laughter that had previously overflowed from the hall had diminished; silence overtook them as they followed their host out into the night. A wind blew through the palm trees overhead and a light smattering of rain fell through the humidity. The entire walkway was lined with lit torches, and wound through a small patch of jungle before sloping up a short hill.

Guests who hadn't seen the temple before gawked when their eyes drew upon it.

It was striped black and red with a small bronze dome capping the cube-like structure. It wasn't large, but there was an elusive strangeness to the building that many couldn't quite put their finger on. If there were any remaining drunken giggles or friendly banter among guests before, everything was silent now. The only sound was the rush of wind through the foliage and crashing of waves from the coast.

A small group of Cubans holding drums and shakers greeted Antonio with hugs and kissed cheeks. The *babalawo* held a cage with a rooster inside. Some of the guests eyed the cage warily, but the Cubans paid their nerves no mind. They beckoned to them with open arms and waved them inside as Antonio pushed open the two doors with a heave.

The drummers immediately set up position around the small benches that surrounded the space. Maxine began to light the candles that provided the only illumination. Guests found themselves handed drinks of rum and lit cigars if they didn't already have something in their hands. In most cases they were given these even if their hands were already full.

"Maybe some of you have heard of *Santería*," Antonio began, beginning loud then drawing his voice inward, to a low conversational level. The guests shuffled onto benches and hung about the walls, while some were given drums and shakers. Antonio beamed when he saw the mysterious woman he'd been making eyes at had followed. She smiled when he winked at her. "*Santería* is a Cuban religion, but most of us prefer another term, such as *Regla de Ocha or Lucumí,* because *Santería* refers to the Catholic saints we had to hide our *oricha* under. Many slaves from West African Yoruba tribes were brought here to Cuba, and although practices change, it lives on. I invite you all tonight to sing and dance with us *creyentes* — believers — as we reach out to the *oricha*. Maybe this seems like strange Voodoo to some of you, but please, respect, and enjoy."

CUBAN CONSPIRACY

Maxine finished lighting the candles at the small altar held at the back of the temple. *Eleguá* was represented by a head made of cement and shells dotting his eyes, nose and mouth. Owner of roads and doors, the temple itself was colored red, black, and white, in his honor to open the door between worlds — nothing could be done in either without his permission. A statue of Saint Anthony sat beside *Eleguá,* who were often associated together, as were each *oricha* with a saint. The Virgin Mary sat there, as well as Saint Christopher for safe passage.

Now they would see if a more personal relationship could be formed.

Antonio gestured to the *babalawo* and he brought out the rooster from the cage, clutching it firmly by the breast and neck. A *creyente* brought forth a knife, and as an uncomfortable murmur rose through the guests and the rooster began to burble as it sensed death, the *babalawo* cut its throat.

Antonio let out an audible sigh as the blood spilled over the *babalawo's* hands and onto the altar. He glanced at his mystery woman. She cocked her head, seeming to connect with him as well. He didn't know why, but something had happened in that instant. He narrowed his eyes, trying to figure out what was happening in the world he could not see.

With life given, the drums began to pound, shakers began to rattle, and the *creyentes* began to sing.

They would see if an *oricha* patron would manifest in an initiated *creyente.*

Marcela was used to cutting chicken throats. She remembered it vividly from her childhood, her father teaching her. She didn't flinch from the act as so many of the uncomfortable dinner guests around her were, but as she watched Antonio, she felt something heavy in the air. Something enticing. Something dangerous. Like a warning.

The atmosphere was getting to her. But she could use this.

Marcela knew if she were to get close to their target she'd have to make a move. She could wait until night fell and slip into his bed. She knew that's what he wanted. But sex wasn't enough. It was easy. That wouldn't make this elusive man spill his secrets. The man was used to sex. So she had to do something he wouldn't expect. And something she knew would drive him truly mad.

She drew her eyes wide in surprise, and planted her feet as she drove her chest forward. She stomped and convulsed, then rolled her body from hips to head. She looked at each Cuban *creyente* drumming and shaking their instruments. Some shrunk back, while others grinned in excitement. She stepped into the circle of the room as many of the island guests gasped. She looked Antonio in the eye.

He sucked on his cigar, then passed it to his female partner. He took a drink of rum from his glass and puffed his cheeks. Marcela knew what to expect next, and closed her eyes.

Antonio sprayed rum at her, and she slowly spun, raising her hands and shaking them. She rose on one foot and hopped, then switched to the other. Antonio's partner spit next. As did the *babalawo* who had slit the rooster's throat, stepping forward and offering a generous spray of alcohol.

And she felt something come over her. A feeling of descent. As if she were falling into a pit. Falling through space, gently, then vigorously, until something inside her connected with a snap in reality. She felt as if there were two of her. As if someone else had taken over. She moved, and danced, swiveling her head, suddenly grabbing Antonio by the hands and dragging him into the circle. He moved with her, his hot breath in her ear, the smell of rum thick in her nostrils.

"Oshun, is that you? Sweet and innocent, vast and powerful. Love, beauty, femininity, sensuality...they are all yours."

Marcela raised an eyebrow, approving of the *oricha* that had apparently taken hold.

Antonio grinned. *"Esta noche es nuestra oricha." This night is ours oricha*

The drums and shakers picked up their tempo. Their voices and beats grew louder. Louder than Marcela thought they could become, echoing in the tight space.

"La noche es mía," Marcela heard herself say. *The night is mine.*

Antonio laughed, and she pressed herself upon him. Many of the other guests were dancing now too, losing themselves to the music and the drink and the haze of cigar smoke that filled the temple. Marcela found her arms around Antonio, and then his partner approached, and she found her arms around her as well. Marcela kissed Antonio, tentatively, then kissed his partner. Marcela felt passion and fire in her belly, she nearly gasped at its intensity, her self-control flagging as the music rose.

What is happening?

She was so entranced, that she hardly noticed when Antonio and his partner broke off from her. She continued moving around the room, brushing past other guests she had briefly spoken with in polite conversation back at the hall. She noticed a gust of fresh air, relieving the room with an almost-audible sigh of relief from the guests, and she saw the doors had been opened. But her mind was fuzzy, even though she'd hardly been drinking, and the dark haze of the room and flickering candle flames made it hard to focus.

She heard a young girl's giggle, and she looked around, trying to find the source of the sound.

She bumped into a short girl who ran underfoot. And then another. A dozen young girls were playing with one another in the temple room even as their adult counterparts danced and drank and smoked around them. One of the girls begged for a music shaker and a *creyente* handed it over, showing her how to use the instrument properly. Another pair of girls stopped and talked to a couple. A man reached out an arm and grabbed one of the girls by the arm. She was pretty, but definitely no older than sixteen. The man moved in to kiss her and the girl seemed to accept...

Marcela stumbled out of the temple as her trance evaporated, pushing past Antonio.

"I need to get some air," she whispered, and Antonio smiled back, as if nothing was the matter.

There were others outside. Other guests talking, many puffing on cigars and sipping drinks. There was another young girl who stood next to a tall cryptocurrency millionaire she had spoken to earlier. It had been brief. But now Marcela nearly gawked at him, seeing his arm around a young girl. A cloud drew over her face. He looked at her, and she faked a quick smile, but he didn't seem to buy it, giving her a dark look then turning back to his conversation.

Marcela pulled out her clutch and leaned forward, making it look like she was looking for lipstick. She pushed the mic in her bra.

"There are girls here. Underage girls. They're for the guests."

She applied the stick to her lips then capped it, placing it back in her clutch and sighed, trying to shake away the dizzy feeling she felt.

It's part of the job. To witness evil. And to destroy it.

She took a deep breath, ready to go back to work. She would get close to this evil man, find out the information they needed, and then she, Mike, and John would take him down. It was that simple.

She finished her internal pep-talk and strode back toward the temple doors. She passed a man smoking a cigarette and felt him staring. It didn't bother her. She was used to it.

"Marcela?"

Her head whipped around involuntarily.

And she found herself staring into the deadly eyes of Juan Puentes.

Chapter 17

Marcela struck out with the heel of her palm under Juan's chin before either of them could say another word or think another thought. His head flew backwards and he stumbled, cigarette flying from his mouth as he toppled to the ground.

Then she kicked off her heels and ran.

She heard him running after her but didn't dare turn back. She had to get off the island.

She made her way towards the boat, but two men wearing army fatigues and red berets rounded her off. She was all too familiar with Juan's men, and recognized the uniforms immediately.

As well as the deadly tactical shotguns they carried.

The first shot exploded as Marcela changed direction. It went wild, spraying into the manicured lawn behind her, a hasty shot meant for speed rather than accuracy. She covered her face instinctively in case a wild pellet made for the eyes, but she still had the element of distance on her side too. A pair of guests strolling by screamed, the man raising his hands in fright and the woman diving for the safety of the grass. Marcela ignored them, swinging her head around and she saw Juan hot on her heels, pistol in his hands as he pumped his legs against the tiled walkway. They'd catch her soon enough; she was in bare feet and a dress that didn't fit.

Maldito sea ese bastardo de la CIA, she thought, knowing she was trying to distract herself from the grave seriousness of the situation that had just unfolded. *Damn that CIA bastard.*

She made for the safest place at the moment — the ballroom. If she could just move fast enough she could cut through and make her way to the boat...

"*¡Mátala!*" Juan shouted, hoarse voice clear in the empty night. *Kill her!*

But she'd have to get away in one piece first.

***

John felt like he was twiddling his thumbs waiting for Marcela to finish her reconnaissance. The night had long grown dark and Mike and John sat in the lower cabin, listening to the occasional radio reports she had made, as she was able.

But that was war. Long periods of boredom, with short instances of overwhelming action.

She had spoken about the Silicon Valley billionaires and a prince from the royal family. But hearing about the young girls that had arrived...

John had stood when Marcela had reported about the girls, ready to rush into action. But Mike had put a hand on his shoulder, pulling him back.

"Too much attention. There's nothing we can do now."

John had turned on Mike and given him a deadly glare. But John knew the other man was right. And John could see a similar cold anger burning in the other man's eyes as well.

John nodded begrudgingly, and the two continued waiting in a tense silence.

The radio crackled to life again with the words no one in intelligence ever wants to hear.

"Abort mission! Abort mission!"

"Shit," Mike said, slipping in his chair that was leaning back on two legs. He fell over with a crash and John stood from his own hunched position, grabbing the receiver and radioing Marcela.

"SITREP."

"*Mierda...*Juan is here!"

"Juan?" Mike asked when he was back on his feet. "Puentes?"

John knew as much as Mike did. He was about to radio Marcela again but she came through first.

"Get me the fuck out of here!"

"I'll get the boat started," Mike said to John, snatching the radio from his hand. "Go get Marcela."

John was up the stairs before Mike could finish. He pulled out his gun and emerged into the dark tropical air, warm and clean in his lungs. He hurried down the ship's ladder, wishing he could simply jump off the boat and into action, but he knew his still-fresh stitches wouldn't survive. He hurried down the dock as best he could, but the beating of hurried footsteps raced toward him from the jungle.

He could only make out silhouettes. If they were enemies, he could fire at them, and probably down both. But for all he knew these were civilians, and couldn't fire blindly like that. But if they *were* enemies, and armed, they'd have a clear shot at him, illuminated by the well-lit dock. He also had no cover whatsoever.

Erring on the side of caution had served him well. The careful agent was the one who made it out alive. So John backtracked, climbed the rungs and fell back into the boat, lying down and pointing his gun out forwards in front of him as Mike started the engine.

"What's wrong?" Mike asked, standing at the wheel and falling into a crouch.

John found himself thanking God that the man had training. Too many of John's missions had become difficult working with poorly trained individuals — or those who were completely lacking.

The silhouettes broke out onto the beach and light reflected onto their dark figures: armed security.

"You on the boat! Come on down, you need to talk to us!"

John passed the gun to Mike as he laid down next to him.

"What are you doing? Shoot them and let's get Marcela!"

John shook his head. "We won't win a firefight here. We don't know how many more are coming and they have the jungle to fall back on, and the night favors them. If they've already sent security, you can bet that a patrol boat is on its way."

Mike rocked his head and grunted, which John figured was the man's way of agreeing.

John dashed to the wheel and put the boat into reverse.

"Hey!" one of the security guards yelled.

John prayed that Mike didn't shoot, because as soon as he did, he knew the others would immediately shoot back. But Mike stayed his hand, stock-still, gun trained on the two men.

As John predicted, more security ran down the path.

"Stop the boat or we'll shoot!" the other security guard yelled.

The boat had reversed enough and John had finished his turn. He slid the accelerator forward and gunned it.

The boat suddenly jumped into motion, the gas hitting the engine and the motor going into overdrive. The loud drone of the engine almost blocked out the sound of gunfire.

"Down!" Mike yelled. He fired back now, and the men ducked off the beach and into the trees. Bullets thunked into the boat's hull and one pinged off the railing.

But that was the extent of the fight, as John drove them past the dock and into a curve that followed the island's sand and foliage.

"You okay?" John asked Mike, wondering if the man had been hit at all. Mike was still laying down on the deck, but now slapped a hand on the railing and struggled to hoist himself up.

"Yeah," he said, his voice shaky. John didn't imagine the man got in many gunfights, and when the bullets flew it was enough to rile anyone up and question their mortality.

"Get down below and find out where Marcela is," Mike said, as John brought the boat's speed down a bit. He didn't want to blow past the villa completely, he just needed to get away from the dock and security. "Find out where she is and if she can get out the east or north exit of the villa. If she can get to the beach we can pick her up."

John left the wheel and headed down belowdecks before Mike could finish. John was still getting over the shock that Juan Puentes of all people was not only alive, but showing up at the same island party they had decided to crash. When he and Barry had been captured by the Cubans, their interrogator had been interested in the data swiped from Isabella Puentes' laptop.

It was all connected.

Everything seemed to go deeper and everything became more integrated the more they dug. Brian's death being a setup. Sandor Puentes and his connection with the CIA. The Nicaragua mission and Barry, who ended up being an asset for both the PAG and the Cubans. Antonio and a mole in the thick of American intelligence...

These thoughts flew by his mind as he reached the radio.

He squeezed the transceiver. "Marcela?"

"A bit busy here John!" her dress rapidly brushing against the microphone told him she was running.

He felt himself tense, but he also felt vast relief that she was still alive.

Now to get her out.

"We left the dock," John said, trying to keep his words brief and clear, knowing what it was like having an annoying voice in your ear while in the middle of a firefight. "Bringing the boat around the east side of the island."

"Okay I can..."

Loud slamming sounds were heard over the receiver.

Gunshots.

"*¡Mierde!*"

"Can you —"

More loud bangs, this time closer and more rapid. "*Bastardos* have me pinned!"

"Where are you?"

There was no reply. John feared the worst. Then there was static and the sound of shuffling.

"If I only had a *maldita pistola* then I could —"

"Where are —"

"The ballroom John!" she snapped, and John could picture the exact pissed off expression she'd have on her face with that tone. "The *maldito* wide open ballroom...they already packed up most of the tables..."

John's face grew dark. "I'm coming."

He dropped the radio and headed above deck.

Mike looked up and recoiled when he saw John's expression. He opened his mouth to speak but John spoke first.

"I'm going in to get her." He held out a hand for the gun Mike had put on the dash. The man handed it over and John moved to the boat's ladder. He frowned and cursed silently.

They were moving toward the east side of the island and John had left the wheel to Mike. What he hadn't accounted for was the swampy terrain and Mike to steer their boat nearly on top of it. It was dark, and the man didn't have the same nautical and directional awareness that John had. An understandable mistake. But one that could ground them.

John didn't have time to correct the error.

"We're moving into the marsh," he said to Mike, who looked back with a confused expression.

"Oh shit." Mike turned the wheel a hundred and eighty degrees. John hoped it was enough to get out. The weeds could clog the propeller, or it might slice them apart. Either way, it was lucky they were turning around before they went any farther.

Mike looked to John. "Where should I —"

"Go to the north side of the island. Less marsh and you can get closer to land."

Mike nodded.

John moved to the edge of the boat. "And watch out for patrols."

Mike nodded again, face growing grim. He knew as well as John the risk they were both taking. The plan had gone belly-up and stakes were life and death. But John was glad to see Mike wasn't about to leave Marcela.

John would never leave a soldier behind.

It was ingrained in his training. Although so much of what he did was driven by pure logic and realistic expectation, some aspects of American training had seemingly nonsensical practices. Risk an entire squad to save one man? Americans would do it in a heartbeat. You never leave a man behind.

With the gun held above his head, John hit the ladder and stepped into the swampy waterscape.

He dropped chest deep into the marsh, cold water soaked through his clothing immediately. His feet sunk into the muddy earth below the water as he pushed through weeds and the muck, wading desperately, as hard and fast as he could, against the brutal slop that was the swamp. Time seemed to move differently for him. His pace was fast, but his legs could not comply.

The rumble of the boat's motor drifted off as John tore painstakingly toward the island, making sure not to spend too long on either foot to prevent from sinking in and getting stuck altogether. Even losing a shoe could complicate his mission.

He managed to feel out areas where the water was lower, and bars of land grew higher and more solid, trying to walk where the spiky grasses of the marshland grew thickest to provide the most support with its root structure. He was nearly at the island's jungle foliage when he heard a splash that wasn't his own.

He wasn't prepared for the crocodile that came at him.

John clenched his teeth hard and pivoted in the swampy mud as best he could, twisting his body around bringing his gun about to aim.

But the crocodile had an animal speed that John couldn't compete with and slithered back and forth in the darkness, its eyes hungry for its prey. It slapped its spiked tail and disappeared under the water, as quickly as it had appeared.

John willed himself to push his hardest against the water resistance and toward the island. He thought he felt a wave push unnaturally against him under water, and dodged as best he could, uncertain where the crocodile could be.

He was mere feet from land when the crocodile surfaced again.

It rose behind him and snapped, managing to snag a piece of John's shirt in its mouth, tugging aggressively and pulling John towards its maw. John was in the middle of his next step, and staggered, falling onto the raised portion of land. His legs dangled in the water and the crocodile fell back an inch and opened its mouth wide, slapping its tail as it thrust forward to bite at his legs.

John spun onto his back and pointed the gun in front of him, his legs scraping against the crocodile's teeth as they slipped into its mouth.

He squeezed off two rounds, sharp pops that penetrated the island air, both zipping side by side over his legs, one entering the crocodile's nose, and the other replacing one of its eyes.

The animal went limp, mouth closing slowly over John's legs. He tossed the gun onto the ground and caught the top of the long mouth before it snapped shut. He pulled the mouth open, pushed the dead animal back into the water, and took a deep breath as the big lizard rolled onto its back, exposing its white belly.

The animal couldn't have known that its prey was, instead, a hunter.

Chapter 18

Mike felt something scrape the bottom of the boat as he reversed out of the marsh. Then the propeller caught on something hidden in the quagmire. He opened the throttle but this only dug deeper into the muck, deep-rooted plants wrapping themselves around the propeller and seizing it fast. The boat continued to struggle as Mike gave it more gas, and in his frustration he nearly didn't see the single bright white light floating on the water and growing larger and in intensity as it moved toward him.

He cut the gas and heard another thrumming motor pushing through the water. As it drew closer he could quickly make out that it was a patrol boat; a large inflatable craft with a mounted spotlight pushing a small wake as it cut through the dark water. The light stood on a stand at the front, sweeping about and finally landing on Mike and his vessel.

Mike ran.

He knew he was stuck in the water, and there wasn't much hope of an escape. He considered going overboard and dashing into the swamp and following John's path, but he'd be caught easily, the patrol boat being much better suited to the marshy waters. Mike also assumed whoever was on the boat was armed. He was not.

He didn't know if the security personnel had spotted him but it didn't make much difference. It's not as if there was anywhere to hide.

Well...

Sal con las manos en alto!" a man with a thick Cuban accent called, his voice amplified with a bullhorn. He waited a moment, then called again in English. "Come out with your hands up!"

Mike ducked belowdecks and swept the room, struggling to eye through the darkness, and frantically looking for a weapon. His eyes locked on the bright red of a fire extinguisher.

He dislodged it from its secure hooks and stood beside the kitchen area, off to the side from the stairs that led belowdecks, and out of sight to someone descending.

There was a long silence, only interrupted by the sound of water sloshing against the hull and Mike's heavy panting. Then there was the sound of movement outside, a low motor hum as the patrol boat moved through the water again. Another sound followed on Mike's boat, coming from the side. He heard the metal *ting* of the rungs being climbed, and the heavy sound of boots on the upper deck.

There were two ways Mike supposed he could deal with this. He could try and talk his way out of things, which was certainly reasonable. He wasn't entirely sure what he'd say but he was sure he could spin some sort of bullshit that would at least buy them all time. But if that failed...

"John?"

The shrill sound of Marcela's voice crackling through the radio penetrated the air. Mike's heart jumped with fright before he realized he'd forgotten to silence the radio.

The man up top seemed to freeze in place also, not certain what to do at first, but then decided to follow the voice. He walked down the steps slowly, and Mike watched the shadow of a pair of arms holding a gun stretch down the bulkhead opposite him.

He was patient. He waited until the man had descended completely before attacking.

Mike swung the fire extinguisher with both hands, shoving it through the air with a force that knew this was a one-way trip.

The end slammed into the security guard's face with a crack and a gruesome wet smacking sound, the feeling of crumpling cartilage and fractured bone reverberating up the cold metal and into Mike's fingertips. He suppressed a shudder as he lost grip of his weapon, and the man fell onto the stairs, the base of his skull landing on the edge of wood. The clatter of the man's gun hitting the floor was the only remaining sound, alongside a heavy clunk following a second later as the fire extinguisher fell and rolled next to it.

Mike let out a breath and wished he could take a quick rest. But he knew he had to get the boat out of the marsh and up north for John and Marcela's escape.

The security guard's radio squawked from the floor.

"¿Has asegurado el barco?" Have you secured the boat?

Mike hesitated, wanting to reply and imitate the guard, but knowing his tone and accent would give him away immediately. That stuff only worked in movies anyhow. They'd be on him again soon if he didn't break free of the swamp...

The low drone of *another* motor in the water crept into the belly of the boat. He was so full of adrenaline the sound hardly caused any fear in him, even though more armed security was already on its way.

Do I think I could pull the same move twice?

Move the body and earn another. But he shook the thought away. The problem wasn't the security, the problem was getting the hell out of here.

Another idea came to mind as he thought about the guard's boat floating next to his own.

Stealing one boat just wasn't enough, huh?

***

"*¡Mierda!*" Marcela hissed through her teeth as another blast of shotgun pellets hammered her position. The pellets slammed into the thick stone pillar at her back and peppered the floor inches from her feet. She wanted to stick her head out to see if her attackers were flanking her or moving towards her but couldn't risk it.

She was lucky that she had moved quickly enough to duck behind one of the ornate classical-styled pillars Antonio had used to decorate and build his villa. There was little cover in the ballroom, and she wouldn't have gotten out alive if she hadn't found something safe to hide behind. The downside was that she wasn't able to move once she was pinned. Moving out from behind the pillar would take her into wide open space, and the nearest exit from the ballroom was at least fifteen feet — far too distant to make a dash for it with Juan and his men ready to gun her down at any instant.

"John!" Marcela hissed again. "Where are you?"

***

Mike swiped the gun from the dead guard and made his way up the steps and onto the upper deck. His leg still wasn't doing him any favors, and he moved with a small painful limp. The cool night air blew at him once he was up, and he realized how much he'd been sweating. There was no time to rest though. He made his way down the boat's ladder.

As he descended, he winced against the pain of his leg, buckling and swinging to the side of the boat. He slammed into the hull and the gun he'd tucked away slipped out of its hastily holstered position.

"Are you fucking kidding me?" Mike said aloud.

The gun tumbled into the water with a small splash. There was no time to contemplate the misfortune any further. He struggled back onto the ladder and made his way down onto the dead guard's security boat.

He moved to the back to start the engine, pulling the cord and hoping the thing would burst into action. But the only thing he heard was a puttering, and then a low moan.

It was still the sound of an engine. But it wasn't his.

Son of a...

Another patrol boat was speeding through the water towards him.

***

John struggled against his wet pants pulling at his legs, as his feet squelched in soaked shoes. But the discomfort was nothing compared to his will to move faster through the jungle and get to Marcela in time.

The dense foliage was dark, and he struggled through shrubs and trees, careful not to trip on roots as branches slapped at his face. The only real guide he had was a series of dim lights in the distance marking the villa and its surrounding properties. He picked his way as best he could with all his limitations, but a voice in the distance caught his attention, and he quickly fell into a crouch behind a thick trunk.

A blob of black in the distance blocked out the lights momentarily, and then it happened a second time.

Two figures.

The sound of snapping sticks and shuffling feet through the underbrush followed quickly as the silhouettes grew more distinct in John's night vision. He could barely make out any more than that. But a pair of dancing lights accompanied them, John not realizing that two of the lights he'd been following hadn't been from the villa at all. The beams from their flashlights danced off the foliage and John stayed stock-still in his crouch, hugging his tree and holding his gun at the ready.

The lights swept over his position but neither of the figures said anything. John focused on his breathing, ready to pounce into action the instant one of them made a move.

But they were off to the right of him and would pass him easily, provided he made no noise.

He didn't have time for another firefight in the dark, and definitely not one against two enemies with flashlights. They'd have him blinded in an instant and have the visual advantage.

"¿Por aquí?" he heard one of the men say. *This way?*

"Eso es lo que dijeron." the other replied. *That's what they said.*

They were probably looking for him. He waited for them to pass, counted the seconds he considered necessary until they would be out of earshot, and then broke from his position, dashing back through the island's jungle.

***

Mike had gotten the boat working and wormed his way out of the swamp, but not before the light in the distance had grown to the size of a golf ball. He cursed himself for not turning off his own. He might as well have lit a beacon and shouted "*here I am!*"

The boat puttered along out of the weeds while he wobbled over to the bow, turned off the light, and wobbled back, nearly losing his footing as the boat shook in the water. It was a small thing, more sensitive to the water surface changes. He plopped down on the stern seat, grabbed hold of the tiller, and turned up the motor's speed, swearing under his breath all the while.

He didn't have a lot of experience steering a boat; maybe he'd done it once or twice years ago when some old pals had dragged him out fishing and urged him to guide their vessel out to their hole. Back when he still had friends. He tried not to think about the sad state of his personal life. It was a shitshow. That was life.

The other boat was still gaining on him, and Mike was forced to increase speed against his will; if he went too fast, he could crash into an unseen submerged log. But if he didn't, he'd be caught, along with John and Marcela. That was the hardest part of being in operations. If he made a single mistake, it cost others as much as it cost him — often more so. It had always been that way in his line of work, and he bared his teeth into the wind and let loose a growl, knowing that no one other than the God he didn't believe in would hear.

He risked increasing his speed as he raced through the darkness.

***

"*¡Deja de disparar!*" one of Antonio's security guards was yelling from the north side of the ballroom. "Stop shooting!" he repeated in English.

Without exposing herself, Marcela was able to see the guard waving his hands at Juan's men, trying to get their attention. His body was stooped over, as if concerned that incoming fire would assault him at any moment, and he'd have to duck and cover. Marcela couldn't blame him for that.

It was also precisely the distraction needed to escape...

Another shotgun blast echoed in the ballroom, and Marcela felt the impact of the pellets through the pillar at her back. Screams and cries of panic came from others in the ballroom. Out of her limited field of view, Marcela could make out partygoers huddling behind the few remaining tables and chairs at the edges of the room, some even lying prone on the floor. One man cried while holding the body of a woman in a cream dress, now stained red with blood where she must have gotten caught in the crossfire. Another man nearby pulled himself across the floor, leaving a streak of blood in his wake from some unseen wound.

Marcela took a few calming deep breaths, uncertain of her next move.

The security guard had his hands up and was moving to where Juan and his men held their firing position. Two more security guards appeared at the north end of the ballroom where the other man had entered, pistols drawn and pointing this way and that. Marcela had no doubt they would've opened fire if it weren't for the more level-headed security guard trying to defuse things.

She could hear Juan arguing with the man, the two of them exchanging shouts, before the voice of Antonio Romero boomed over them.

"*¿Cuál es el significado de este?*" *What is the meaning of this?*

The argument continued. Marcela picked up bits and pieces of it as more and more yelling continued over one another.

"*No entiendes...*" *You don't understand...*

"*¿En mi isla?*" *On my island?*

"*Conozco a esa mujer.*" *I know that woman.*

"*¡Haré que los maten a todos!*" *I will have you all killed!*

"*¡Esa puta es una espía!*" *That whore is a spy! DEA!*

Something seemed to shift in the air. A chill went down Marcela's back. That was sure to get Antonio's attention, and maybe even his understanding.

"*¿Señorita?*" came Antonio's voice, the only one left after the flurry of words and argument.

"*¡Si salgo me disparan!*"Marcela called. Her voice caught as she spoke loud enough for them to hear on the other side of the ballroom. *If I come out they will shoot!*

"*Si no lo haces tú, entonces lo haré yo. Si no lo.*" *If you don't, so will I.*

Marcela swallowed hard, raising her hands slowly and edging out from behind the pillar.

***

The enemy boat was overtaking him.

Mike tried to push the throttle as far as he could now that he was free of the marshes, but every time he tried to push the speed he found he would start to lose control of the rudder. His tail clearly had more experience than he did and was able to go at a higher speed; the distance between them was shrinking.

The search light glanced past his boat once again as he kept the rudder as steady as he could, following the black waves and hoping the darkness would keep him hidden, or at least difficult to trace. He swore as the phantom light illuminated him and his boat for an instant, a flash that made him grit his teeth, then it swept on, struggling to center on him once again.

He had pushed farther out into the ocean but now moved closer to the island once more. He didn't want to go so far that he'd get lost. He also had no way of knowing how far he had to go to reach the north side of the island. Their previous boat at least had a compass along with its digital map. This boat was more like a dinghy.

And where the hell on the north side of the island am I supposed to dock? Mike thought to himself, growing increasingly grim with the turn of events. The island was big enough that a single cardinal direction didn't provide enough to make an exact location. He searched the dark trees crawling up off to his left, but the island simply stretched on, giving up no answers to his silent questions.

The searchlight on the previous boat swept over him again, and Mike instinctively ducked, although no incoming fire followed. The enemy boat was getting closer; the sound of its motor droned louder and louder until it seemed to synchronize in tone with his own, and the light grew more and more steady until it barely wavered, and Mike was bathed in constant light.

Oh, fuck this, he thought.

He swerved the rudder and felt the boat slip through a tall wave, gaining air and nearly flipping for the third time. He slammed back into the water with a crash and drove on, defiant against the wind blowing in his face and the spray of water that had long drenched his shirt and pants.

He turned into the island and fell back into darkness once more. He swiveled his head around briefly, and saw his tail take a hard turn, matching his own a second behind, and return to searching the water.

Enough was enough. Mike drove straight at the island and began to lower his speed.

He was going too fast.

Mike killed the motor altogether but the dark trees ahead grew in shape. There was no beach to slow to a halt on, just a raised lip of dangling roots and a mess of foliage to greet him.

He turned the boat to its side, hoping to skid the remaining twenty feet, and the boat skipped across the water, but it was still a dangerous speed. He grabbed a hold of the ropes tied into loops on either side of the boat and braced for impact.

The side of the boat slammed into the lip with such force that Mike lost his grip immediately. He flew up and over the side of the boat and onto the ground, nearly flipping in the air and crashing into a tree like he'd just been launched from a catapult. His chest collided with bark and he half-wrapped around it, spinning with a dizziness that was nauseating. Winded by the impact, his legs gave way and he collapsed to the ground.

The drone of the enemy motor slowed as it puttered to a safe spot, sidling up next to Mike's boat bouncing in the water. Mike attempted to log roll further away into the jungle, but mostly flopped around until he hit a shallow slope, leading into a short ravine. The searchlight slid over his head smoothly as the pain of his collision began to register.

His chest and ribs felt bruised but he tested his bones and didn't seem to find anything broken. But his arm was sticky and hurt like hell; running his other hand along it revealed a deep gash that he'd have to worry about sometime or other. The pain in his leg where Sara had stabbed him was excruciating.

But what else is new?

The enemy boat cut its motor and Mike could hear the man shuffling out and onto land. The swath of light from the boat continued to play above his head, but it stayed in place. A moment later a smaller, faster beam of light danced through the trees.

Of course he's got a flashlight.

And the guard was armed. Mike hugged his hill, back sliding quietly up next to a tree that had decided the slope was a good home. He peered around the trunk and watched the silhouette of the man creep slowly forward.

The guard began to do a basic sweep. The problem with being the seeker lay in that a hidden person could be anywhere, and could have gone in any direction. Picking one and following that route could lead to a mistaken route indefinitely.

But the guard knew Mike couldn't have gotten far. And indeed, he hadn't.

Mike sifted through his options. He could try and wait it out, fighting if it came to it. He'd have the element of surprise. But he wasn't sure he could win a fight, and the guard had his gun even if Mike did get the jump on him. No, unfortunately the best option was the least appealing.

Mike rose into a crouch. He waited until the sweep of the flashlight crept into the distance at the edge of the guard's patrol. The light in the distance shrunk and the crunching footsteps of the guard receded.

Mike broke cover and ran.

He was on all fours for a moment, running like a scrambling gorilla to get out of the shallow ravine, but by the time the guard was shouting Mike was in a true run, galloping over roots and rocks and crashing through low-hanging branches and vines. He kept his arms in front, protecting his face, and swung past tree trunks with his hands when he veered too close.

He heard the guard behind him and saw the sweep of the flashlight...

It glanced off him. Mike spotted the obscured dots of light ahead, indicating the villa. He used them like a compass, guiding his way through the foliage.

"¡Deténgase!" the guard barked. *Stop!*

A loud pop sounded out somewhere behind him and a sharp splitting sound came nearby.

The man was firing into the trees.

Mike huffed and puffed as he picked up speed, knowing that cardio was not his forte, but his life might very well depend on it.

***

John found himself at the edge of the villa's property; a lip of concrete jutting out over a slope of dirt and roots leading back into the dark jungle behind him. He was still hidden in between the lights of the villa surrounding the property and illuminating the night. He crept up the slope and onto the concrete bed, careful to stay in the darkness as much as possible.

Movement flickered off to his right, John was in a crouch and watched as security guards ran past twenty-five feet away. Following the sound of gunshots, no doubt.

John had heard some himself. It sounded like shotguns and pistol fire. He remembered well the weapons that Juan's men carried.

He walked along the property's wall until he found an entrance through a series of open arches. He slipped inside the open hallway. Its ceiling was high above his head, two parts meeting at a peak, and reminded him of a Greek forum. A soft pricking sound rang out off the clay tile roof. A light tropical rain had decided to accompany his steps, which was good — it was easier to make less noise that way, and he was silently thankful he avoided being caught in the jungle where he could slip in mud.

He edged along, moving from arch to arch, stopping in between gaps, pistol held at the ready. From his memory of Teddy's floor plan, John knew he was getting close to the ballroom. He continued until he reached a glass-paned door on the wall, warm yellow light pouring out and onto the outdoor hallway. He edged up to the side and crouched, grunting as the wound in his side protested the movement. He peered through the glass.

The ballroom was large and extravagant, with a taller ceiling than even the one John found himself under in the forum-like hallway. Warm lights came from chandeliers hanging from the ceiling, and ornate pillars lined the walls of the room, standing ten or fifteen feet apart from each wall and one another.

His eyes honed in on Marcela.

She was standing straight as a rod up against one of the pillars, about halfway along the wall and far from the door.

John traced a path across the room from Marcela, to see her attackers.

Juan stood there in a cream suit, accompanied by two of his personal guard, both in uniform. Each held a Remington Model 870 tac-14 shotgun at the ready; one pointed at Marcela and Juan held a silver handgun in that direction as well. The other soldier pointed his shotgun off to the north side of the ballroom where John now spotted three security guards, guns drawn and taking up positions against pillars, pointing at Juan's position in the western entranceway.

John wasn't sure how to play it. If the two groups could be distracted enough with each other that Marcela could make a break for the door...

He stood back up slowly, back against the wall, and his hand slithered out to turn the delicate glass doorknob. He twisted until the door gave way, and he gave it a soft nudge with his foot. The door popped open. He peered through again. No one had seemed to notice.

Marcela put her hands up and came out from her pillar. A security guard jogged across the ballroom over to her, while the others seemed to have found an uneasy ceasefire. John wondered if he could shoot one of them, sowing discord and making them turn on one another again. They'd relied on the tactic back in Antigua, when they manipulated Juan to turn his men against Pablo. And even in Nicaragua, when John and Barry had been captured, they managed to turn Juan against Cuban intelligence.

John watched closely where their weapons were pointed, and assessed the risk. If a stray bullet rang out, Juan or his guard might just discharge their guns on Marcela in reflex. He'd have to do something to get their attention.

He still had the element of surprise. But to save Marcela...he'd have to give it away.

***

Mike heard the gunshots ringing out from within the villa before he had reached the building proper. It was an ugly mix of shotgun blasts, pistol fire, and the rattle of an AK-47.

What the fuck did Marcela get herself into?

He checked himself. What the hell did he let *himself* get into? All of them. The mission was a clusterfuck, and what did they have to show for it?

Finding out the island is a pedophile haven for a start...

The gunfire continued. But Mike had other more pressing concerns.

"¡Oye! ¡Para ahora mismo!" Hey! Stop right now!

The guard was still at his back, sending fire his way that Mike had long ago decided weren't warning shots. Another tree made a harsh cracking sound as another bullet struck at head height, moments after Mike ran past. The guard was gaining on him.

And as Mike drew closer to the villa, the safety of the darkness around him faded with it. The lights shone around the building with a soft glow, illuminating its surrounding jungle.

Mike did his best to hug the last remaining shadows, took a deep breath, then burst forward into the light. His feet slapped onto the tiles of the property as the jungle gave way to stone. He found his way through an open-arched entrance and into a tall-ceilinged outdoor hallway.

The guard's footsteps hit tile a moment later. Mike was being outpaced and had nowhere to go.

Mike turned the corner and hugged the edge of the adjoining hall. His last hope was to trip the guard and see if he could wrestle him down.

At least I have my bodyweight to thank for that advantage, he thought to himself.

"You!"

A sharp British voice rose on the air. At first Mike thought the voice was referring to him. But there was no one in sight — they were farther away. Mike heard the rustle of a series of footsteps. He didn't peer around the corner.

"You! Did you not hear me?"

"Gun!" another stern British voice cried.

"¡Baja tu arma!" That was the guard. *Lower your gun!*

It was too late. Three shots from two different guns sounded out in rapid succession.

***

Marcela stayed close to the pillar and tried her best to place the security guard running toward her in between herself and Juan's position. She locked eyes with him. Even from across the long room she could feel the heat in that stare, the intensity making her raise her eyebrows involuntarily. She suppressed an urge to give the man a flirtatious wave. She didn't exactly want to be shot.

The security guard approached her, looking sheepish but trying to remain stoic.

"*Señorita, discúlpeme, pero por favor venga conmigo.*" *Miss, my apologies, but if you will please come with me.*

The man had his gun holstered but the holster was unclipped, ready to wield it again. It was understandable. But for Marcela it could be an opportunity...

But what could she do with so many enemies against her?

More security guards poured into the ballroom, confusion surrounding them when they saw the scene. They talked amongst one another, filling the newcomers in on the situation.

"*¿Señorita?Por aquí.*" *This way.* He gestured for her to follow him.

She complied, giving one last sweep of the room, trying to figure out how she could escape the situation. The guard turned his back for an instant...

And an explosion of glass came from the east entranceway as the door burst open and slammed into the wall.

It was John.

Relief had hardly enough time to wash over her.

Marcela reached out and yanked the guard by the collar, so hard that his head snapped back hard enough to give the man whiplash, along with a nasty red ring around the front of his neck. Not that these things would matter.

The guard stumbled back towards her and she swiped his gun out of its holster. He fell to the ground as Marcela flicked off the gun's safety.

She put a round through his chest before he had even broken his fall.

She spun back behind the pillar to avoid any incoming fire.

But none came, with all the attention on John. He sprinted into the room, firing his gun as he went, receiving panicked and surprised shots from their enemies as he grabbed cover behind a pillar along the wall, down from Marcela.

Marcela managed to further take advantage of the distraction, moving one more pillar closer to the doorway, and her eyes locked with John's.

"What took so long?" she yelled, as a shotgun blast splattered the back of her pillar and the surrounding wall in front of her.

John scowled. "Crocodile."

"Crocodile?" Marcela furrowed her brows but clearly that was a story for another time. "How are we getting out?"

"North side," John said, a series of sharp pops interrupting him. He was standing with his back against the pillar like Marcela, trying to peer around the side.

"John, that's the opposite side from us! You want us to pillar hop all the way over there?"

"To what?" John called over the gunshots. He waited for a short break in between incoming fire. "If we can get out this doorway, we can loop around the hallway and make a break through the jungle."

Marcela had no choice but to nod. There wasn't much more they could try and do anyhow.

John gave her a countdown, then peered out from his position. The floor beside him shattered as a volley of pellets ripped a hole by his feet. Shards of stone burst from the pillar beside his face, but John fired back, causing their assailants to yell and duck for cover. Marcela knew it was tricky because he had to divide his shots between Juan and Antonio's security. That also meant he was spending double the ammo he would usually use...

She hopped a pillar and narrowly avoided a few rounds that she saw pock the wall in front of her, small bursts of wallpaper and plaster puffing from each hole. Another shotgun blast rang out and John ducked back to cover. She was two pillars from him now, and could see sweat dripping down his forehead.

**

Mike heard two things: the sound of his heavy breathing, and the sound of a slumping body hitting ground.

He nearly decided to make another break for it. This was a distraction he needed. But to what end? Prance into the ballroom unarmed, wave at John and Marcela and tell them their ride was waiting?

No, he'd need to take a chance.

Mike peered around the corner this time. He saw two men and one woman, all with guns drawn and scanning their surroundings for new threats. They watched each other expertly, covering various lines of fire, with proper gun control. He noticed earpieces and proper stance before they were able to make him out.

"Don't shoot!" Mike cried, as the three of them brought their weapons up, all synchronized in their movement.

Damn, these guys are good, Mike thought.

"Come out slowly, hands up," the woman said. She had a British accent like the other two.

A small group of tightly trained Brits, Mike thought, putting the pieces together. It didn't take him long.

"MI5?"

The three of them tensed involuntarily. One of the men looked at Mike with murder in his eyes, while the other two looked merely surprised.

"And who the bloody hell are you?" asked the angry-looking agent.

"CIA if you'd believe it."

The woman narrowed her eyes and didn't lower her gun. "International signature?"

That would be a rotating password shared between allied agencies — or at least agencies willing to work together once in a while. But there was a reason it rotated, and Mike didn't have access to it anyhow. It's not as if he had every password memorized for every particular situation, as the movies might make people think intelligence officers did.

Oh sure, a duress check is one thing to know by memory, but an international sig? Come on.

"I'm out of rotation. Retired."

"Sure," the angry man rolled his eyes. "Come on, he's a partygoer."

"Who would know there's a rotating sig?" the other man asked. He was tall and lanky, with a haircut that made Mike embarrassed on his behalf.

"Plenty of people know —"

Another salvo of gunfire coming from the nearby ballroom interrupted them.

"Look, there's no time," Mike said quickly. "You're here for the prince. I know where he is. I can help you get him out."

"In exchange for?" the woman asked, lowering her gun.

Savvy, Mike thought. He kept his hands up regardless. "I've got two agents stuck in there as well. Need them out."

"We'll do what we can," the woman said, cutting off the protest of the angry agent with a wave of her hand. "That's Tony, this is Graham," she said, pointing to the angry looking agent first and then the one with the bad haircut. "I'm Diane."

Aliases for communication, most likely, but Mike didn't care much. "Mike."

"Lead the way, retired CIA."

***

"Again?" John asked. He traded fire with both groups of security but was quickly forced back, spinning his back flat against his pillar once more.

Marcela nodded.

John focused on the weight of the gun in his hand. Focused on his breathing. He looked to Marcela, and found her eyes full of confidence and full of life. As if this was all just a part of the game.

He almost smiled back. He counted down on his fingers, and they both poked out from their positions, Marcela firing on Antonio and his security and John firing on Juan and his guards. The enemy hunkered down and Marcela scurried across the floor to hug her body behind another pillar. They were only one away from each other now, escape close at hand.

"Ammo?" John asked.

Marcela frowned. She removed the magazine from the gun she had stolen off the security guard and checked her count.

"Five," she said, a stern look smothering her previous expression.

John checked his own. He had been counting down the fifteen-cartridge mag, minus two for the crocodile, but it never hurt to check if one could. Miscounts could be deadly.

Two measly rounds lay stacked upon one another. John felt his face tighten up. He looked back at Marcela, who flinched as a matched pair of holes opened up in the floor next to her bare foot, puffs of dust evaporating in the air. He held up two fingers.

"Mierda."

John couldn't hear her but read the word on her lips.

There was no good solution. They'd have to make a break for it.

They made eye contact again, and John began to count down.

Two security guards dashed in through the entrance John had come in through, not fifteen feet away.

John and Marcela's reflexes were like lightning. Both of them swung their guns over to the two intruders and gunned them down. John fired one burst at each of the men and

Marcela added another three rounds to the flurry they encountered.

The security guards crumpled like marionettes with their strings cut, one of them crying out briefly, spitting blood as he fell.

John gave Marcela a grim expression. *Out of ammo.*

She gestured with her gun. She'd have to provide their covering fire with her remaining shots, and the two of them would have one chance to duck out.

Marcela counted down from three...two...one...

John sprang into action as Marcela spun out from her pillar and ran toward his own. John ran from his position and sidestepped the two newly-dead bodies on the floor, diving for the doorway, flying through the air. He began to tuck and tumble, conscious of the broken glass nearby from when he had kicked the door open, making sure to shield his eyes with his arms. He hit the ground outside and fell into a roll, somersaulting and coming up on the balls of his feet again, gasping at the spike of pain from his wound and putting a hand on the wall beside him as he panted.

Marcela wasn't behind him.

An eruption of gunfire came from the ballroom once more. John put his back to the wall as he had before and peered through the entrance.

Marcela had gotten stuck on her pillar, apparently not even able to make it one over to where John had been. She must've gotten pinned again, and John assumed she was out of ammo.

She'd have to make a break for it without any covering fire if she were to get out.

An eerie silence fell over the ballroom. There were a couple harsh shouts in Spanish thrown around, and a few more stray shots that rang through the air, but the firefight had largely calmed.

John eyed the two dead guards that lay close to the doorway where he lingered. If he could snag a pistol and sidle up next to the closest pillar again maybe...

The sound of rapid footsteps sounded in the ballroom. At first John thought Marcela was making a clean break for it, but she wasn't wearing shoes, and it was coming from the far end of the room. John couldn't see from his vantage point, but it sounded as if one of the men from Antonio's group was running into a new position.

With no return fire from Marcela, more shuffling occurred. Someone else made a break for another closer position. John could see one of Juan's guards across the room edging into the entranceway and taking up cover behind a pillar. A moment later he edged out further, and another guard took the pillar opposite.

Marcela stood stock-still on her pillar. Another shot rang out. Then Juan appeared in the doorway opposite John, gesturing to his men to move forward.

There was hesitation, then Juan himself took the lead. He moved forward slowly, and with a slight limp, out of the safety of the doorway and away from the pillars next to the wall behind him, out into the no-man's-land of the empty space in the center of the massive room. He fired as he walked, and was soon flanked by his two guards, one reloading his shotgun while the other fired again, blasting Marcela's position. She looked over to John.

He saw fear in her eyes.

All the playfulness he had known in her was gone. Death was staring her down, and she knew it. There was little he could do about it.

Well shit... he thought idly, as he dove back into the ballroom a second time.

Juan and his guards weren't as well trained as Marcela and he, which helped. Their reaction time was slow but they still swung their guns towards the sudden movement. They were also farther, which meant the effectiveness of the shotgun and general aim was going to be harder. One of the men was still reloading, so it was only really up to Juan and his solitary guard.

Bullets whizzed overhead as John tore into the fray, running crouched with an arm outstretched and pointing his empty gun. Although he had nothing to fire back, Juan and his men didn't know that, or at least acted reflexively as if he did. After their attack they sprinted the rest of the way to find cover on the same end of the hall as where Marcela lay hidden.

John tossed his gun aside and scrambled to scoop up a new one from one of the guards they had gunned down. He grabbed it as he ran and took up a new position on a pillar on the south wall this time, still close to the entrance but farther from Marcela on the eastern wall.

Out of the corner of his eye he saw Marcela break for the entrance as he'd hoped, but she was intercepted by the guard struggling to reload his gun while he ran for cover. Shells scattered on the floor as she broke from cover and put her back to the wall, snaking around him through a narrow gap between body and wall, and giving him a kick in the back. She ducked and covered herself with her arms reflexively, guessing what would happen.

The man shook in front of her as a blast of shotgun pellets tore a chunk of the man's torso off, splashing blood onto the wall where Marcela had slipped by. The other guard had seen Marcela and tried to gun her down, not accounting for her quick thinking in the heat of battle.

Juan yelled to his remaining guard and John cried for Marcela to stay low.

She did, running for the entrance as John fired right over her head at Juan and the other guard. But the angle was off, and John wasn't about to hit anything. Meanwhile, Juan and the other guard had a clear line of sight in a straight firing pattern for Marcela as the other guard fell to the ground dead, blood pooling on the floor.

Marcela didn't make it to the entrance, but she managed to swing behind a closer pillar, leaning against a narrow space on the ribbed stone that blocked Juan and the other guard's fire. But she also struggled to cover the line of fire from Antonio and his men, who had been slowly advancing onto the eastern wall as Juan and his guards had moved forward.

He fired once across the room at Antonio and his men, seeing if he could slow their advance, but the immediate threat was Juan and his guard. They were still out of his line of fire, but John fired a warning shot in that direction too, hoping that would stall them.

It didn't.

The guard and Juan simply charged.

The guard entered John's line of sight and he was about to gun the man down, but Marcela peered around the opposite corner, spotted Juan coming up the ballroom side, and had to make a decision. Because rolling onto Juan's side would also expose her to Antonio's men, she rolled the other way back toward the wall.

Right into John's firing line.

"Move!" John yelled.

But there was nothing to do. He changed aim and fired at Juan, but the man ducked behind Marcela's pillar, and his shot hit air.

The guard with the shotgun had the gun pointed and ready, but Marcela was wise to it. The first thing she did was give a mighty kick to the man's arms and the shotgun pointed upwards. The guard discharged the weapon reflexively, and she followed up with a punch to the gut.

The guard staggered back, but Juan pushed him aside, and lunged at Marcela.

Again, John tried to get a shot off. But Marcela was too close to the other two, and they were moving too erratically, too quickly for him to get a secure mark. His pillar suddenly exploded with a series of sharp *pings* as the distinct rattle of an AK-47 retorted and forced him back behind the pillar once more.

Antonio's backup had arrived.

He watched the unfolding fight with frustration, unable to do anything to aid his partner.

Juan brought his gun down to fire. Marcela was quick, and bat his arm away. He punched with his other arm, and Marcela took a backwards step, leaning back and dodging the blow by inches. The gun came back around and Marcela grabbed the gun hand with both of hers, grappling Juan.

"*¡Puta sucia!*" Juan yelled, teeth bared and saliva spitting on Marcela's face. *Filthy whore!*

John tried to leave his position again, only to be greeted by more gunfire from the assault rifle. He swore again, then aimed high above the heads of Marcela and Juan and fired a couple times at the wall, hoping it would cause Juan to back off, or at least second-guess himself.

He didn't. Rage was the only thing driving him now, and his bloodlust was bulletproof.

The guard regained his composure and tried to aim his shotgun, but it was too unwieldy and he couldn't get a shot off, just as John was struggling. He shifted his grip and rammed the stock at Marcela's face.

Marcela had just delivered a kick to Juan's crotch but he hadn't loosened his grip of the gun, which he fired twice, both shots hitting the wall as he roared in pain and anger. The stock of the guard's shotgun slammed into Marcela's face, connecting with her nose and forehead, and making her stagger backwards, blinking, as blood began to crawl from her nose.

John watched with detached emotion. It was all cold calculation to him. And finally, the attackers and Marcela were separated by this blow.

John fired off a series of rounds less than a foot past Marcela as she staggered back, and all three of John's shots connected with the guard who continued his attack, trying to ram Marcela again. He died instantly, crumpling on the spot, falling awkwardly into the pillar, blood streaking down its side as he slid the remaining height to the floor.

Unfortunately the blow that did connect had left Marcela reeling. She was trained to shake hits off, and she was managing just that, when her feet connected with one of the bodies on the ground. She tumbled to the floor, landing hard on her tailbone and elbows.

She rolled away just in time. Juan fired and John fired back, forcing the man backwards. But Marcela would be exposed to assault rifle fire if she continued backing away, scrambling to her feet and ducking close to the wall once more, trusting John's covering fire as she stayed low in a crouch.

Her calculation was right. The Ak-47 rattled once more, a brutal staccato of bullets ripping up the floor where she had been a moment earlier. John took the opportunity to fire at Antonio's position then, and managed to spot the advance of a few guards, snaking their way onto the eastern wall where the fight had broken out. A lucky shot made one of them panic and stagger, and John killed the man caught in the open with ease. John was forced back once more and turned his attention back to Marcela.

She was grappling Juan again, but this time advanced her aggression. She pounced on him like a tiger, driving him to the ground. He lost control of his gun and it went flying into the air, bouncing off the pillar and sliding inches away from Juan's reach.

He instinctively grabbed for it, but it was just as Marcela expected, and she stomped on his hand and ground her heel, crushing tendons to the sound of Juan howling. Not satisfied, she kicked him under the chin and his head snapped back, but he grabbed her other leg with his free hand and yanked hard enough that she slipped to the floor once more. Blood coated her face, arm, leg, and chest, most of it from the guards, but more spilling from her nose. Juan kicked reflexively as he struggled to crane his head back up, and a heavy boot pummeled Marcela in the chest even as she was trying to get her footing once more from her pulled leg.

She tried to catch the boot but her arms moved too slowly for the rapid kick. The blow sent her sprawling once more and Juan slung an arm across his chest and grabbed the gun his other injured hand could not.

John's face grew grimmer. The two of them were prone and he couldn't get a safe shot off. He was in position to get a perfect killing shot if Juan regained his stance, but with the gun in the man's hands, Marcela was forced to stand once more, putting herself in the crossfire.

She rolled awkwardly at him, hoping that would give John the vantage he needed, but Juan wasn't able to get to his feet as she hoped, or he was wise to the sightline. She grabbed his gun arm with one hand and the gun with the other, pointing it towards him. Juan dropped the gun and wrapped an elbow around her throat instead, pulling her up as he limped to stand. His other hand pulled a knife from his belt.

Marcela struggled in the chokehold, desperately driving her elbow into his ribs. He ignored her assault on his battered torso. She was about to change tactics and spin him about, attempt to bowl him over her shoulder but he lifted his elbow and held the knife to her throat.

Her eyes went wide when she felt the metal pressed against her skin, and froze, uncertain if continuing to struggle would be better or worse for her situation.

John held his gun out, trained on the two of them. He followed Juan's head carefully. Juan shifted, tucking behind Marcela, putting her in between him and John. Juan lifted his eyes and met eyes with John. They were full of fire, and determination.

"Para ti, John Carpenter," *For you, John Carpenter.* He spat on the floor in front of him.

Then Juan pulled the knife in a sudden jerk, slitting Marcela's throat.

Chapter 19

"What's with the gunfire?" Graham asked as they sped along the open hallway. Another burst of gunfire interrupted whatever he was going to say next, taking the words out of his mouth.

"Cartel violence," Mike said quickly. "Guatemalans interfering with Romero's affairs."

"That why you're here?" Tony asked.

Mike nodded. *Let's keep things simple for our friends across the pond,* he thought to himself.

"Heard a rumor about some Guatemalan cartel a little while ago," Diane said. They hit a corner and she checked for them while the others swept their six and flank. "Big moves out of Antigua. Wouldn't know anything about that, would you?" she gave them the go ahead and the four of them turned the corner.

Mike grunted in response. Intelligence gossip always rankled him.

"Where's the prince?" Diane asked instead.

"Last intel puts him in the ballroom," Mike said.

"Right where the action is," Tony grimaced.

Mike nodded. "Gun?"

The woman cocked her head and Graham passed Mike a pistol. He flipped off the safety and chambered a round, aware that Tony was giving him a glare but neither of them said anything.

They approached the east entrance. Both male agents put their bodies up against the wall on either side of the door, while Mike and Diane crouched, ready for entry.

"What are we looking at?" Diane asked.

Graham replied almost before she'd finished asking the question, peering inside and not looking back as he spoke. "Guards shooting from the north entrance. Snaking up along the east."

"That's us," Mike said.

"No shit," Tony grumbled.

"Firing line...they're shooting at the southeast."

"So we're heading into a crossfire?" Diane asked.

"No...not exactly, it looks like —"

"Oh, fuck you guys," Mike said, standing, opening the door, and diving inside.

Mike fired his gun as he burst forward into the ballroom, grabbing the first pillar he could see. He put that between him and the main group of guards on the north entrance, and threw a few blind rounds up ahead of his entrance, making guards duck behind pillars as he advanced.

"Go! Go! Go!"

The Brits poured in after him, Mike having given away their careful entry in favor of getting the job done. Tony looked like he was about to blow a fuse as the veins in his forehead bulged in rage at Mike, but not before he grabbed a pillar in front of the group and laid down covering fire. Diane and Graham took Mike's six and flank, grabbing their own pillars next to him and firing down the room.

Mike glanced about. The place was crawling with activity.

Partygoers were screaming with fear, crying, shouting in pain — it was a horror house.

Bullet holes pocked the floor and walls, and the scent of blood was thick on the air.

He turned around and caught sight of someone in a cream suit firing and limping their way out an exit near the corner of the room.

He recognized that man.

It was Juan Puentes.

He moved past a small pile of bodies; a couple of his bodyguards and a woman...

Jesus, no. It can't be.

Mike fired a round in the man's direction but he was already ducking out. He turned, ready to pop back out into the hallway and chase the man down, but the MI5 woman leapt to his pillar and pulled him close.

"The prince!"

"Opposite corner!" Mike yelled over an incoming salvo of assault rifle fire. The pillar thudded like a jackhammer was hammering into it, and it rattled his back with a harsh vibration.

"We move down this way," Graham indicated in front, where Juan had taken flight.

"And get those bastards to stop shooting!" Tony called.

Diane nodded. "Let's be about it."

The two men poked out from cover and began to bellow at security, trying desperately to explain that they were here for the prince.

But Mike only had eyes for the body of the woman down on the floor, in a dress remarkably similar to the one Marcela had been wearing.

"Covering fire!" Mike called.

The other agents swore as Mike made a break for it, dashing haphazardly between pillars, and Diane waved her hands for the guards to see.

Mike heard gunfire following Juan's exit from a pillar on the south block of the ballroom, and as Mike drew closer to the pile of bodies, he saw the dark figure of John Carpenter rush out in the same direction.

Mike knew it was Marcela on the ground at his feet before he knelt down before her. He looked up at John.

The man's eyes were filled with ice. His face was pale as a ghost. And Mike had never been more terrified of someone before.

He cleared his throat and somehow managed to speak. "I've got her, go after that bastard!"

John stopped short, as if he were a robot suddenly given new direction. He nodded curtly and spun on his heels, hungry for vengeance.

***

John Carpenter was out for blood.

Seeing Marcela's throat slit had unlocked something deep within him. It reminded him of when he had read the message confirming Brian's death. He knew he was in shock. His mind and body couldn't comprehend a partner like Marcela dead, killed right in front of his eyes while he stood there helpless. And at the hand of a hated rival, no less.

He shook off the desire to go back to her, and focused on the feelings that would drive him forward. A fire burned in his belly. Rage boiled up inside of him, consumed him. He was a force of nature. No man could escape his wrath.

All his senses were attuned to the present moment, his breathing, his movements, and his mind ticked ten steps ahead.

Every path led to Juan's death at his hands.

John took the hallway, peered around the entrance, expecting his enemy to look back and fire.

He did. John leaned back behind the wall as the shot whizzed down the open hallway, burying itself somewhere in the tiles past him.

John poked out again, and squeezed off two rounds, but Juan took the corner, and the shots clipped the wall.

John moved out into the hall, expecting the second attempt. He hugged an archway and pushed his shoulder up to it, gun held up and ready.

He was right again. Juan fired around the corner, hoping to catch John in the middle of the hall. John moved on the outside of the hallway, picking his way carefully, hugging each arch but making steady progress on his hunt. He moved like a panther through the shadows, and another shot from Juan whizzed harmlessly down the empty corridor.

John heard the man shuffle again. His gait was uneven. He had a limp. John could use that. He consumed every piece of information. Placed it in his calculated thoughts.

Executed his patterns, perfected by years of training. Every moment led to this fateful pursuit. As it had plenty of others.

"¡Vete a la mierda hijo de puta!" Juan screamed through the hallway, his cracking voice a mix of pain, fear, agony, and an animal anger. *Fuck you motherfucker!*

John let the words feed his movements. Let them indicate how far Juan was ahead. Heard him panting. Heard him struggling. Like a blooded deer trying to outrun a wolf.

John broke from the cover of the arches and dashed across the hallway, sidling up to the corner Juan had been at a moment before. Strings of light danced on the walls and ceiling from floodlights reflecting off the luxury pool on his flank. He took a breath and the air caught in his throat as a sharp pain gripped his chest.

His wound had opened up again, and he felt at his shirt. Thick and sticky blood had soaked through easily, and he spotted red droplets splashing on the tile underfoot in the twinkling lights. He frowned, realizing he had been moving slower than he usually did too.

He peered around the corner. Juan was limping ahead, his lumbering figure moving in and out of shadows, occasionally catching a flash of the dancing reflected light from the pool. John aimed his gun at one of the flashes and fired.

The first shot missed, but the second would have hit, if Juan hadn't moved behind one of the arches in time. John ducked back behind the corner of the wall, and two more shots came his way; one went wild and the other clipped the wall high above his head. Small chunks of plaster and stone chipped away and fell on his head with a shower of dust.

"*¡Está muerta, bastardo. Gracias a ti!*" She's dead, you bastard. Because of you!"

John let the words slide off him like oil. His emotions were tucked away, deep inside, hidden in a separate compartment of mind and body, one that couldn't be reached right now. The only thing that mattered was the hunt.

Another incoming shot went wild, then John sprang into action once more.

Juan was moving along the hallway, using the arches for cover. He may be limping, but John was also struggling, and it would be a losing race at this rate. Between Juan firing backward every other moment, and John's increasingly worsening hole in his side, Juan had the better of him.

John needed to cut him off.

He fired off a round, then took to sprinting across the pool. A small arching bridge led from the lip of the tiles to a larger luxury garden. Juan limped to cover as John crossed the bridge, and as the man's arm poked out around a corner to return fire, John put two rounds in the wall, inches away from the man's hand, and he missed his opportunity to sling anything John's way.

John tucked himself behind a marble statue, and waited. *One...two...three...*

John poked out a split second before Juan did, firing another round that narrowly met air as Juan hid again. John took the moment to dash into the adjoining hallway, running through the arches and sidling up against the wall again, his breathing becoming noticeably haggard. Juan was on the other part of the wall, joined at the corner.

John slid up the side quickly, knowing Juan would be able to hear him. He had to move fast...

Juan spun out and brought his gun to bare, but John was too quick. He ducked and pushed Juan's gun arm upwards as he gave a kick to Juan's ankle, guessing at which one was wounded.

The howl that followed confirmed his choice.

Juan's gun discharged, and John tucked his own gun back, ready to fire from the hip. But he stumbled with the effort of ducking, which had folded his wound, and he gasped in pain as well, wavering his aim. He missed the first shot as Juan fell on top of him.

The weight of the man was too much to bear. John crumpled and struggled to aim a second shot but Juan let go of his gun in order to shove John's gun aside, slamming it into the wall, and punching at his hand and wrist to let go.

John held on, hand pinned against the wall as they slid together to the ground. Juan was on his back, and John tried to roll out from under him, but Juan somersaulted over.

John took his gun in both hands and aimed...

A kick connected with John's hands before he could pull the trigger. His gun flew through the air and clattered on the tiles, sliding toward the pool edge, too far to retrieve. John ignored the pain in his hands and kicked out, aiming for Juan's wounded ankle again as he pulled his knife.

Juan awkwardly hopped back, avoiding the blow, but collapsed onto his knees. His own knife appeared in his hands. John stared at it. Marcela's blood coated its edge.

John decided it would be better to take the opportunity to stand, but as he did so, Juan swiped with his blade. John grabbed Juan's wrist, and Juan responded by grabbing John's raised leg and pulled John down. Off balance, John rolled and Juan followed, John kicking and Juan scrambling and clawing at John's clothing, scratching his chest and trying to reclaim his knife-arm from John's grip.

They crashed into an arch, John hitting his head. He shook off the blow and began to stand again. Juan twisted his way out of John's grip and crawled his way up, stabbing for John's throat.

John dodged, and Juan's knife connected with the stone archway. John arced his own knife up as he moved, slashing the man's wrist. Juan's knife clattered to the floor.

The man was sustaining injuries, but they weren't stopping him.

John went for the killing blow, swiping for Juan's throat. But Juan kneed John in the side at the same time.

Stars burst across John's vision as his eyes bulged with the sharp pain, like he had just been knifed himself. He gasped and keeled over, and Juan fought to disarm him as he was distracted. He moved to knee him a second time, sensing the weakness there. John did what little he could do to stop a second blow, having to choose between his knife or passing out. He grabbed the knee with both hands and Juan fumbled to catch the knife, and it slipped through his fingers. John's grip was weak from extended exertion, and Juan struggled on his one leg. The two fell apart for a moment. John stumbled forward, arm dragging and his other hand covering his wound.

They stared at one another, exhausted, wounded, angry.

Juan bared his teeth and spit at John. John's face twitched as the spittle hit his face. He winced as he leaned forward to try to pick up the knife at his feet...

With a roar, Juan lumbered into an exhausted charge to tackle John and John moved forward instead of backwards as the man expected. It still resulted in a collision, and the two of them tripped and tumbled down a set of stairs leading into the pool.

They splashed into the water.

John somersaulted heels over head as he hit the water, taking a desperate last-minute breath that ended too soon before he was submerged. The mess of limbs and fabric that was Juan crushed on top of him, pushing him down in the water. Juan managed to grab air and the water was shallow enough that he stood on top of John.

John tugged at the man's legs, but this did little to stop the man from continuing to press his weight as best he could in the water, keeping John under. John grabbed one of the man's hands and pulled hard on the thumb, dislocating the finger with a sharp pop that he could feel as much as he could hear.

Juan shrieked with pain, and John moved to the next finger. Juan's distorted screaming continued, but still he held John under the water.

John moved onto the next finger.

Again, a sharp pull. A pop. A scream.

The next finger...

Juan's will was tested, but the man didn't let up. He pulled at his hand, trying to free it, but made no move to allow John back to the surface.

Unfortunately for Juan, John could hold his breath for a long time. And even with his hasty gasp, John was trained to be submerged. He knew how to suppress the panic of drowning.

John popped another finger. When this still made no change, he moved to snap the wrist.

Something changed in Juan then. Whether it was pain, or some realization, Juan decided it would be better to shift position. He kept standing, but bent down, his hands reaching out to choke at John's neck.

It was the wrong move.

John grabbed both hands and tugged Juan under, using the momentum to pull himself above the surface.

He breathed in deeply but carefully, making sure not to choke, and careful to stop breathing as soon as the inevitable return to below began. As expected, Juan grabbed him by the hair and yanked his neck back.

John flipped himself in the water and bucked his legs, hitting Juan somewhere unknown. As John managed to breach the surface again, he heard someone yelling.

"¡Ahí está!" There he is!

The words came from nearby. Probably Antonio's security chasing after the gunshots he and Juan had exchanged. But John couldn't spot them before he was plunged back under the surface.

Juan used the momentum from John's kick to move him closer to the stairs, and began to crawl up them, gasping for air and a break from the vicious deadlock with John.

John wasn't about to let the bastard get away.

He windmilled an arm to grab Juan's collar, but the man was slippery, and John only managed to grab his suit jacket. He yanked, which made Juan stumble, but he slipped off the jacket and pushed himself out of the water with his desperate remaining efforts.

John dropped the jacket with frustration and moved to lunge at Juan's ankles, but Antonio's security was closing in on the pool.

Juan spun around and pointed at John while soaked, seated on the ground. *"¡Dispárenle idiotas!" Shoot him you idiots!*

The security guards opened fire.

***

The ballroom echoed with yells from the MI5 agents and Antonio's guards, the two forces moving around. Miraculously, the shooting seemed to have stopped, the reluctant silence broken by a barked order or the sobbing of a guest.

Mike put a hand to Marcela's neck, attempting to stop the flow of blood. It spurted out and sprayed him in the face as he knelt down in front of her. She coughed, blood spilling from her mouth. Mike put pressure on the cut, but it was wide and his hand hardly covered it all. He wasn't even sure if he was doing any good. He felt like he was choking the poor girl. He grimaced as more blood oozed out between his fingers and began to pool onto the floor.

Marcela looked him in the eyes, panic and fear in them, and Mike did his best to hold her frightened gaze.

"It's alright," Mike lied. "It's alright."

She tried to say something. She coughed again, blood staining her lips, then she managed a single word.

"Mierda."

Her lips curled into a haunting smile, and then her eyes glazed over, the light fading as her head lolled to the side in Mike's hands.

"Fuck, fuck...fuck!" Mike yelled. He held her head a moment longer, taking his hand off her neck as the blood continued to trickle out, slowly now, like a hose had been turned off but letting go of excess pressure. Then he put her down slowly, wiped blood on his pants, and wiped his face in his sleeve.

Fucking bastards. I'll make 'em pay. And if I don't, well, I know John will.

***

John dove back into the water, crashing under the surface as the bullets whizzed over Juan and into the pool. He spun and retreated, keeping calm as he moved away from the security guards and towards a pool edge.

The water was shallow; he hugged the bottom as best he could and put distance between him and the incoming fire. Although some debated whether bullets really slowed enough in water, John doubted those individuals having those debates had ever been shot at. The Hollywood 'myth' was very much true: water was denser than air, and the opposing drag force slowed bullets to a crawl at a few feet.

John knew from experience.

Between a moving target, the obscuring darkness, and the water, John would be safe for as long as he could hold his breath.

The guards would find an edge and wait for him to surface. *Like shooting fish in a barrel.* John wasn't about to wait for that fate to come.

He approached the pool's edge closest to where the guards were approaching. Then he sank to the bottom of the shallow pool and bent his legs like a coiled spring.

He unleashed the tension.

John launched himself upwards, pushing hard on the pool's bottom and up through the water, the sound of bubbles cascading announced his emergence as he broke the surface. His hand was outstretched, and grabbed at the gun he knew would be there, from when it had been knocked out of his hands.

He aimed and fired before he could see through the blur of water shrouding his eyes.

He heard a yell from one of the security guards, as well as a pair of gunshots sounding from their direction. One bullet he heard whip past him and into the hedges by the pool, while another spat into the tiles somewhere off his flank.

Most individuals didn't realize how hard it was to hit a moving target, especially in the dark and at a distance. But that didn't mean John was going to push his luck. He had to push his advantage.

John's eyes cleared and he spotted one of the guards on the ground, writhing in pain from some unseen wound. John ducked behind the lip of the pool as the other guard fired again. The able-bodied guard had begun to drag his friend into the cover of a hedge, but John was quick on the trigger. He put two rounds in the man who'd decided to try and save his friend, making him twitch with the impact and crumple like a folding chair, head collapsing over his knees and falling onto the side of his head, pushing into the stone tiles, rear raised like a dog digging for a bone, then fell over entirely.

The other man on the ground screamed, whether from his wound or from his partner being killed, John didn't know, nor did he care.

He did a sweep to see where Juan was. He wasn't at the foot of the pool steps anymore. John didn't like taking his eyes off an enemy still alive, even if wounded. A man with a gun on the ground and a bullet in his gut was still able to kill you. But Juan was the more pressing threat, and so John turned away from the guards, searching for the don.

He followed the sound of ugly coughing; water clogging one's lungs. Juan was limping, hand held tight at his stomach, searching frantically for something on the ground.

His gun.

The man had found it, and limped over to it, coughing and spitting as he went.

John brought his gun up to point at Juan and called out.

"*¡Detente!*" Freeze.

Juan swiveled his head as he was halfway bent to the ground. When he saw John pointing his gun, he did indeed freeze.

John trudged out of the pool, taking the steps slowly, wincing at his wound and ignoring the mix of faded red color shining in front of one of the pool's lights. That was a problem for later.

Juan needed to die.

Unfortunately, John had been counting rounds, and he knew he was out.

"Te veré en el infierno," Juan spat. *I'll see you in hell.*

The air had grown still. The sound of the pool lapping against its edges covered the night breeze, along with the low moans from the wounded guard on the tiles.

John continued to move, making his way over to him, eyes held on Juan.

The bluff couldn't last.

At some point, Juan either realized John wasn't going to shoot him, or he might as well try and kill John first, against all odds. John saw the change in the man's posture, and Juan broke from his freeze and fell to the ground, snatching up his gun, hoping to dodge a bullet if he needed to along the way.

John tore into a run, or as much of one as he could manage one with the hole under his ribs. He grabbed the gun the dying guard was clawing towards, ending the man's hope for redemption, and blind-fired at Juan behind his back in an underhanded gesture before he could turn around for a clear line of sight.

Juan fired too, but between an awkward firing posture and using his injured non-dominant hand, he missed. Before John could get another shot Juan scrambled back towards the open hall for cover.

John also threw himself into cover, back against a tall statue next to the hedges that the guard had been trying to drag his partner toward. The sound of feet running through the night made John turn around again. Pinned between two enemies once more, another guard came out of one of the hallway arches, from the path of the ballroom.

John squeezed off two rounds, killing the man before he realized where John was, then John pointed his gun at the man on the ground, and pulled the trigger, ending his life in an instant without looking, scanning the arches for Juan.

Juan hadn't returned fire. He allowed himself a few heavy breaths.

John had been keeping track of Juan's ammunition as well, counting the shots the man took, but there was no way to know what he had spent in the ballroom fight before John arrived. John waited, listening, the night still once more, when he caught the sound of Juan shuffling in the distance.

He was getting away.

John scooped up the remaining gun from the guard and tucked it in his waistband, then got back to work, taking to the arches and hunting Juan once more.

The man wasn't hugging corners and firing backwards anymore. John suspected Juan was out of ammunition, but it may have been that he was simply afraid.

He had good reason to be.

John continued down the hallway, hugging cover as he moved, sweeping each new entryway and listening for guards or Juan along the path. But being careful was costing him time, and Juan was getting away. His shuffling had broken out into a desperate jog and although John could hear his grunts of pain, they were growing more and more distant with each passing second. John clutched his side as he picked up the pace. He had to finish things himself before he bled out.

John entered a particularly shadowy stretch of hallway, swept the lights surrounding its exterior, then broke from the hallway altogether and onto a large lawn. He hugged the darkness; as the wind gusted off the ocean he could hear crashing in the distance, the grass bristled in anticipation. He took to a wide circle, aware of his lack of cover in the open lawn, but was protected by the dark and the ability to take to the ground at any instant, while not having to worry about enemies chasing at his back. Across the dark lawn rose the vast west entrance of the property; beyond it the lights of the island's airfield glowed.

There was a long strip of runway lined with equally placed lights to guide pilots into the airstrip. About a dozen private planes sat neatly lined up at the end of the landing strip, some with lights on, some dark. John saw a few figures milling about, some more frantically than others. In fact, it looked like the number of people was growing. One of the planes actually started up and began moving onto the strip.

People were leaving — escaping — the island. It made sense. When the bullets had begun to fly, John was sure many of Antonio's guests had fled for the promised refuge of their private planes or yachts.

Not only for safety, but also for liability...

Important people were injured or dead. A Cuban island, where political favors were bought and sold, where some of the world's richest and most powerful individuals had been visiting for God knew how many years, and one full of open pedophilia.

There was no way any of this was staying under-wraps.

Unless they worked hard to cover it up...

John focused his mind. That was a problem for the spin doctors and the politicians.

His only thought was Juan.

John scanned the growing crowd and watched a small dark figure in the distance jogging awkwardly, with a hop and a skip in his step. John honed in on the figure and made his way down the short hill from the villa's lavish lawn and over to skirt the edge of the small airfield.

The distance was too far for an accurate shot, and there were people milling about. Besides, it would give away his position.

John tucked his gun away and moved onto the airfield, joining the crowd. People were running and shouting all about, reuniting with loved ones and making sure they were safe, or waving down their staff. One of the planes had started up and filled the air with its whine.

Some of the frantic partygoers gave him a glance; he wasn't wearing a tuxedo or suit but he could well have been someone's security, and although he was haggard and visibly wounded as he ran, most were busy enough with their own evacuation plans.

Which was fine by John. He needed to blend in with the crowd and find Juan.

He rushed as best he could over to the lineup of private planes at the beginning of the strip and back of the airfield. He felt noticeably weaker; blood dripped down his side and created a sticky puddle on his clothing all the way down to his thigh. John had noticed a growing pulsing headache — having his head smacked around would do that — and besides the normal exhaustion someone fighting and running in a high stress environment might naturally take on, he was getting dangerously close to losing consciousness if he continued to work himself as seriously as he did.

He had no choice.

There could be no rest until Juan was dead.

John surveyed the scene. People were boarding their planes. There was a heightened tension in the air. John pushed past a couple yelling at one another and nearly bowled over another woman tripping over her dress. He approached the planes and began running past them, trying to figure out which one would be Juan's. He still had the man in his sights. But he wanted to beat the man to his destination if he could.

He honed in on Juan and began to tail him more purposefully, ready to make his way to a plane at the slightest inclination.

Juan turned around and checked the crowd, looking for John. John ducked behind another couple who hurried past him. The couple passed...

Juan was looking directly at him.

The man froze for an instant, then something seemed to shake him alive, and Juan rushed forward toward one of the planes. John abandoned all pretense of blending into the crowd and broke into an uneven run.

Juan's plane was nearby; the staircase was lowered and he limped up the steps while gripping both rails, yelling to someone up inside the plane.

Juan didn't pull out his gun. He was almost certainly out of ammunition. Either way, it wouldn't stop John's pursuit. He pulled out his gun and made ready.

Juan made it up the stairs before John crossed the tarmac and approached them himself. A plane tore by behind him, screaming loudly as it turned on the strip and picked up speed, getting ready to launch itself into the air. The wind was picking up, and it whipped at him as he took the first step. As soon as the plane had passed John was able to hear Juan yelling from inside the plane.

"*¡Ponnos en el aire!*" he roared. *Get us in the air!*

Someone said something else that John couldn't make out. There were other voices; one was female and the others sounded younger.

"*¡La escopeta!*" Juan coughed. *The shotgun!*

John struggled up the last of the steps and prepared himself for combat once more.

The plane's turbines started up and the scream of them filled the air, cutting off anything else he might hear from onboard.

He approached the doorway with haste, knowing that Juan was trying to summon a weapon. He reached the top step and began to 'pie the corner,' a technique to take corners incrementally, increasing field of vision as one moved.

He sensed movement behind him toward the cockpit as he simultaneously stared down the aisle towards the tail-end. Juan was there, standing in the middle of the aisle, facing forward.

A man ran out of the cockpit area holding a shotgun. John pulled the trigger twice, shooting the man as he flew past. Both bullets hit at point-blank range, killing the man and sending him face down on the aisle without him ever knowing John was beside him.

The shotgun clattered to the ground. Juan wasted no time diving to the floor to pick it up. John took another step into the plane, lining up his shot on Juan...

But as John crossed the threshold a series of passengers huddling in their chairs came into view, some peeking out from above or the side of the aisle.

The girls, thought John.

A dozen or so girls, no older than their teens sat at the back of the private plane with a woman in her late twenties herding them and trying to keep them calm. She saw John and cried out in fear, and the girls began to scream as well.

John couldn't risk taking a shot at Juan and hitting one of the passengers. He was normally unaffected by unforeseen instances — he always had to roll with the punches — but the entire scene took him by surprise, making him hesitate.

Juan was scrambling for the shotgun in the middle of the aisle when the plane sprang to life. The engines cried with unseen energy and the floor began to rumble under their feet.

John shot his gun into the air, making the girls cry out in fright and duck behind their seats even further, and making Juan flinch back for a moment before he realized the bullet wasn't for him.

John charged forward, hoping to get a clean shot on Juan that wouldn't have any firing line involving the other passengers. If he could somehow shoot the man from above or the side, he could make quick work of things.

But John also had the shotgun to worry about, and Juan brought the gun up as he stood, rocking the pump action as he rose.

John hit the floor and slid, kicking out at Juan's feet like a baseball player racing to home before he could get a clean shot. Juan fired and the shotgun roared with anger as the girls screamed and cried at its sound.

John ignored the ringing in his ears and brought his gun up to aim at Juan under the chin or crotch, but Juan stepped on his arm as he tripped over John. The plane had hit the runway and was starting to pick up speed.

As Juan loomed over him, John grabbed the barrel of the gun and wrenched downward, at the same instant John lurched his head forward in a vicious headbutt as Juan was pulled onto his knees. The headbutt slammed into Juan's nose and Juan reared back in pain. John shoved the weapon off to the side as it bucked and spat its deadly hot metal, pellets cracking a window, shredding a seat, and penetrating the plane's hull.

John shook off the pain ringing in his skull and brought his own gun around to aim at Juan's ribs, but Juan realized how close death was for him and was wise to John's injury. He swung the shotgun's butt down and slammed it into John's side, directly onto his wound.

John cried out in pain, unable to control his arm's movement as lines of agony speared up his ribs and into his armpit. His hand slid under a seat without him realizing, and when he finally worked his mind over the pain and hoisted his gun hand up again to aim at Juan, it collided with the seat above. At the same time, the plane bounced on the runway. Surprised and disoriented, John lost hold of the gun. It fell out of his hands as the plane finally lifted off, sliding down under the seats as the floor became a steep incline.

John wanted to reach for the other gun in his waistband but was still on his back, and Juan still had a shotgun. John grappled with Juan, reaching out for the gun and the man's hands, pushing and pulling to try and break the thing loose. Juan had the upper hand being above John; John had gravity but no leverage. Juan yanked and then bashed the gun into John's face, and John felt a distinct *crack* of pain in his nose as blood began to spill from his nostrils. John let one of his hands go and clawed at Juan's fingers, finding the broken ones he'd busted up in the pool and pulled at them without mercy.

Juan howled as one of his hands was pried from the shotgun. John punched him in the cheek hard and finally ripped the shotgun away with his other hand. He tried to shove Juan away so he could bring the bulky weapon underneath his throat or gut before firing, but Juan honed in on John's wound once more, delivering another vicious jab to the wound.

John coughed, nearly throwing up with pain. Juan scrabbled for the shotgun while John was distracted, and John tossed it away towards the front of the plane, convinced it was better to deny the weapon altogether. Their eyes followed the gun and where it landed, clocking the motion and end position so they could continue the fight over there if need be.

That was when John noticed a wind blowing inside the plane; a dangerous whipping sound like the wind were tearing at the hull. John saw then that the door hadn't been closed. The staircase must be hanging off the plane like an open maw, never to be shut now that they were in the air.

The plane bounced again and the incline steepened as they continued to gain altitude. John forced himself to suck in a breath against the pain and kicked Juan in the crotch, forcing the man off him and rolling backwards to put space between him and his opponent, place him closer to the shotgun, and finally get to his feet.

Juan was holding his crotch and struggling to stand, grabbing a seat to aid him. John was slower to get up, using a nearby seat much the same, and slowly walking backwards towards the gun. The air grew more violent as he drew closer to the open door.

A gunshot rang out loud and true, and John ducked, surprised and trying to find where it had come from. Juan had no gun in his hands but John instinctively reached for the second gun he had tucked in his waistband from one of the security guards he'd killed and pointed it, initially at Juan, who thought he was going to die in that instant. But when John didn't take the shot, Juan turned around and saw the girls, then turned his head back to John with an ugly smile. He moved in front of them, making sure to put them directly at his back, making John hold his fire.

Another sharp pop as the sound of gunfire rang out, and the bullet *pinged* with a metallic sound off a chair or the hull, John couldn't tell. He heard the young woman yell something incoherent during the gunshot.

He looked over Juan's shoulder and identified the threat.

She was holding the gun and firing at John.

She must have retrieved it as it slid under the seats and to the back as the plane took off. She was further away from the girls, finding a line of sight off to the side, so John risked a shot.

The plane bounced then, and his shot went high, and also reminded him of the dangers of shooting at all. If he hit one of the girls he'd never forgive himself.

As if to remind him, the girls screamed and cried once more, reacting to the gunfire, although he couldn't see them hidden in their seats. It was little consolation. This was the sort of thing no child should witness, let alone be a part of.

"*¡Fuera del camino!*" the woman yelled to Juan. *Out of the way!*

Juan moved off to the side giving her a clear line of sight, and John dove into the nearby seats.

Blam! Blam! Blam!

The woman fired as quickly as she could, a reckless display of power for one untrained in shooting a gun. Two shots went wild, although the third penetrated the seat near John's head. He saw a blur of motion as a hole suddenly tore through the seat and the bullet whizzed inches in front of him, forming a new hole as it continued as able, penetrating anything in its path.

"*¡Dame ese!*" Juan yelled at the woman. *Give me that!*

She fired twice more as John rolled onto the floor, doubting she would think to fire that low. But Juan would ferret John out.

The plane tipped again as it began to level out. John curled up in the seat and peeked out the side into the aisle.

Juan snatched the gun out of the woman's hands and whirled on John, firing as John ducked back to cover.

It was the worst situation. John was under fire, with cover that hardly provided protection, and was unable to fire back.

He threw himself out over the aisle and into the seats opposite; a reckless move in most situations, but it might force Juan to angle himself away from the girls, giving John an opportunity he couldn't waste. Juan fired twice, and John got lucky; Juan had to fire left-handed because of his injuries; between that and the unpredictability of the plane's motion, the onslaught couldn't connect.

"¡Hijo de puta!" Motherfucker!

John let out a breath, not realizing he'd been holding it, and tried to plan his next move. But an angry sound came storming up the aisle.

Juan was charging him.

Realization dawned on John. The man must have run out of ammunition.

Now with no more options, Juan was upon him again.

John hurried to his feet. He fired a carefully angled shot as the man tore up the aisle. John was used to hitting moving targets, and this was nearly point blank. The round speared through Juan's shoulder but by the time John was firing his second round, Juan clotheslined him awkwardly, slamming him against a seat, and leaving his gun aim flailing.

Juan slammed John's head against the seat. He was lucky it wasn't a hard surface, but the impact still jostled him. He fired once at Juan's feet but missed as Juan kicked him in the shin. The man grabbed John in a bearhug, taking advantage of his awkward position in between seats where there was little room to maneuver. John found himself slammed onto the aisle, a sharp pain in his back as he landed half on the shotgun that had been discarded earlier. Wind whipped around them from the open door as Juan stepped on top of him, scrambling for the weapon.

The plane banked hard. The shotgun slid across the aisle, bounced once against the hull, then tumbled out the door. Juan swore and spun on John just as John was lining up a shot with his own gun.

Juan grappled his hands, pushing the gun off to the side, able to use more of his bodyweight because Juan was on top and John was prone on the floor. His arms splayed out to the side, and Juan took the opportunity to plant a knee on John's nose, slowly pushing in and breaking what was left of the cartilage there.

John breathed through the excruciating pain. He turned the gun around but Juan stepped on his hand next, crushing his wrist. John kneed Juan in the crotch for a second time. While Juan loosened the grip of John's gun, they grappled over it, swinging side to side, bucking and kneeing and kicking and elbowing as best they could to each try and get the upper hand.

John finally conceded the contest, feeling the wind bellow and blow fabric near his head. Behind him lay the curtain between the pilot's cockpit and the rest of the airplane's cabin.

He got his knees up under Juan, pushed himself up the aisle on his back, and managed to free a hand and reach for the curtain. Juan managed to get the gun in his offhand, but not before John tore the curtain free and tossed it over Juan's head.

Juan fired the gun at the floor and John pulled himself out of the way. With his limbs free, John grabbed at the curtain and twisted the fabric tight, enveloping Juan's head, making him look like some comical ghost at a Halloween party.

Juan fired in front, where he thought John would be. But John was up now, and moved to the side, spinning the fabric like a spider with its web. He noosed the curtain tighter so it choked Juan, then yanked the man up the aisle towards the cockpit. The wind tore at the sheet, sucking it into the open air. Juan felt the danger of the situation and pointed to shoot a third time, still focusing on killing John instead of freeing himself. John had moved close when Juan blind fired, inches away from his ear and pushing him towards the open door.

Juan spread his arms as the wind pulled the sheet out, as if he had a long wig of hair blowing wildly. He gripped the door's edges, but one hand held the gun and the other hand was mangled.

"Adiós," John whispered.

He kicked Juan out the door.

The man screamed as he flew into the nothingness, suddenly sucked out of the airplane, like the hand of God Himself had snatched him into the abyss. Juan's cry of surprise and anger faded into the air as quick as he fell, lost in the rage of the wind.

***

Mike looked up and saw Graham running to the opposite corner of the ballroom, with Tony hot on his heels. Diane was talking to Antonio's security guards — standing fifteen feet away, and although her gun was pointed down, it was still in her hands.

"I don't care if you were responding to a threat, you're putting others in danger!"

One of the security guards seemed to be the head. He was simultaneously trying to calm his men and respond to Diane. He said something Mike couldn't hear.

She pointed a finger towards him. "That's not my job, that's yours!"

"He's over here!" Graham called.

Diane turned her head when she heard the call. Mike laid Marcela's head down gently and stood, stepping around the blood on the floor and careful not to slip. The puddle there continued to grow, as if it were alive and slowly consuming the ballroom floor. He made his way over to the corner the two other agents approached.

When he arrived he stopped involuntarily, frozen. He blinked twice before processing what he was seeing.

The prince was naked, scrambling to pick up his scattered clothing. But more shocking were the two young girls, also naked, huddling under a tablecloth, peeking out at the agents. They were obviously underage, and Mike couldn't imagine the trauma they'd just been through — sexual and otherwise.

"Fucking pedophile island," Mike said aloud.

The prince stood, indignant while pulling on a pair of underwear, opening his mouth as if to say something, but then he nearly tripped and the agent with the bad haircut gave him a hand, stopping his fall. Tony crossed his arms, looking similarly upset. He exchanged a glance with Mike, unreadable in its message.

"Get those girls some clothes," Mike said, turning away and waving over Diane. A series of men standing and staring was the last thing the girls needed at the moment. He wanted nothing more than to get them away from all this; get them home and safe.

He looked around to clear his mind — or perhaps to distract himself.

Bullets riddled the ballroom walls and chunks of pillars had been torn and blasted apart, spilling onto the floor. Most of the guests had fled by now, running when the shooting had stopped if they hadn't gotten out earlier, although a few casualties were being tended to. The security guards began securing entrances and exits, confused about what to do next. The threats had been neutralized in the area, but a few guards were savvy enough to go after Juan and John, slipping out into the outdoor hallway before Mike had a chance to stop them.

Antonio was nowhere to be found.

Bastard, Mike thought.

Their target had gotten away. What was supposed to be a simple reconnaissance mission had taken a deadly turn, killing one of the few people Mike trusted in this whole affair, and blown their chance at capturing Antonio. The man would be whisked away to Cuba, avoiding any charges the United States or the international community might throw his way. He was a Cuban asset and would be protected, and any revealed secrets would only hurt rival countries.

But things weren't over yet. Mike knew John would be burning for vengeance, and Mike wasn't done yet either. There were still wrongs to right.

Diane rushed over, oblivious to Mike's brooding thoughts, and was quick to put an arm around the girls' shoulders, looking for their clothing. Mike gave her a moment, then he gestured with his head, indicating he wanted to talk to her privately.

"We're getting the hell out of here," Mike said.

Diane nodded curtly. "Agreed. Your agents?"

"One is in pursuit of that drug lord that started all this," Mike said, eyeing the security guards warily. "The other is KIA."

"I'm sorry," Diane said.

Mike nodded. "Let's hit the airfield. Your men will help with the body?"

Diane nodded back. She spoke to the prince and other agents quietly, eyes furtively glancing at Mike as she finished. The others nodded and the agents ran over to Marcela's body with a thick tablecloth. Graham helped her onto Tony's shoulder and the two waited for further orders, both looking around anxiously at any potential threats. Diane took the girls by the hand, as they made nervous looks at the prince. The agents pretended not to notice.

Mike wanted to get out before the security guards could get their act together. But he didn't want to leave without John.

He could only hope he'd taken care of that bastard Juan.

Chapter 20

John finished duct-taping the woman who'd shot at him into a seat. She struggled at first, but was quickly subdued, especially after seeing how John dealt with Juan. Which was fortunate, because John was badly injured and tired, and needed medical treatment soon. The woman probably couldn't fight him, but it wasn't exactly something John wanted to test. Once he finished, he turned to the girls.

They huddled in near-silence, some whimpering, cowering and flinching when John's cold gaze swept over them. He didn't know what to do to calm them. Didn't know what to say. He must look terrifying. He just kicked a man out of an airplane after a violent gunfight.

He wasn't good with kids. But they reminded him of Pablito — the half-brother of the man he had just thrown out of a plane. Kids shouldn't be involved in this sort of thing. These girls were already abused, to traumatize them further was a sin.

"Anyone hurt?" John asked. His voice came out hoarse and he cleared his throat. He repeated himself, forcing his voice to come out gentler and slower. As much as he tried, it didn't appear to have a soothing effect.

"We're okay," one of the girls said, sticking out her chin, a look of defiance on her face.

John nodded. "That's good. Let me know if that changes."

"Are we going back to the island?" the girl asked. Some of the other girls looked to her, then to John. John saw one girl, blank-faced, eyes glazed over, staring out the window. Another girl was asleep or had fainted.

John felt his face grow dark. The girl shrunk back.

"We have to turn back," John said. "So I can get my friend. But then we're going someplace safe."

The girl mustered some more of her courage. She was about to speak, but the other girl looking out the window spoke instead, not turning to face John.

"Promise?"

Her voice was like a ghost speaking. John looked at her, face tight, and nodded.

"Promise."

He left the girls and went to confront the pilot.

It wasn't hard to convince the pilot to land the plane. Someone holding a gun could convince most people of what they wanted. The pilot said it was a bit tricky because of so many planes trying to get in the air from the airstrip at the same time, but eventually they descended, and as soon as the door opened and the staircase was lowered, John poked out, gun ready, ready to go hunting for Mike.

He hadn't needed to go far. Mike was already at the airfield with a small group of others, John initially mistaking them for Antonio's security. He was devising a plan of action to take on the group but Mike approached the plane without trouble. One of the men following had the unmistakable figure of a body slung over his shoulder, wrapped tightly in a cloth, blood seeping through near the neck.

John knew who it was immediately.

They brought Marcela's body on board and left Mike. The man watched the group warily until they closed the plane door.

"Who were they?" John asked.

"MI5."

John nodded, as if this was the most natural answer in the world. Mike looked over to him.

"You look like hell."

John didn't say anything. He wasn't looking back at Mike.

He was staring at the wrapped-up body, lying on the seats.

There was silence for a little while. Mike surveyed the rest of the plane. His eyes widened when he saw the girls at the back, poking their heads out with fear and curiosity. He was more surprised by them than the woman duct-taped meticulously to a seat on the other side of the aisle.

John finally broke his stare and went to tell the pilot to get them in the air again. He was anxious to leave before security decided to board the remaining planes and investigate. Mike flopped in a seat and put a hand to his forehead, sighing. John could hear a million words in that sigh. He sat across the aisle from Mike and held a tissue to his broken nose, eventually stopping a determined bleed. He didn't say anything until they had taken off, pulling up into the sky.

"Did you get Antonio?"

Mike bit his lip. He turned to face John, a grim expression of resolve overcoming him.

"No. Got away."

John didn't say anything. He suspected as much. There was nothing they could do about it now.

"Where are we heading?" Mike asked.

"Antigua."

Mike's eyes widened with surprise. "Antigua?"

John nodded. He gestured to the girls with a tilt of his head. "It's where they're from."

"John…"

"And close to where Marcela is from."

John looked out the window, face impassive.

Mike took a deep breath and let it out. "They won't be safe there," he said, deliberately ignoring the statement about Marcela.

"They won't be safe anywhere," John said, examining the dark mist surrounding the plane as if it were the most interesting thing in the world. "But they need to go home."

"John…"

John swiveled his head suddenly, and Mike drew back at the intensity of John's stare and expression.

"We can't protect everybody."

Mike put out a hand but John looked like he'd snap it between his jaws, they were set so hard. Fury blazed in his eyes.

"Alright. John. Listen to me."

John blinked.

"Let me take care of this. I've got some non-CIA contacts in Guatemala, we'll watch the girls. Bury Marcela. Lay low."

"What do you want me to do?" John asked. He was falling back into what he knew. Orders. Mission. Debrief.

"Go home," Mike said, with a softness to his tone John hadn't heard before, nor believed the man could achieve. "Wherever that might be for you. Get patched up, take some R&R. Contact me when you're ready."

"For what?"

Mike smiled. It was a hungry curl of the lips that spilled over his mouth. "To bag Antonio. Once and for all."

Chapter 21

John walked up the steps to the house in front of him, hardly remembering the drive. It'd been long and rainy — it still was — and the cold chilled him to the bone. A light mist fell over the village of Trinity. It had started to roll in as he'd gotten off the highway, the orange glow of the outdated streetlights diffused into the dark cloudy night.

He took a deep breath full of moisture, and reached out a hand to knock.

The door swung open before he had a chance.

An older woman stood there, graying hair tied up in a bun, wrinkles creasing her eyes and cheeks with age. But her eyes were sharp as a hawk, even if they were poised behind a pair of glasses, and her lips were pursed tight. Her expression was unreadable. That at least, hadn't changed.

"I suppose you'll want to come in," she said, before John could say anything.

He blinked, staring back at the woman. She looked familiar and different at the same time. She had aged in a mysterious way that crept over John, like a spider's web had fallen over his memory.

"If that's okay, Mom," he said, before he let her answer get the best of him. It wasn't unkind, but it wasn't welcoming either. He didn't know why he'd expected otherwise.

She nodded, turned around, and walked toward the kitchen.

"Take your shoes off," she said to the hallway, not facing him as she moved. It was a slower motion, he noticed. She always asked him to take his shoes off, even though he never kept them on inside. Few households in Canada left shoes on indoors.

He obliged, meticulously untying his shoes and taking them off, realizing he was self-conscious that she might be watching him. She always used to bother him about how long he took to tie and untie his shoes, how long he took to put on an outfit, how long it took him to leave the house. Maybe that's why he'd left so soon. Maybe that's why he'd rarely returned. He finally learned how to move quickly.

He hung his coat on an unfamiliar coat hook on the wall: one of a trifecta of 'jellybean houses' — colorful tall rowing houses Newfoundland was famous for — with hooks where their doors should be. He walked down the hall passing more familiar paintings of boats on the ocean hanging in their spots along the wall.

She was rummaging in the kitchen cupboards when he entered the kitchen.

"I don't have much. Wasn't expecting you."

John didn't respond. Then her eyes snapped up to meet his, and she arched an eyebrow, as if he'd just insulted her.

She always hated when John didn't answer her remarks. But that was because she rarely asked direct questions, or ever particularly wanted to hear what John had to say. At least that's how it felt.

"That's fine," John responded. "Don't need much."

"You never did, did you?"

"No."

His mother sighed. "I was just about to make cod bites. I can make more."

"Alright."

"You can help."

John nodded.

The kitchen was as he'd remembered it, light brown cupboards that were out of date but homey. His mother might be cold, but the kitchen was warm.

She already had a large codfish out on a cutting board, halfway through filleting it. The head, chopped off before John had arrived, stared up at him with a bewildered expression.

"Is there —"

"Fresh one in the fridge," his mother said before he could finish, picking up her fillet knife and cracking her neck, staring down at her victim.

John found a bag with another bloody codfish in the fridge, and found a plate where they were usually kept. That much hadn't changed. He found a knife that'd work alright, and set up uncomfortably close to his mother on the counter.

They worked in silence, the only sounds coming from their knives, and the tearing of fish flesh and bone. His mother looked over once or twice to examine his work. She didn't say a word but he knew she was surprised he remembered how to fillet a fish, and so well. She didn't need to give him instruction.

She'd only shown him once, after all. After he was shown anything once, he was expected to master it. And if he couldn't master it...

Then I couldn't do it, he thought, as he sliced off the tail with a single chop.

They tossed the remains in a bucket, but not before removing the tongues and cheeks off the heads. These would be cooked separately, and carefully, as the choice parts of the cod.

"Get a pot," John's mother said. "Under the —"

He opened the lower cupboard and found a large pot, interrupting her. He filled it with water from the tap. She pursed her lips and began to dice an onion with slow methodical slices of the knife.

John moved on to peel potatoes.

"Not in the sink," his mother said when he began, "do it over the compost."

The compost container was small, and it was hard to land the potato peels accurately inside. If you weren't good enough at it, that was.

John placed the container in the sink and got to work. Whenever a peel hit the sink, his mother looked over and frowned.

The water began to boil and they cooked up the potatoes, onion, and cod. Once finished, they mashed it all together in a bowl with butter, salt, pepper, egg, and flour, then used the same burner and pot for the oil.

"That's too much," his mother said, snatching the oil from him as he poured it in. "What a waste."

John darkened, but didn't respond.

They made tablespoons of the mixture and placed them inside the oil. The smell and sound of frying filled the kitchen. His mother watched the balls like a snake watching a mouse. John began to do the dishes, handing her a dry one once she was ready.

"Paper towel," she said.

He was already reaching for it, but didn't say anything as he ripped off two pieces and handed them over. She plated and dabbed the cod bites, and John set the table for two.

They had to wait for them to cool. John looked at his mother. She looked back.

"So, you're in town," she said.

She had never been good at small talk. That was fine by John, he wasn't either. He liked to think he'd gotten better. He didn't know if that was the case.

"Yeah."

"What brings you in?"

"Healthcare," John said, attempting a weak joke, with some truth.

His mother smiled, but it was a strange thing, like a pair of strings were hooked into the corners of her mouth and then suddenly jerked upwards. It disappeared in an instant.

"Trouble?"

"Yeah," John said. "But the doctors say I'll be alright."

"Right," she said.

He didn't know how much she knew. He never knew how much she knew. He had never told her anything. Not outright. But mothers knew things. And their relationship had always been 'don't ask, don't tell.' In all things.

She took one of the cod bites onto her plate and tore it in two. John followed. It burned his fingers, and he set it back down as she ate.

They were silent for a few minutes. He yearned for a fork but dared not ask or get one himself. He tenderly began to eat when the food had begun to cool.

"Something on your mind?" she asked.

John stopped chewing. He nodded.

"Go ahead," she said.

"I lost someone," he said, before he could decide against his better judgment to say or not say the words. "Someone close to me."

His mother didn't respond right away. She took another cod bite from the serving plate, again tearing it in two.

"Was it your fault?"

John frowned. "I don't think so. No. But you know how it is...it always feels that way. Feel like I could've stopped it."

"Maybe you could've."

John grabbed another cod bite. He bit into it and it burned his tongue. He chewed through the pain and swallowed, letting the hot crispy material cut his throat. "Maybe I could've."

Silence again. The cod bites were gone.

"Can't save 'em all." She clucked her tongue, then stood, piling the plates for cleaning and examining the cheeks and tongues left on the cutting board. She'd cook them up next.

John watched her, wondering what she was thinking. Wondering why he cared.

She turned to face him. "Your room's ready upstairs." Then she turned back around to clean the dishes.

When John awoke, it was to the sound of pounding on the front door. He hurried to get dressed and retrieved his Glock from the nightstand before he heard someone running up the stairs. An aggressive knocking followed on his door.

John swooped behind the door as it burst open.

"Hi cuz!"

John tucked his gun away, and he stepped out from his hiding place.

Connor jumped with exaggerated fright. "There you are! Auntie Lynn said you were home! I couldn't believe it!"

John attempted a weak smile. But he had a lot on his mind.

"Bad time?"

John's cousin Connor was one of the few people who could read him well. It was hard to hide anything from him. They'd been close growing up together, and remained close even after they took their separate paths.

"Weird being home," John replied.

He wasn't lying. While his old posters and action figures had been long given away or tossed by his mother, the walls were still the same deep blue, the desk was still in the same spot by the window, and the bed still felt the same. Everything seemed smaller though. It was like his mother; familiar and different at the same time. It left an uncanny feeling in his stomach.

But Connor could tell he had more than home on his mind. The man sometimes had a sixth sense for people and their thoughts. It was no surprise he had become John's closest confidant.

Connor held out the handline he was holding in his hand. He grinned. "Come on. The fish miss you too."

CUBAN CONSPIRACY

The sun was just rising by the time they pulled their little motorboat out of Fisher Cove and swung around the small little cape of Trinity, eventually pulling up to Fort Point and sneaking past Admiral Island. Then they were out in the true blue, the Atlantic Ocean opening before them. The sunrise painted the horizon in front of them with splashes of oranges and yellows against violet and navy, like someone had spilled a series of paint bottles into the sky. The golden orb of the sun slowly lifted, and the last of the seagulls from land cawed before turning back, hoping to find better pickings on the coast than the water.

John and Connor got to work with their handline jiggers, letting the boat drift. They could've used rods just as easily, but they'd grown up with handlines from Connor's dad and John's uncle, so they kept up the tradition. They tossed their lines in and unwound the spools, allowing the hooks to be pulled in by their weights, splaying out for their catch like a jellyfish spreading its tentacles. The ocean was fairly tame, with only the occasional wave pushing their boat astray.

Calm, quiet, relaxing. John found himself uncomfortable. He wasn't used to this.

"Auntie Lynn says you were in the hospital," Connor said, eventually breaking the silence and opening up for conversation. It was a statement, not a question, allowing John to answer or leave it as he chose.

John shrugged. "Yeah. Bullet wound."

Connor's eyes widened. "She didn't tell me that part."

"She doesn't know," John replied.

Connor didn't know everything about John's work life, but he knew more than most. John kept what secrets he needed, but told the ones he could.

"Was lucky," he said, raising his shirt for Connor to see when he saw the man grow curious. "In and out clean, didn't hit anything important."

"Wow," Connor said, a mixture of fascination and disgust overcoming him as he stared at the ugly scar in John's side. "Looks like the doctors did okay."

John nodded sagely. "They were pretty upset when they found out I'd torn the stitches more than once and that I'd been running around and getting into fights, but I think they were more surprised I was able to in the first place than anything else."

Connor chuckled. "That's my John."

John gave a weak smile in return. He felt better now — physically at least. He was finally able to operate at full capacity. The rest had done him well. But he still felt uneasy about the work. They had to get Antonio. The Cubans weren't going to extradite him, and the CIA weren't too keen on bagging the man, what with the PAG wanting to keep things under wraps. The way he'd last spoken to Mike, it sounded like they'd have to do it themselves if they expected any results. Force the brass to conduct an internal investigation. Audit everything.

A darkness fell over him then. He still hadn't gotten his revenge. The spirit of Brian haunted him. Killed during the first Antiguan job, Brian had known something was wrong from the start. Brian's death had been John's motivation in everything these past couple months. He couldn't sleep at night, couldn't trust others the way he used to...and now, with Marcela gone, it had all gotten worse.

He may have killed Juan, but without Antonio, things were left undone. He would put their spirits to rest. Or die trying.

I swear to God, he thought to himself.

"The Pope says hi."

John shook himself out of his reverie. Then his eyes widened once he realized what Connor had just said. "You met him?"

Connor rocked his head back and forth as he tugged on his line. "Basically. Didn't have a chat with him, but I did shake his hand."

John felt a smile creep across his lips. "Did he say anything to you?"

"Said I was doing God's work. And I thought, yeah, no kidding, I'm a priest."

They both laughed at that.

An easy silence fell over them. John's dark thoughts threatened to surface once again, but he fought them down. He tried to enjoy this moment with his cousin. But it was hard to enjoy anything these days. Not with all the corruption and evil in the world. Too many people would get away with their insidious deeds while working for the very institutions he had trusted. John was privy to too much of it. He often found himself wishing things could be like they used to. Follow orders. Complete the mission. Do good and sleep well at night. His mind wasn't built for ambiguities.

"Oh dang, here we go," Connor said, yanked his handline.

The line was taut, and quivered, pulling back as Connor fought with it.

"Oh, he's a big sucker," Connor said. "John grab the gaff!"

John was already moving across the boat, grabbing the big hooked stick at the bow and moving to Connor at the stern.

"Hurry!"

John stepped over the middle bench and poised with the gaff, watching the surface closely. Connor pulled in his line, hand over hand, and within moments, a green shape began to emerge in the deep, writhing and struggling, slowly growing brighter as the sun reflected off its shiny, speckled skin.

"Come on..."

John stabbed at the water but missed the thrashing fish. The surface splashed as its tail kicked and Connor heaved the line.

Connor's hands flew high up and over his head as the line broke and the sinker and hooks whipped over them, plunking into the water opposite them with a small splash. The fish disappeared as quickly as it had come, wriggling away back into the depths of the ocean.

John looked at Connor. They exchanged a glance and laughed.

"Ah, it was close..." Connor said as their laughter tapered.

"Was huge too," John said.

Connor brightened once more. "It was! The ones that get away are always the biggest."

John's smile faded. Connor pulled his line back in and checked the hooks and tackle, then dropped it over the side once more.

"A fish got away from me recently too," John said, the words out like a whisper, not certain what he was saying until he had already spoken.

"Yeah?" Connor was staring at the water, a pleasant expression on his face. He had such a way of enjoying the world around him. John loved that about him.

"Yeah." John jigged his line, but nothing was biting.

Connor leaned over, nudging John's shoulder and looking him in the eye, as if trying to see something under his gaze. "You're like Auntie Lynn. I can never tell what you're thinking."

I'm glad of that, John thought. He didn't want people like Connor being touched by the darkness he faced. Like the girls. Like Pablito. The world deserved better. But someone had to fight for it.

"I hope you find it," Connor continued, tugging at his own line.

"Find what?"

"The reason you came home."

John felt a nibble and yanked his line in an attempt to set the hook, but nothing took. "I can't stay."

"I know."

They sat in silence for a long moment after that. There were a couple nibbles, but no catches. The sun rose then shrunk behind a pair of clouds, and a soft rain followed, and they decided to turn in.

That was fine by John. It was never about catching fish anyway.

Later, John found himself driving back through St. John's, and decided to go to Cape Spear. Most tourists liked Signal Hill, where Marconi received the first transatlantic wireless transmission, but John preferred it elsewhere. There was construction making it difficult to get there, but it also meant most skipped over the first quiet parking lot in the area. He pulled in, all to himself, and got out of the car.

Cape Spear was the Easternmost point in all of North America. South America had it beat with Cape Branco, but John could still enjoy the view. It had been pouring when he'd finally said goodbye to Connor and his mother and left Trinity, and evidently the town had gotten some rain along with the bay. The lingering mist and hesitant droplets fell from a cloudy sky, and John's shoes pushed through mud as he made his way to the edge of the cliff.

To the right of him was the great lighthouse and tourist attraction. But he was content with his spot. He stared down at the crashing waves below, angry in their cycles as a violent wind whipped into motion. He didn't know how long he stood staring out at the deep gray-blue water and sky. It didn't matter.

Eventually he went back to the car. He called the number Mike had given him, and with his new operative phone.

"Esteban?" John asked, using the more formal code name for his handler.

He thought he could hear a smile on the other end. "Go ahead."

"Where's Antonio?"

Chapter 22

Antonio Romero was in Havana.

Unsurprising, perhaps, but Mike hadn't known that. Not before he'd gotten the phone call he'd been waiting for.

Mike was in Jaco Costa Rica. It was a tourist beach town, with plenty of surfing, restaurants and expats to go around. A lot of people spoke English and half the people there seemed to be Canadian or American . It reminded Mike of Miami.

He'd written a letter in code to Barker and sent it to the man's address. Part of the decoding included knowing Barker's Starbucks order, so Mike felt fairly confident no one would be cracking it anytime soon if they were searching his mail. In the meantime, Mike had been enjoying his exile. He'd found one of his secret accounts hadn't been shut down, or at least not yet. He was on his second Piña Colada and enjoying the sun on the beach when his phone rang.

"Hello?" Mike answered.

"Hiya boss," came Barker's unmistakable tone; a creepy-sounding squeal of excitement, followed by the sucking back of phlegm from his nose. Mike could picture the man's leer vividly in his mind's eye.

Mike grinned. There was no one on this sweet earth he'd rather hear from. "Hey Barker. Good to hear from you."

"Likewise! That letter was some real spook stuff, huh?"

Mike rolled his eyes. "Yeah, yeah, glad you got the number." He didn't have to ask if Barker was on a safe line.

The man was good at his job if anything else. "What's going on back at the Farm."

"I'm in charge of Blackthorne!" Barker exclaimed. "I don't think I'm running it quite as well as you did, but boy is it cool to be in charge!"

Mike smirked. That was something. But he wasn't altogether surprised. "Good to hear. I'm sure you're doing great. Linda on the warpath?"

"Yep."

"Figures."

"They filled the desk too."

"Did they now?"

"Lauren Lopez. PAG transfer."

"Oh fuck."

"Right?"

Either Linda doesn't believe a word I say about the PAG piggybacking G2's plans or things are even more out of control than I thought.

"Boss...when are you coming home?"

Mike took off his shades and rubbed his eyes. The words had affected them more than they should've. "That's what I'm calling about. Well, sort of. I need to pin Romero."

"There was talk about some action on the island, but the stuff coming out of the rumor mill is anyone's guess. Care to fill me in?"

"Not now." *The less you know, the better.*

"Alright. Antonio Romero."

"Yeah. I've been doing some thinking while I've been down here. And I think I figured things out." There was a pause on the other end, Barker allowing Mike to fill it. "I was investigating a mole in the CIA. But I may have gotten things wrong."

"What do you mean?" Barker asked, genuine surprise in his voice. "I thought —"

"The Russians gave me the lead that the Cubans had an active spy program. And with our own uncovering of PAG interference, we seemed to confirm it. But I'm thinking that less likely now. It all comes down to Romero. He's the Cuban's asset. The PAG is working off him. He's our guy. There doesn't have to be some boogeyman hiding out in the CIA for those things to add up. I'm sure the Russians are enjoying us chasing our tails."

There was a long pause this time. Mike could almost hear the gears working in Barker's head. Barker was a smart man. For this long of a pause, the man must have steam pouring from his ears.

"That seems...sensible."

Mike nodded even though there was no one there to see him. "We get Romero, we prosecute him, he spills the beans, probably for some shitty protection deal, and we button this thing up."

"And Linda will let you come back."

And Linda will lift the hit on my head. Mike thought, not keeping his hopes too high. "That's the idea."

"No way the Cubans will extradite him."

"I don't plan on extradition, Barker. We're the fucking CIA."

"Spook stuff?"

Mike grunted. "Spook stuff. I need a location."

"Havana."

Mike sat stunned.

"Sir?"

Mike collected himself. "Further intel?"

"He's let a lot of his guard down. He's got a driver and an armed guard, but it's not as if he's hiding out in some secure villa like his island. And I'm sure I can work the resources here to get you whatever you need."

Mike rubbed his temple thoughtfully. "Good Barker, that's good."

"But he's still in Cuba. We don't have any agents there. The safehouses are all compromised. I'm not sure how you plan to get him. I'm not even sure how you plan to get *in* there."

Mike grinned. "Carpenter."

***

It had been a while since John's last HALO jump.

Standing for high altitude — low opening, John had practiced the technique during his Navy SEAL training. He had earned his military freefall certification at Fort Bragg, North Carolina, and remembered the first week of training in a wind tunnel set vertically, learning how to properly fall and what to do with his body before the real thing.

But nothing could quite prepare an individual for a proper HALO jump.

The cargo door slowly lowered open, making the whine of moving machinery as the metal bars extended in place. The roar of the four six-bladed propellers droned through the air, punctuating the sound of wind tearing through the craft's now open door. John and the three other men walked down toward it, waiting for the all-clear from the jumpmaster.

"Check equipment!" came the bark from the jumpmaster for John and the other operatives to make sure their gear was good to go. Of course they'd done extensive equipment checks before they'd even gotten wheels off the ground, but another last-minute check was always important in case something had changed.

He was in the darkness of a C-130J-SOF, the only illumination coming from a series of harsh red lights. They'd decided a HALO jump would be the most appropriate thing, considering how limited their options were. John needed to get into Cuba. After considering sneaking on a tourist plane or boat, Mike decided they were leaving little to chance. The HALO jump meant they'd be bypassing radar, the jump was happening at night to limit a visual on entry, and the sheer speed of it all reinforced the nature of the job.

All the risks were on John, as well as the other operatives who would be acting independently from him.

"ETA one minute!" the jumpmaster called.

"One minute!" they called back.

They cruised through the air at over three hundred and seventy miles an hour before slowing for the drop. The C-130J-SOF was the newest craft in the Super Hercules line of military transports, introduced only a few years previous. Meant for intelligence, surveillance, and reconnaissance, among other special operations, the SOG R&D department had suggested the Lockheed Martin plane for exactly these sorts of purposes. Equipped with an enhanced cargo handling system, the C-130J-SOF allowed for precision air drops.

John gave a wry smile internally as he thought about it. He was surprised they were giving him the good stuff. He was expecting some mothballed thing from 'Nam.

"Thirty seconds!"

The sky outside was black. A pure abyss of dark ink, with no distinguishing features like the clouds or moon. It was as if a giant black maw had already swallowed the plane and everyone in it, and the jumpers were expected to dive into its sinister throat.

"Ten seconds!"

Most recreational skydivers jumped under fifteen thousand feet, and opened their parachute at around three thousand feet. The operatives were diving at forty thousand, and their 'chutes would open at around eight hundred if they could get away with it.

"Green light! Go! Go! Go!"

John didn't hesitate or entertain a second thought. Those got you killed.

He ran at the open sky and sprung off the hatch into empty space.

The wind cradled him at first, but then began to blow violently as he fell. His stomach flip-flopped as his body reacted to suddenly having the ground pulled out beneath him, and adrenaline began to pump into his system.

He had spent about an hour in the pre-breathing period, breathing pure oxygen to get rid of the nitrogen in his blood to prevent the bends. Still, he had to breathe from an oxygen bottle and mask as he dove. The temperature was around negative fifty Fahrenheit and the air bit at the few unprotected areas on his face, threatening to freeze them. He had a polypropylene-knit bodysuit to prevent the worst of the cold, along with his helmet, pack, and military-grade protection gear.

John felt like a speeding bullet. He spread his arms and legs, hips pushed forward and chin up. It was a neutral, stable position resulting in a comfortable arch. He had learned it long ago, that first time he'd done a proper jump, and every time after. He checked his altimeter as he sped past one hundred miles per hour and saw he'd dropped five thousand feet. Another thirty plus to go.

He was above the clouds. He could make out the curvature of the horizon. He mentally calmed his body, and his body slowly came to terms with an eternal fall. Terminal velocity was achieved, and John hit one hundred and twenty-five miles per hour.

Clouds sprayed over him. He fell through the mist and moisture battered his face and speckled his goggles with drops of water, blurring his view. He slowly moved a hand to wipe the droplets clear, carefully moving back into a relaxed position, outstretched. With the clouds gone, he had a better view of earth down below.

Dark as it may be, there were shapes amidst the black, and lights shining down below. The shallow hook of land looked like a crocodile basking in the Atlantic, the Bahamas and the tip of Florida to the north, a smear of Jamaica to the south, and still hidden behind the horizon was Haiti and the Dominican Republic to the south-east. The other landmasses began to shrink from his field of vision, as if slinking away into the bowels of the ocean. The main island of Cuba began to swallow all, and soon the ocean melted away so there was only land.

The ground continued to rush up toward him. The cold of the air was starting to numb him now, and he wiggled his fingers through his gloves to give them as much feeling as possible. He couldn't have his body falling asleep now. Not with such a crucial entry.

The lights down below grew from pinpricks to circles, and the roads and buildings began to take shape under the cover of darkness. He checked his altimeter. Another thousand feet flew by in an instant. He readied himself, bracing his body and preparing to pull his secondary emergency 'chute if anything went wrong.

Four thousand...three thousand...two thousand...one...

His primary parachute exploded from his pack automatically at eight hundred feet. It flew up with a burst of energy and unfolded like a blooming flower, and John was shot upwards with it, pulled by the powerful cords and nylon. His harness hoisted him by the chest and groin, tugging his legs up with it. He felt like a rag doll at the whim of a child's temperamental hand.

Although the pull slowed the altimeter greatly, the ground was still coming up towards him. He continued to fall at speed, and he spotted the field that was the designated DZ. He took a brief moment to look away from his target to make sure his lines had unfolded properly.

There was a tangle.

He reached up and gave the lines a tug, trying to see if that would sort them out. But they were stubborn, twisted in such a way that wouldn't be undone by a simple pull. Tangled lines were dangerous. Most people were concerned about the parachute springing, but tangled lines could be just as deadly. They messed with steering and could mean a hard landing if the jumper lost control.

The ground continued to rush up towards him, another hundred meters disappearing in seconds.

He pulled hard to try and put some drag on the drop, but the pull was lopsided because of the tangled lines, and he listed dangerously off to the left, straight for a copse of trees. He pulled the other side to offset the veered direction but it did little good. He was on a collision course with the brush and rough trunks of trees.

He tried to relax as best he could, and allowed himself to drift closer to the ground, even if the speed was still too dangerous. He pulled a knife and began to cut the lines.

The right side snapped loose, separating and swinging him to hang from the left. He prepared to cut again but the trees were coming up fast, and a fat trunk was rushing up right in front. He watched the ground, dropping further and trying to time it so he wouldn't collide with the tree...

He sliced the lines and dropped from the parachute, freefalling fifteen feet and landing in a crouch and rolling quickly to distribute the impact. He landed in a sitting position, legs splayed in front of him, the tree within spitting distance.

The entire drop took less than two minutes.

He let out a heavy breath he hadn't realized he'd been holding and watched the parachute tangle into the brush. He stood on shaky legs and began to calm his body, clear his mind. Adrenaline made his limbs buzz, but he didn't want to stay in one place for too long. While he didn't think anyone would have detected his entry, it wasn't good practice to stay put after insertion.

The others landed nearby, and he checked in with them.

"Sprained ankle," one of other operatives said, testing another's foot as he hopped on the other. "We're fine."

"Happy hunting," another operative nodded to John, unclipping his helmet.

He had his job, and they had theirs.

John worked quickly, gathering up his parachute and folding it together, tucking it under a spiky bush. Then he unclipped his harness, helmet, and goggles, ditching those as well, and finally stripped into his plainclothes. He was dressed like a tourist in a loose-fitting white shirt and shorts, and had nothing but a phone, wallet with cash, and a gun in his bag.

It was all he needed.

Chapter 23

Antonio Romero had had a busy month. Besides the usual business, he'd experienced and survived his first gunfight. Not that he'd been at the center of it, but it had been harrowing to have his island of pleasure become a place of carnage. His home had been invaded. His sanctum breached. Its shelter had been sundered forever. So many of his security guards had been killed by only a few insurgents, and for what? The G2's informant in the CIA had told him that the whole thing had been either a reconnaissance or assassination attempt, botched by a Guatemalan drug lord Antonio had dealings with. It was only because Juan Puentes had been there to recognize the CIA infiltration that it had been thwarted, but that had also been the reason unbelievable violence had broken out.

Antonio considered himself a man of class. Such barbaric ferocity was beneath him, but he'd been furious to find out some of his clientele had been killed and wounded during the incident. It was supposed to be a lavish but straightforward party. He had held them before. And now? Who would come to his island? Who would want to deal with him? Besides the reputation for danger, it painted too obvious a spotlight on what would otherwise remain private affairs. Antonio had been working all month to salvage the situation, but it had been difficult to bribe, silence, and threaten so many people and moving parts.

Cuban intelligence had brought him to Havana immediately for safekeeping. If the CIA were infiltrating his island, they wouldn't allow him to remain there. The island was now under lockdown, with G2 patrol boats and hidden jungle agents prepared for anything the CIA might think to throw at them once more. In other words, his favorite place — his home — was forever gone.

They'd kept him safe and secure in a guarded hotel for the first couple weeks, but Antonio had demanded he be let go. The Americans had ordered him to leave the island and stand trial for various crimes, but Cuban Intelligence had no plans to extradite him. He was their agent, and he was important. And they'd never bow to American imperialists. Besides, even if the right pressures were applied by the international community, the risk of what Antonio knew was too great. He was one of the few people in the entire world that knew a Cuban mole remained active in the CIA.

This had at least given him a bit of leverage to eventually break his constricting stay-at-home order. He was now able to come and go at his leisure. Followed perhaps, but he was no stranger to security detail.

Antonio hadn't met John Carpenter. He didn't know who he was, or that he was in Cuba, or that he was hunting Antonio. But most of all, Antonio couldn't conceive the sheer will John had to capture him.

He'd find out soon enough.

Dusk began to fall on Havana. With Mike's intel, John was able to locate Antonio. Amidst all the vintage cars driving around thanks to America's embargo, Antonio was riding a flashy 1958 Ford Thunderbird, bright red. John also quickly identified the two G2 agents that were tailing Antonio as the man went about his business. Antonio thought he was safe in Cuba. He knew he wouldn't be extradited, and didn't believe the CIA or any other agency would try — or be able — to get an active agent into the island. Even if they did, Antonio wasn't worth much dead. He had to be taken alive. And that seemed to make things difficult.

John thought otherwise.

He pretended to take pictures with his phone, acting the part of a tourist. The enemy agents were good, and it had taken John a while to identify them, but they still hadn't realized he was tailing them. John hadn't gotten this close before. But now that Antonio had decided to wander this far from Havana's downtown, John decided it was time to strike.

They weren't too far from Old Havana — the old stomping ground of Ernest Hemingway. A prostitute flagged John down but John waved her off. Prostitution was common in Cuba. Castro tried to arrest them all once, but didn't have enough jail space so he had to let them go. Mistresses were common too, although more discreet in the country. Family might be big in Cuba — it was the number one thing in Latin American culture — but once the woman got old, the guy sometimes just went to a younger woman.

It was hot. Humid. There was the constant wind off the ocean, but John was still sweating through his single thin shirt. He saw Antonio's T-Bird driving slowly past a series of prostitutes, but soon enough the window rolled up and the car began to move on. John knew the man preferred his women younger , and tonight 's wares didn 't suit his tastes . That worked well enough for John.

He continued down the sidewalk, watching the two G2 agents from the corner of his eye. They saw Antonio's car roll away and made their way to their motorcycles, ready to pursue and watch from a distance.

John timed his walk carefully. Steadily, he drew his gun as the two agents approached their bikes.

They wouldn't get a chance to mount them.

John shot the first man in the head, the back of his skull exploding from the impact of the bullet streaking through the evening air.

Prostitutes screamed and ran. A car's tires squealed as rubber burned asphalt and the car tore away, wanting to get as far as possible from a conflict involving a gun.

The second agent was trained well enough that he didn't turn to his partner as his body hit the road. He drew his gun from his belt instead and locked eyes with John.

The man wasn't quick enough.

The second shot took the man in the chest, followed by a third through the neck. The man spun awkwardly, convulsing in place before falling onto his ribs. John stood over the man ready to put a final bullet through his head, but both G2 agents were good and dead. He wasted no time in his mission.

John rifled through the suit jacket of the first agent and found the keys. After hearing the satisfying growl of the engine, John took to the streets.

Antonio hadn't gotten far.

His driver was taking his time taking Antonio back to the hotel. John had watched Antonio's car mosey along other nights, moving slower in the evenings than it did during the day, making frequent stops. It all factored into John's hunt, and he had meticulously calculated the variables for this instance.

John tore through the street and weaved through the other lazily moving cars that had no business rushing anywhere. Cubans didn't move with the directed hustle New Yorkers were famous for, and John found the driving easy. But he dared not let himself think his plan was successful until he had his quarry.

Antonio and his men didn't seem to think anything was off. The T-Bird continued through a changing traffic light and John ran the red. Antonio's driver didn't speed away or make a hasty turn as if it knew a dangerous tail followed. So John made his move.

He pulled into the right lane, slowly pulling alongside the other car. He waited for a traffic light that would make the next step work. They passed through two greens before a red stopped them.

John pulled up next to Antonio's car.

He dismounted, and walked up to the driver's side window, gun out and pointed at the glass.

He fired three times, shattering the window and decimating the driver's head. The bullets flew through the air and into the security detail next to him in the passenger's side seat. Neither had time to react. Neither had time to scream. Neither knew they were dead until it was upon them.

Antonio Romero was the only one able to yell.

"¡Mierda! ¡Mierda! ¡Mierda!"

Darkness swallowed John's face as he opened the driver's door and unbuckled the seatbelt of the corpse inside. He pulled the body off the seat by the shirt collar and swept the seat of any glass before taking its place and calmly putting the seatbelt back on. He ignored the cowering of people in the cars surrounding them, and the flurry of activity as a few cars pushed past and ran the red or took hasty U-turns away from the scene.

John turned in the seat and looked at Antonio.

He hadn't seen the man up close before. He'd only seen the man in his briefings.

He didn't feel a thing for him.

"If you say another word I'll shoot you," John said calmly. The matter-of-fact tone cut through the man's screams.

"*¡Vete a la mierda! ¡Se que me quieres vivo!*" *Fuck you! I know you want me alive.*

"I said I'd shoot you," John said. John shot the man in the right knee, blowing out his kneecap.

Antonio howled in pain. John pointed the gun at the man's left knee.

Antonio spat in John's face.

John shot the man's other knee, and Antonio let loose a blood curdling cry for help.

No one would be able to save him.

John locked the doors and stepped on the gas, the light conveniently changing green. He drove past the violent scene and eventually found himself alongside other vintage cars, blending in with the other bright or pastel-colored vehicles enjoying the sunset. An ambulance and a pair of cop cars rushed past. John continued to drive calmly ahead. He turned onto the *Avenida de la Independencia,* occasionally looking at Antonio in the rearview mirror. The man was whimpering, contemplating his doom. An icon of Saint Christopher, patron saint of Havana and travelers hung from the rearview mirror.

Saint Christopher wouldn't be taking care of Antonio today.

They eventually came up on the airport. John drove to where a series of helicopters sat waiting for tourists and the like. He drove up to a sky-blue chopper with branding for helicopter tours, and put the car into park.

He got out of the car and opened Antonio's door. The man cowered, but John grabbed an arm and dragged the man out. He cried out in pain as his legs were suddenly needed to support his weight, but a wave of John's gun shut him up. John leaned over and pulled the man onto his shoulder. He was happy to see his own strength had returned after his injury. There was nothing worse than having to operate at limited capacity.

The helicopter door slid open. A man in dark tactical gear had his arms outstretched, ready to accept the quarry. John dumped Antonio into the man's arms, and a second man appeared, beginning to apply bandages to Antonio's wounds.

John nodded to the pilot lurking behind the window and turned on his heel, ready to ditch the car somewhere.

"Aren't you coming?" the man in the tac gear asked.

John looked over his shoulder at the man. The man had his head tilted, confused.

"I'm not done here," John replied.

Chapter 24

The mole sat at her office window, staring out at Langley's campus. It was a sunny day outside, and she could hear the sound of birds chirping through her window. She idly wished she could open the sealed window and let in a breeze, allowing her to hear the musical sounds more clearly. But windows were sealed at Langley.

She liked the sound of the birds. They sang freely.

She slumped deeper in her chair. The birdsongs drifted into the back of her mind until she could no longer hear them, her mind swirling with mangled thoughts and choppy internal dialogue. The day might be cheery, but it was a sharp contrast to how she was feeling, and it could do nothing to elevate her spirits. A pit in the center of her stomach had opened up, and began to absorb all feeling.

She had received a message from the *Dirección de Inteligencia*. It had been a letter disguised to look like a harmless flyer to anyone unaware of the code embedded, should someone rifle through her mail. She didn't often receive messages from them. It wasn't as if she required management — she mostly acted on her own, especially now that she'd been undercover for so long and proven herself to be highly capable. Her loyalty was unquestioned. So when she received messages they were usually important.

This one wasn't just important. It was personal.

She expected to feel despair. Instead, she felt nothing. A numbness that crept from the pit in her stomach and swallowed her thoughts. She had repeated the words she'd read in her head again and again until they spun together and dissipated into nothingness.

She clicked her pen, exposing the ballpoint at the end. She clicked it again, concealing it once more. She did this a few more times, slowly, methodically, with intention. It made her feel in control of something.

She stood from her computer and office desk and began to pace the room. She was used to being in control. When something slipped from her grasp, it confused her more than anything else. It was a character trait she'd — ironically — fought for control of all her life.

She considered the words once more as they formed in her mind. A message — an order — from G2. The unthinkable had happened. The unthinkable was required to rectify the situation.

It was what she had signed up for all those years ago, when she first left Cuba and created a false identity in America. Infiltrating the CIA hadn't been as difficult as she'd expected. But maneuvering to be in an effective place to make the best use of her position had been tricky. It had taken years. It had, admittedly, almost broken her more than once. She had given her life to the cause and in return, what did she really have to show for it?

She shook her head. She couldn't think like that. She forced herself to think of other things. She sometimes thought of Cuba. Thought of the parents she never knew. She'd been raised by an aunt and uncle before anonymously immigrating to the United States. A position with the CIA opened up for her. She brought much to the table. She lied about being Cuban — that would be too close to home —

but a Puerto Rican wanting to work with the CIA? Her language and cultural skills were incredible assets; she would become known for her work ethic and drive even more.

She was old. Almost too old for the job — she'd be retiring soon. But she'd established much, and the wheels of the Cuban plans were finally in motion. The Political Action Group had been quickly cowed into a position that worked for their purposes, and other than some minor irritants, the plan had worked. The CIA was in league with Latin American drugs and human trafficking; its politics synonymous with Cuban interests.

But now...

Now all that hardly mattered.

We keep going, a voice told her. She thought it was her brother's at first, but she quickly realized it was her own. It was what she often found herself telling *him.*

We keep going.

She slumped back in her chair. She stared at her computer screen. She wheeled around and watched a pair of curious birds chirp at one another.

Free. Not a care in the world.

They don't live in the same world, she reminded herself. Her grip tightened on the pen she held as she clicked it, and she snapped the clip clean off.

She stifled a yell, threw the pen across the room, then picked up the phone.

She dialed a number and set another plan into motion.

For Cuba, she told herself through the tears welling in her eyes, *always.*

Antonio lowered himself gingerly from the chin up bar before dropping back into his wheelchair. He was eager to progress with his mobility, but without a double knee replacement he was mostly confined to his chair. He settled in and stretched out his arms, relishing in the feeling of working strength in his muscles. He'd always been a fairly fit man, and he intended to keep it that way, even through this newest bout of imprisonment. True, the cell wasn't quite as comfy as last time, and he wasn't able to leave during daylight hours, but that last arrest so many years ago had been a joke anyway. This time around, it wasn't about his taste in young girls. This time it was about intelligence. About his *real* secrets. His cover was blown, and G2 would be furious. He was too closely connected with their CIA mole. But the CIA didn't necessarily know that.

Did they?

Antonio knew the CIA wanted to keep things quiet. Too many of its own officers were involved in his affairs, and too many related politicians had been to *Isla de Anticipación.* He was too well-connected, knew too much, and other than having him under lock and key was all they could really do. They might prosecute him under pedophilia, certainly; his reputation was damaged, and many of his contacts were dropping like flies, cutting communication. But that only meant more opportunities for threats and bribes.

This was all ignoring the fact that he was a Cuban asset.

And the G2 plans were already in place. They couldn't remove those. The tech bill might prove more stubborn now, but imprisoning Antonio didn't prevent all the damage they'd already done to the CIA and the manipulations in American politics they'd achieved.

Antonio sighed as he signed in with a banal-looking guard and was escorted to his cell by another endless lamb in the United States correction system. He didn't know how long it would take for his people to get him out, but he knew he had nothing to worry about. He brushed his teeth and lay down on his bed, fixing his sleep apnea machine around his mouth and strapped it to his head. The sound of pumping air lulled him to sleep.

Antonio wouldn't wake up.

Chapter 25

John watched the news from his hotel room. He felt a darkness slowly descend on him as he watched.

"Cuban socialite Antonio Romero was found dead in his Florida prison cell yesterday, only days after Cuba accused the U.S. of kidnapping the man on Cuban soil. Romero was found dead in his sleep just after four a.m. from natural causes, but this has sparked harsh criticism and skepticism from reporters and even some officials who have been following the situation over the past few weeks..."

John's phone buzzed and he felt pulled from his trance. It was his Blackthorne phone, and he muted the TV and answered immediately.

"Are you watching the news?" It was Mike.

"Yeah."

"Shit. I'm sorry John."

John didn't want apologies. He wanted answers.

"What happened?"

"They got to him. He knew too much."

"We should've seen this coming." An edge entered John's voice. What they both knew was that *Mike* should have seen it coming.

"It's a clusterfuck," Mike said. "Two cameras cut out on his empty cell during the day. Guards tried to falsify records...well it doesn't matter. They're ruling it a natural death. They moved the body before anyone could lock down the scene for an investigation, and I doubt the autopsy is going confirm the carbon monoxide they would've used to kill the guy."

John's face tightened. "They'll buy the story?"

"It doesn't matter. He's dead, and with him, our case. They'll pay out the girls from his fortune and everyone else will scurry away. It'll be in legal hell for the next ten years. I've been on the phone nonstop since four a.m."

"You knew about this before the story broke." Not a question.

"Of course I did John, I'm the fucking CIA."

"I thought you quit."

"I'm working through some shit here John, trying to —"

"You knew."

"Why do you think I have anything to do with this?" Mike asked, more than a little irritation in his voice.

John didn't care if the man was irritated. John could care less about Mike's feelings. John had completed the mission. Mike had failed him.

"John, it was out of my control. Listen, I've been thinking. The Russians fed me the Cuban infiltration program and I thought there was someone further on the inside too. But I'm not so sure now."

"Tell me," John snarled.

"Antonio might've been it. What if there is no mole?"

John's world suddenly fell silent.

No mole? But that was everything they were after. If there was no mole, that meant...

"Antonio set up the deals," Mike continued, oblivious to John's silence. "He had his perverted little fingers deep into the PAG. It may have just been him all along."

"And now he's dead. We don't have answers."

"We'll never know for sure but —"

"We don't have justice."

"He's dead John, what more do you want?" John heard Mike take an exasperated breath. The next time he spoke it was softer. "What more do you need?"

John set his jaw. "It's not over."

He hung up the phone.

He sat for a long moment, hearing nothing but the soft ringing of silence.

Mike was a CIA goon. He'd crawl back with the information Marcela had dug up from *Anono* and offer it to his superiors as a bargaining chip. Like a cat bringing home a bird. He'd show his superiors what they needed to know and quietly cover up the rest in an effort to buy back his job. All while the real culprit continued on, as if nothing had changed. With Antonio dead, the double agent would go underground like a rat who'd swiped the cheese right off the trap.

John felt his anger bubbling up from beneath him. It sat in his gut and roiled up into his throat, about to come out as a mighty yell...

He stood up suddenly instead, turned off the TV, and tossed the remote on the couch. He was breathing hard.

He thought of Brian. Thought of Marcela. Their dead faces danced before him. Phantoms unable to rest.

He thought of the young girls caught up in a conspiracy that they couldn't understand. Thought of the Latin American lives burning for political plays the people had nothing to do with, nor any desire to become part of.

There might be no boogeyman at the top. Mike could be right. But John didn't think he was. And that inkling of thought was the difference between them. Mike was willing to settle. John would never stop. If there was even a sliver of a chance that their culprit was still at large...

John's eyes drifted around the room. His mind craved a distraction. Something to get his mind off the pain. He needed to refocus. Figure out his next plan of attack. He was on his own. He was used to that.

He saw the Bible sitting where he had left it on the bedside table. He stared at it. He looked at his watch. Then he slowly gathered himself and walked out the door.

Havana Cathedral was small, but its history went back to the mid-eighteenth century, built by Jesuits. Some of the construction was done with coral stone, which meant John was able to marvel at the fossilized marine life in the very brick itself. Havana Cathedral was also known for holding the mortal remains of Christopher Columbus for just over a hundred years. The Cuban War of Independence saw them shipped back to Spain, but some still believed the bones to be held in the Santo Domingo cathedral in the Dominican Republic due to a mysterious box of bone fragments and label alluding to Columbus being discovered there.

The service was good. The sermon was about presuming God's intention. John found it fascinating. He always found the depths of his faith held more than he previously considered.

"So many people say that 'God doesn't like something,' or we even determine who will go to heaven or hell," the priest had said. "But even the Bible doesn't *say* anything. We interpret. That's all we can do. And with God, we may never presume His ends. Do not replace your faith with claiming to know something you cannot know. Place your faith in the Lord."

After Mass, John meandered as others exited, eventually finding himself in front of a small shelf of votive candles. They sat flickering in front of a statue of the Virgin Mary, the patroness of the cathedral. He lit a candle for Marcela and stood for a long moment, staring into the flame.

"A candle? Pah!" He could almost hear her say. *"Have a drink for me instead."*

He made his way into the annex and smiled when he gazed upon his old friend. It had been a surprise, and a sight for sore eyes.

Father Francisco had been the village priest when John had first been posted to El Gigante on a Nicaragua job. John had attended Mass there and befriended the priest quickly, initially as an asset to integrate with the local population, but John soon found he genuinely appreciated the man's company. He was an old man who'd reached the point in his life that he could speak his mind and shrug at any repercussions. A good conversationalist and theologian, Father Francisco had been one of the reasons John had made his El Gigante base the closest thing to a home he had in Latin America.

That was of course, before it had been burned down.

Father Francisco had been transferred to another parish in Nicaragua and they'd lost touch. John had no idea the man had then moved to Cuba — promoted obviously — and he couldn't help but be proud and happy for his friend. He didn't have many of them left after all.

Seeing Father Francisco preach once more was a rare treat that John didn't suspect he'd get to enjoy again. The priest had given John Communion with a wry smile and wink, and both had known they'd say hello after the service.

"John!" Father Francisco laughed when John approached.

"Hello Father," John said in Spanish, dipping his head respectively.

"What are you doing here," Father Francisco asked, shaking the hand of an older parishioner, giving the woman a smile and a nod of thanks as she went on her way.

"Coming to Mass," John answered.

Father Francisco laughed. "Of course, of course, I meant here! What are you doing here in Cuba?"

"I could ask you the same," John said, dodging the question easily.

"Come," Father Francisco said, smiling to another parishioner who gave a wave as they left the annex, *"café?"*

John blinked, not registering what the priest was asking for. His mind was still swimming with thoughts from earlier that day, although the service had helped.

But Father Francisco smiled. "Do you have time for a coffee, John?"

John pursed his lips. He had work to do. But he was also tired. After watching the news earlier that day, he felt drained. He felt like he'd failed. The Cubans, the rich and powerful, the CIA — it may as well have been the world against him.

And yet, something still pulled at him.

"John?"

John blinked again, clearing his mind and finally taking his friend's outstretched hand. "Coffee would be good," John said.

Fifteen minutes later, after the parishioners and volunteers had gone, and Francisco had made his rounds seeing to the church's various affairs, the priest beckoned John into the back room. He moved slowly — even slower than John had last remembered — but the man refused to retire.

The room was half kitchen, half office. It was practical and surprisingly humble for a cathedral room. Father Francisco offered John a seat on a small couch against a wall as he got to work on the espresso machine. Coffee shops in Havana and Varadero were quite modern and sported espresso machines, but coffee had been hard to find and expensive. Cubans made an average of twenty-five dollars a month and often couldn't afford the luxury.

Father Francisco dumped the measly remains of a container of coffee grinds into the machine and exchanged a glance with John. John raised an eyebrow.

"No more coffee?" John asked.

"Es Cuba," Father Francisco replied, without missing a beat. He turned back to filling the coffee maker with water. *It's Cuba.*

John nodded sadly. *'Es Cuba'* was a popular phrase that summarized most of Cuba's problems. It wasn't that Father Francisco had run out of coffee, it was that *Cuba* had run out of coffee. There would be no more on the store shelf. It was a fact of life in Cuba that one couldn't get what they wanted or needed at the store. There wasn't necessarily a solution to it either, unless one wanted to find someone to smuggle something in.

Es Cuba.

The espresso was understandably weak, and they drank from *tacitas*, small cups accustomed to the unfortunate supply and demand. They drank it black and without sugar, the flavor a bold sting on John's tongue. Father Francisco asked John again what he was doing in Cuba, and John gave him an easy answer about the expat life, which was all Father Francisco suspected of John anyhow. They did the song and dance of small talk catch-up and talking about the nasty weather that had cropped up recently (bad winds), until the priest mentioned the very subject John had come to get away from.

"Are you following the news of Antonio Romero?"

John suppressed the feelings that stirred within, and gave a noncommittal nod.

"Sorry, perhaps not the most polite of conversation..." Father Francisco sighed and sipped his espresso. "But I find myself compelled to talk about it. What an awful man."

John nodded again, not having anything to contribute to the conversation — nothing he was willing to reveal, anyway. But Father Francisco's next words made John's eyes widen in surprise.

"I've been asked to preside over the funeral."

John put his cup of espresso down slowly after the words interrupted his sip. "You have?"

The priest nodded sagely. "It was in his will."

"For the priest of Havana Cathedral?" John asked.

Father Francisco gave a sad smile. "No, for me specifically."

John's face fell. "You knew Antonio."

"Yes," Father Francisco said. "But not the way you probably think. I don't brush shoulders with celebrities John, you know that. Besides, I'm old. There's a picture of Romero and his partner with the pope floating around there somewhere though, no word of a lie. That'll be buried quick."

John waited patiently, controlling the pit in his throat, trying not to picture Father Francisco and Antonio Romero in league with one another.

"I was his family's priest when I was in Cuba a long time ago," Father Francisco said, and John raised an eyebrow, intrigued. "Another parish — a smaller church — I presided over their parent's funeral."

"They?"

"Yes...Antonio had a sister. I don't suspect they mentioned her in the news."

Wasn't in our briefings either, John thought. "No."

"You know, he turned out to be a bad man, there's no denying it, but his childhood was a thing of tragedy. First his parents die — shot dead by Americans during the Bay of Pigs — and then some years later he loses his sister."

John didn't say anything in response. He found it difficult to find remorse for a man like Antonio Romero.

Father Francisco took a deep sip from his cup. "But here's the real interesting bit, and again, they won't mention this in the news: I never saw the body."

John was staring into his cup, gazing into the dark brown liquid. But the words made him furrow his brow and narrow his eyes. He looked up at Father Francisco. "Which body?"

"The sister. Lisandra, was her name. Lisandra Romero. Apparently she was killed in some car accident. They said her body was too mangled for an open casket, which I found strange, considering how good embalmers can be, but it was also a different time, they've gotten so good these days you know..." Father Francisco took another sip of espresso and smacked his lips before continuing. "But the thing I always found strange was that I never saw the body. There were some paperwork issues too but that happens sometimes...oh! Are you okay?"

John's cup had snapped in two clean pieces in his grip. Blood ran down his palm where his skin had been split. He didn't feel it. He was staring at Father Francisco.

"John?"

John blinked and looked down at the red of blood, and deep brown of espresso pooling together on his hand.

Parents killed in the Bay of Pigs. And Antonio's sister fakes her death.

"Here," Father Francisco said, fishing through some drawers before finding a napkin and handing it to John. John cleaned up the mess and bound his hand. "Are you okay?"

John took a deep breath, then released. "I think I am now," he replied.

Chapter 26

John waited patiently for Antonio's funeral. In the meantime, he dug into everything he could regarding Lisandra Romero.

The police record of the car crash was murky. The hospital records were non-existent. He had located some extended family in the United States. John could've contacted them, but they might have tipped his hand. He still had the jump on her. He intended to keep it that way.

He didn't bother calling Mike either. This was his fight. If he got what he was after, he'd enlist the bastard to help him.

But first he had to attend a funeral.

John trudged under the triple arch of *La Necrópolis de Cristóbal Colón*, holding a small wreath of flowers he'd picked up at the local craft flea market off of Obispo Street earlier that day. The market was nearly canceled because of the nasty winds that had been picking up recently, but the covered stalls with their vendors were out and hawking their wares; all sorts of souvenirs and handcrafted items like jewelry, paintings, shirts, bags, and leather goods were present. The stall owners were fairly polite and didn't resort to pushy sales techniques, letting their craft speak for itself. Tourists loved the market, and John fit right in.

The *Colón* was a massive and unique cemetery, considered one of the most important in the world, and certainly in Latin America. Named for Christopher Columbus, it covered fifty-six hectares and had over fifty-three thousand tombs and monuments. This was no simple matter of row after row of tombstones; elaborate mausoleums and sculpted memorials of marble and granite covered the space where the state finally buried its citizens. But space was at a premium. The deceased were only given three years in a tomb before the remains were moved to storage.

John walked by the Firemen's Monument — the tallest in the cemetery at nearly seventy feet — commemorating twenty-eight firemen who had died heroically in 1890, and he passed a small queue of Cubans lined up in front of *La Milagrosa*, a miraculous tomb where offerings were sometimes left, and prayers were hopefully answered. Other tombs were long abandoned by families who fled from the revolution.

He placed his wreath gently on a random tomb and crossed himself, pretending to pray as he looked out the corner of his eye under his sunglasses at the funeral gathering for Romero.

The crowd was massive.

But John didn't care who was here, or how many admirers the man had in death. He clocked in his mind where the grave was, and continued on his way, leaving the cemetery by the north-west.

He came upon the Rio Almendares — a river mouth that cut into Havana by Miramar and he stared over the Straits of Florida as he moved north along the *Malecón*. The seagulls cried in indignation as water crested the seawall, peppering

John with saltwater as he walked on by. Piles of dirty seaweed had collected on the wide pavement of the esplanade, drying out on the pavement. Sometimes after a big storm, the entire road would be covered in seaweed, and the highway would have to be shut down. It would take a day to sweep and traffic would be rerouted. A wind picked up and John continued to look out over the water as he moved.

He was certain he had her. The true name of the mole — Lisandra Romero. But even that information wasn't enough. He had to find out what her cover was.

There was a chance Antonio never knew. Perhaps he really believed his sister had died all those years ago, before she was given a new identity and sent to the United States.

But John thought they had been working together. A public face and a private one for Cuban intelligence; infiltration and exploitation.

They must have been quite the pair.

Regardless, they couldn't interrogate Antonio now. He was dead. But he still had something available for questioning. And it only worked because they were related.

DNA.

John walked for a short while until he found a pair of fishermen. They looked destitute, and John could see hunger in their eyes each time they cast their rods. Officially, there was no unemployment in Cuba. But bribery was common.

"*¿Hola, cómo va la pesca?*" John called to them. *Hello, how's the fishing?*

Both looked over, surprised someone was speaking to them, let alone a *gringo* tourist. The one scowled, but the other nudged his friend, and mimed taking a picture of John.

John smiled back and pulled out his phone. He approached the men and stood beside them, using his phone to take a picture. The fishermen put on false grins as a spray of seawater crested over the seawall.

The men laughed and John looked at the photo, nodding. Then the smiling man held out his hand, and John stared at it, pretending to be dumbfounded.

Es Cuba, John thought, and nothing was free.

He pulled out his wallet and fished out an American five-dollar bill. The scowling man's face lit up with surprise at the amount, while his friend continued grinning, taking the bill and giving John a wink.

John fanned through the rest of the bills in his wallet and eyed the two men. They both watched the precious paper.

"¿Cómo les gustaría a ustedes dos ganar algo de dinero?" John asked. *How would you two like to make some money?*

The wind blew hard and another wave crested the seawall, splashing out over onto the esplanade.

The men weren't happy when they found out about the work. But John promised them to make it worth their while with a hundred dollars American each. That was the equivalent of four months wages a piece, and it was hard to turn down. So much money at once could put them ahead. But if they got caught, they'd be behind bars...

"Here," John said, shining his phone light on the tomb.

It was night, and they stood in the *Necrópolis Cristóbal Colón.* The two fishermen had sheepishly followed John into the cemetery, nervously looking over their shoulders as John forged ahead.

Now they stood over Antonio Romero's grave.

"Let's get to work," John said.

They cleared the wreaths laid out for Antonio. The two fishermen carried long wooden poles, and began to work the lid off the tomb. John knew they would have a lavish mausoleum built for the man, but for now, he was just another body in the ground.

It was humid, even at night, as was the expected weather in Cuba, but a wind had been growing the last few hours, and now it blew something fierce as the men began to pop the lid. John covered his eyes and moved upwind, finding a grip with his fingers and joining the two men.

The wind continued to blow, swirling around the cemetery like an angry beast knew what they were doing, prowling around waiting to strike. But eventually, the sound of stone scraping against stone sounded, and John helped slide the lid carefully off the tomb. It was heavy. He wiped his sweaty brow as they stared at the standardized wooden coffin revealed inside. A small window showed the calm visage of Antonio at rest.

"*Nosotros hemos terminado,*" the fisherman said, lifting his pole over his shoulder. *We've finished.*

"*Todavía no,*" John said. *Not yet.*

He climbed into the open tomb and fell upon the coffin with a soft thunk and moved to swing open the cover.

There lay the body of Antonio Romero.

John didn't spend time gazing upon the man. He was here for one thing and one thing only.

He reached into his pocket and retrieved a pair of pliers. Then he knelt and opened the dead man's mouth.

The fishermen peered over the edge of the open tomb, staring down to see what John was doing. When they saw, they both recoiled, exchanging glances and refusing to look back down. The one man crossed himself.

A moment later, John closed the coffin and reached a hand upwards, and the men helped him out of the tomb. Neither asked what John was doing pulling teeth from a dead man's mouth. But they weren't given the chance even if they wanted to.

A calm voice rose through darkness, breaking through the vicious winds of the night.

"Hello, John."

John spun around but knew the voice before his eyes fell upon him.

Dimitri stood twenty feet away, holding a gun casually at his hip, leveled at John's chest.

Chapter 27

John reached for his gun but Dimitri raised his eyebrows and his gun as one, giving the weapon a little wag.

"Ah, I'm sorry *moya mysh,* I don't think so."

John allowed the surprise to wash off him and the calm intensity of crisis took its place. "What brings you to Havana?"

Dimitri smiled, caught his hat as it blew off his head, and rubbed his forehead with the back of his wrist, sweat soaking his hair. "Business, unfortunately."

John hadn't heard the man coming with all the wind. It was making them both unsteady on their feet. The two fishermen dropped their poles and slowly put their hands up, understandably nervous at the sight of the weapon, and both wondering what sort of mess they'd allowed themselves to get into.

"*Ustedes dos se acuestan,*" Dimitri said calmly. *You two lie down.* He had to raise his voice over the wind, but the two men heard and began to comply.

"Why haven't you killed me yet," John said.

"Professional courtesy," Dimitri shrugged. "I'd expect the same."

"Don't think I can guarantee that," John replied coolly. "I'll ask again."

"Why do you think?" Dimitri continued to smile. "You're my asset, John."

John kept his face neutral, considering Dimitri's words. It was true the Russians used John for rare communications, and it was also unfortunately true that they had used him to kidnap the Silicon Valley billionaire Barry Bridges in their operation not so long ago. John didn't know what Dimitri was getting at.

"Asset for what?"

"To find out who the mole is, John," Dimitri struggled to keep his hat on his head and rolled his eyes, throwing it out to the wind. The dark wind snatched it up in a whirl of blowing air and it disappeared into the night sky. "But I also need to stop you from getting to them."

John's face grew dark. Again, the restless spirits of Brian and Marcela seemed to rattle their ghostly chains, demanding vengeance. A revenge that would never come if Dimitri left him dead in a Cuban cemetery.

"Russia wants to know what you know so they can use it as leverage. The CIA keeps blood samples of all their employees, as do we. That's what you're counting on right? For some reason you think they're related to Romero. I want to know why."

"Over my dead body," John growled. The crashing branches of trees clashed in the distance as the wind continued to pick up. A massive splitting sound called out from the dark as some struggling tree broke under strain.

Dimitri fired his gun at the ground, inches from John's foot. A PSS-2 silenced pistol, 'Vul' or 'Wool' in English. A favorite for Soviet special forces, and now Federal Security Service agents. The two fishermen on the ground cowered, one shouting out involuntarily.

Dimitri glanced at the men, then returned his eyes back to John. "That may very well be, if you're not careful, *moya mysh*. You will give me what I want, or I will tie you up and leave you outside G2 headquarters. I'm sure the Cubans would love to talk to you."

John set his jaw. He was dead either way. By Cuban or Russian hands, it didn't matter. He had no choice but to give Dimitri what he wanted, or the Russian would make sure he wished he were dead altogether.

Dimitri closed his eyes for a brief moment, something like sadness replacing his smug air. "There are no second chances John. Not in this business. You know that." He sighed, then opened his eyes once more. "This is the end."

He took a step forward...

The tornado came out of nowhere.

A wall of wind sent the four men staggering. The fishermen were nearly lifted into the air, losing their footing and falling to the ground, rolling and slammed by the air. They tumbled into a tree and reached out to hold on for dear life.

Dimitri stumbled and caught himself on his feet once more, but his arms wavered enough for John to dive behind a mausoleum nearby. He heard the suppressed gunshot from the Wool ring out, but just barely, as the sheer white noise of tornado winds blasted at his ears.

Dimitri fell to the ground and John pulled out his gun.

He leaned out of the edge of the massive stone angel to aim and fire, but the wind sucked his arm away from Dimitri, as if the devil himself were set on keeping his rival alive. John watched a stone cross topple over in the distance and crack in half as it crashed on its tomb. John gritted his teeth. He rooted his feet and held onto a groove in the angel's flowing robe, the wind threatening to pick him up and fling him into oblivion if he wasn't careful.

Dimitri somersaulted against his own will and collided with a tall spire off to John's right. John aimed and fired but Dimitri had found cover, and leaned into the spire with his weight, the wind pulling John, but pressing the Russian agent into the stone securing his position.

Another rush of wind whooshed forth as John held on for dear life. His fingers began to lose grip, but that may as well have been the least of his worries. Debris from the cemetery flew through the air on the wings of the storm, and smashed into the mausoleum's angel statue. The head of the angel and one of its wings tore loose and fell to the ground, and John dove out of the way.

He found himself out in the open.

Dimitri missed his first shot and John fired blindly, twice, forcing the man back behind his spire. But the wind suddenly reversed, as unpredictable as a rabid animal, pushing John back to the ground as he struggled to stand, and pulling Dimitri out of cover.

John fired again, losing his shot to the winds as Dimitri struggled to stand. He aimed at John and pulled the trigger...

A tree branch whirled through the air and slammed into Dimitri from behind, knocking the wind from him and leaving him dazed. He dipped to his knees once more as his shot went wild. John dug into the earth with one of his hands and rose steadily to his feet, aiming his own Glock in response. But then the winds reversed again, and John was launched forward, tumbling through the air, and crashing into his adversary.

They both grunted as John tried to lead with his feet but failed, opting for a last-minute hit with his elbow and shoulder. The blow connected and Dimitri's ribs cracked with a satisfying peppering of pops.

He was more concerned about John's gun. He grasped John's right hand with both of his, and squeezed, aiming to mangle the fingers and wrist so John would be forced to let go. To his credit, he managed to ignore the pain bursting from his ribs, but John still had a free hand when they tumbled to the ground together.

John chopped at the neck, and Dimitri blocked with a hasty forearm. John felt his fingers pried apart and kicked for the shins.

He missed as the wind took hold of them both and whipped them with debris.

They were stuck in a whirlwind, punching, kicking, grappling whatever was solid, tangible, stable. John noticed Dimitri had lost his gun and was about to leverage the advantage, when a golf ball-sized piece of debris slammed into his temple.

The wind moved on, suddenly leaving an abrupt nothingness in its place, throwing them both off balance in its wake. John landed on his neck and head, seeing sparks and hearing nothing but a distant ringing as sharp inner pain spiked through his brain.

Dimitri was quick to go for the gun, which John had held onto all the while.

John's fingers didn't respond fast enough, and Dimitri pulled the gun out, turning it inwards...

John flipped himself over and behind Dimitri, kicking him in the back and launching him forwards, slamming him into the spire that had given him cover before. At his feet, he toed the Wool, and swiped it up off the ground before Dimitri returned to his senses and fired off three crisp rounds in John's direction.

John had poked behind the spire just in time.

They had switched guns, and switched sides. But Dimitri was still out in the open.

John blind-fired around the corner of the spire before poking out properly himself, and spent the last shot of the Wool. It took Dimitri in the shoulder and he fell backwards in surprise.

John dove into action, following up.

The Wool only held six rounds. It wasn't meant for extended firefights — it was an assassin's weapon. But Dimitri wasn't dead, and he had the Glock.

Dimitri lifted the Glock but John dove to ground and launched a kick into the air, snapping at Dimitri's wrist with a sharp crack as the bone fractured. Dimitri cried out and the gun went flying through the night. John caught it and turned it around as the man tried to stand, struggling on a knee.

John stood in front of him, panting, gun trained on Dimitri. They were back where they had started, standing in front of Antonio's grave, switching positions once again. Dimitri's hand held his wound, blood slipping between his fingers. John didn't think about the irony of the situation. He was only thinking about the mission. The people who needed him. And the work that needed to be done.

"We don't like to kill agents John. Makes things messy. Retaliation and all that," Dimitri said, giving a weak smile, but a lion's courage still sat behind his eyes. "You have to say 'check' when your opponent catches you," Dimitri continued, wincing at the pain. "But we never kill the king."

John felt acid at the back of his throat. Felt his eyes burn through Dimitri's.

"We're not kings, Dimitri. We're pieces on the board. Expendable."

Dimitri laughed, but he began to rise to his feet. "Where would we be otherwise? There would be no more games to play."

"I'm done playing," John said.

Dimitri's eyes held cold realization for a brief second. His smile faded, and for the first time — and the last time — John saw his rival full of fear.

John kicked Dimitri in the chest and sent him tumbling into the deep, open tomb behind him, limbs sprawling and landing awkwardly on his back. John loomed over the man from above as he struggled to stand, tripping over Antonio's coffin.

"*Moya mysh —*" Dimitri started.

John hammered the trigger of the Glock, allowing the rounds to shred his quarry down below. Dimitri shook as the bullets dotted his body, spasming as if he were having a seizure and coughing blood before two bullets blew through his skull. John stopped before he emptied the magazine, staring down at the carnage he'd wrought. He grimaced, tossed the emptied Wool in his other hand into the tomb, and turned to see his Cuban fishermen cowering in the dirt, apparently still hugging the ground instead of running off when the fighting had broken out.

John tightened his lips, pulled two hundred American dollars from his wallet and broke the bills apart, holding a hundred out in either hand toward them.

"*Sellarlo,*" he said, gesturing behind him with a rock of his head. *Seal it.*

The fishermen nodded nervously, obeying perhaps more out of fear for John than desire for his money. But they took the bills nonetheless and got to work.

It was time to go back to America.

Chapter 28

It was a rainy day in Washington DC. Linda stared out the window of the sleepy little cafe that hugged the corner of the street just before things got busy with political officials and tourists. It was her favorite place, almost sacred. Home had been lost to the invasion of her career long ago — she took far too much of her work home. But the cafe was one place where work was off limits. The one refuge from her career. No one really seemed to know about it — certainly none of her colleagues.

"Linda."

She turned with a start, nearly spilling her tea as the metal stool next to her screeched in protest as it was dragged roughly across the floor. Mike tossed a wet jacket on the window counter and leftover rain droplets sprayed. He flopped down on the stool a little too close to her as he struggled to balance on the thing.

"You've got to be kidding me."

Mike grunted. "Yeah, I missed you too. We need to talk."

Linda sighed, placing a bookmark in the book she was reading, sliding it away from Mike's jacket and wiping away the moisture that had fallen upon it.

"Oh, a reader? You are a reader, aren't you?"

"Yes, I admit it Mike, you've caught me off guard. Now, do we have to talk here or can we do that back at Langley?"

"I'm good here. Why? Are you itching to get back to the office?"

Linda pinched the bridge of her nose. "It's time to come in, Mike. Tie up loose ends."

"I'll say."

"Fine, we do it your way." Linda checked her phone. She'd already stayed too long.

"Off the record."

Linda smirked. "Both of us would prefer that. For now anyway."

Mike nodded. "We got Romero."

Linda's expression grew dark. "You did. Not that you got anything out of him. *I've* just been dealing with furious Cubans for the past three weeks. And they say the Cold War ended."

"I was too young for the good ol' days," Mike said.

Linda glowered. "Careful, Mike."

Mike licked his lips. "Fair enough. I want to know if anyone is bothering to prosecute the bastards involved with Romero."

Linda frowned. "There's a lot of high up people, Mike. It might be a little less secret, but there's not a lot of proof."

"Bullshit. The girls."

"You know how these things go. A lot of that is going to depend on if the girls want to testify or not."

"They have to."

Linda gave him a weak smile, as if Mike were a toddler struggling to understand something only the adults could come to terms with. "They're teens. They don't see themselves as the instrumental keystone in closing the biggest corruption case since Watergate."

"What will they do then?" Mike spoke through clenched teeth.

"Probably settle out of court, mostly. These girls can get millions by doing nothing other than promising not to speak of it. Not a bad deal."

"That's bullshit."

Linda laughed. "Oh Mike. I missed you. I really did." She decided to change the subject. "I can talk to the brass. Get you a slap on the wrist."

"You'd do that for me?" Mike was genuinely surprised.

"You've been competent enough in this gig that I think I can manage a get out jail free card. No promises though," she said quickly.

Mike smiled. That meant a lot coming from Linda.

"Mike, look, admit it. The Russians played you."

"We found the mole." Mike slid a folded piece of paper over to Linda.

There was a long pause. Linda stared at the note. Then she opened it and glanced down. She didn't budge.

"Impossible. There's no mole. And certainly not someone that close to home."

Mike nodded. "I was skeptical myself. But John Carpenter had other ideas. Gave me some DNA from Romero — no, I don't want to know how he got it either, all I know is the Russians are mad about something or other — I gave it to DNA analysis and cross-referenced it with the blood samples of our officers on file."

Linda's eyes were slowly growing wider as he spoke.

Mike nodded, as if understanding the shock she was experiencing. "We got a match."

"We need to process them. Immediately."

Mike stared at Linda blankly. "You can try."

Linda moaned. "Order John to stand down. Jesus, *I'll* order John to stand down."

"Oh, I didn't do anything," Mike replied truthfully. "John doesn't work for us anymore."

"What?" Linda nearly stood from her seat.

Mike shrugged, barely hiding his satisfaction. "One more thing." Mike handed Linda a thin manila folder.

"What's this?"

"My two weeks."

This time Linda stood. "What? You —"

"Some big players are putting together a taskforce. A large one. Something with the funding and authority to make a difference. My name was mentioned."

"Sounds political. Didn't take you for the type."

"It might be. But that's not why I'm doing it."

"What's it for?" Linda asked sharply.

"To round up every son of a bitch who brushed shoulders with Romero, looked sideways at a girl, or anyone under the PAG."

Linda's nostrils flared. "You're going to deep dive the PAG?"

"Who better to do it, other than the bastard who found out they were playing dirty in the first place?"

"The CIA will shun you, Mike."

Mike gave a vicious smile. "How is that any different from how I'm treated now?"

Linda pursed her lips. She didn't reply. He was right and they both knew it.

"I think that's going to be a lot harder than you think."

"Maybe. Oh, but speaking of, I also wanted to give you a heads up."

"Of what?" Linda didn't like surprises. She rarely experienced them.

"Bombshell report coming out today. Do you remember a certain reporter...Edward Robbie? Ted?"

Linda blinked.

"Teddy? Ah, well. One of these crazy fringe reporter guys. He somehow got his hands on a list of everyone in touch with Antonio Romero. Including flights, transactions, conversations and chat histories that were supposed to be anonymous, the whole little black book...that tech bill was playing some part in keeping that *Anono* app quiet but looks like things have gotten rather loud all of a sudden."

Mike had never seen Linda's face grow so red and flustered. He didn't know it was possible. He took an odd pride in this fact but managed to curb a smile.

"You bastard. How long have you had this? When does this drop?"

Mike checked his phone. "It takes, what, twenty minutes to get to Langley from here? You should be fine."

Linda snatched up her tea, promptly threw it in the nearby garbage and stormed out the door.

Mike sat there for a moment, wondering if he should feel bad. He'd made a mess, and Linda was the janitor. But that couldn't be helped.

He looked around the cafe until he noticed a small TV playing above the main serving area. He moseyed over, pulled up another one of the rickety stools, and waved the barista's attention.

"Mind turning it to the news?"

And as the TV played in the background, revealing the fallout from the Romero event, Mike felt more and more confident that what he was about to embark on would be a good and rewarding part of his life and career. After all, there was plenty of work for a bastard like him to do.

He folded his arms, and smiled.

"I'd like to order a donut, too."

Chapter 29

Lauren Lopez sat through the rush-hour traffic the nine-to-fivers usually had to endure, and cursed her luck getting out of the office when she had. Intelligence never rested, but she'd been up all night dealing with the damage control the office had been slogging through. Linda had finally made her go home just so she could sleep.

Lauren didn't feel particularly haggard, nor did she look that way. She had perfected the art of overtime and knew how to condition her body to the extra work. She was a CIA officer. A little work couldn't hurt her, or her image.

Coming home was always a disappointment. Lauren was a workaholic. She felt like if she wasn't continuing to work at home, she was staring at four walls keeping her in against her will. But even workaholics had to take a break so they can continue to work optimally. And Lauren was past her optimum this time around; she couldn't help looking forward to a glass of red wine and the couch.

She walked up the concrete steps of her place, reminding herself for the second time that month that she'd have to get a contractor in to replace them. They were cracking and had never matched the house the way she'd wanted them to. Her house was a tall three-floor townhouse in Georgetown. The tight shrubs on either end of her property were getting scraggly and she reminded herself to trim them as well. She missed the days when she had rented a bachelor's. Home ownership was too much work.

She unlocked the door and entered the dark house, tossing her keys in a dish on a table by the door and hanging her coat on a hook as she closed the door behind her. She glanced around for Snookie, her fluffy Persian who usually greeted her at the door like a dog might. She took off her shoes and placed them meticulously on the shoe mat and pursed her lips, making a kissing noise.

"Snooks," she called softly.

There was no reply, but a pair of eyes poked out from under the couch as she moved through the living room. Lauren smiled and got on her hands and knees, reaching with an arm under the couch and trying to coax the cat out.

It took a moment, but soon enough Snookie was out and meowing for dinner, curling around her feet as Lauren stood. She pet the cat affectionately and moved to the kitchen, retrieving a slightly more expensive bottle of wine than she would normally choose and a large wine glass.

Her place was lonely other than Snookie. She liked it that way.

She rummaged in a drawer for a corkscrew and uncorked the bottle of wine, eventually pouring herself a generous glass and looking back at the living room for her cat. Snookie had retreated back under the couch, her wisp of a tail twitching as she crawled away into the darkness.

Lauren took a deep sip of wine and was about to turn on the kitchen light, when something struck her. Intuition sprang upon her, and she placed the wine glass next to the wine bottle on the counter, slow and deliberate. She looked around the kitchen, eyes scanning entrances and exits. She reached for her gun, tucked away in its holster at her side.

She unclipped the leather top and pulled her gun out slowly, spiraling with her feet as she did so, looking in a three hundred and sixty degree arc.

The air was silent. The only sound was the wind rushing through the trees, muted outside in her backyard.

She padded carefully on the tile of the kitchen and onto the hardwood of the TV room. She considered how she had been meaning to get a contractor to blend that hardwood into the kitchen, and pushed the idle thought to the back of her brain. Her eyes darted to the washroom.

She stood outside for a moment, off to the side, before springing the door open and flicking on the light, gun trained on the bathtub. The curtain was closed.

Had she left it like that? Didn't she normally leave it open?

Such a minor detail eluded her in that moment somehow. She pulled the curtain aside.

Nothing.

The tap dripped once. Twice. Lauren cocked her head. It dripped a third time.

She turned off the light, walking slowly through the TV room and kitchen, moving to the stairs. They creaked softly under her weight, and she winced, stopping at each start of a creak, and moving like molasses to the top step.

She checked the upstairs bathroom, and she heard Snookie meow from downstairs. She checked the guestroom and found nothing. She moved to her bedroom.

The door creaked open as she opted for ever slower and subtler movements. She moved like water flowing around rocks, slipping into the room and training her gun in the corners.

She moved past her bookshelf, making sure to check behind the door, then onto the closet. But before she could get there, she realized something was amiss.

There were a pair of papers on her dresser. She eyed them, slowly approaching the dresser and raising a tight eyebrow. She leaned in, to read the words, sensing the trap a moment too late.

It was her original Cuban birth certificate, listing her original given name: *Lisandra Romero.*

She began to spin and point her gun but the unmistakable click of a round being chambered rang out in the silent room. The first sound to truly pierce the evening's silence.

She froze, flicking her eyes to the mirror on the dresser. With the angle, she could see a patch of darkness hovering above the bookshelf.

A pair of eyes met hers, like Snookie's a moment earlier.

But these weren't the eyes of a cat.

These were the eyes of a killer.

She'd been caught.

After nearly forty years of infiltrating the Central Intelligence Agency, and making it all the way to SOG Latin American desk head, 'Lauren Lopez' — Lisandra Romero — had been caught.

She breathed a sigh. It was heavy. It came out with a stutter. She wondered if this day would come. She'd been meticulous. She'd been perfect. Recent events had shaken some things up, but no one had been able to figure it out. Not unless they dug far into the past...

The figure slipped down off the top of the bookshelf, Glock trained on her all the while. She watched him continue to stare at her through the mirror. She dropped her gun, and it clattered to the ground.

It was growing dark.

She turned slowly. The man didn't say anything.

She didn't know who he was. He could've been an independent, ready to blackmail her for wealth or information. More probably, it was a CIA asset, meant to pin her down before they could arrest her. She'd have to lawyer up. She knew the game was up, but that didn't mean she couldn't legally fight things. Besides, spies were turned over all the time. Cuba would reluctantly trade for her. She'd go back in shame, but revealing the incredible blunder of the CIA for allowing such blatant infiltration would be a victory in itself. A nervous smirk touched her lips.

The first bullet ripped through her chest before another thought could enter her brain.

Her mouth opened in shock as the burning pain of a fresh bullet wound blossomed, and blood began to drip down her chest and stomach and onto her legs.

The second bullet was even more surprising somehow, tearing through her chest alongside the first, blood filling her mouth and spilling from her lips as she coughed for air.

She wasn't quite dead when the third bullet was fired into her forehead. A last panicked thought raced through her mind before the round left its chamber. The hot breath of fear from her brother Antonio on her hand clamping his mouth, huddling beneath a tarp in a marsh in Cuba during the American invasion of the Bay of Pigs.

The sound of the third gunshot rang out, and all went black.

Epilogue

Tyler Christiansen watched a pair of teenagers skateboard down the street in front of him. He was sitting in his favorite chair, drinking a light beer, and killing time in the afternoon. The kids waved to him and he waved back.

He'd made the porch himself. Well, him and an old carpentry friend to make sure he didn't screw it up. They'd put the whole thing together over one warm spring and enjoyed that hot summer drinking beer and eating peanuts and talking baseball. His friend didn't come by anymore — he was in a retirement home now, but man, those were the days.

His house was old and was decidedly a fixer-upper now. He let too many things slide by when he should've worked on them. Junie was always on his case about that. But nothing to do about that now. His wife had passed from a bad case of pneumonia six years ago. He had the lonely house all to himself.

He fished for a peanut out of the bowl on the little table next to his chair. He cracked it open and chucked the peel over the railing and onto the lawn. He eyed a squirrel skittering down the big oak in the front yard.

Just the peel you little bugger. You'll have to fight me for the peanuts.

The squirrel gave a chitter and ran back up the trunk.

That's when Tyler heard the gate open and a mail lady walked into the front yard. Tyler raised an eyebrow in surprise.

"Hey...Mr. Christiansen?" the mail lady asked, looking at the envelope in her hands.

Tyler smiled at that. He never much cared for people calling him mister anything. But he was old now. Old people didn't get called by their first name. He was getting used to it.

"That's me," Tyler said. "I got mail?"

The mail lady gave him a sweet smile. It had been a long time since someone had smiled at him like that. "You've got mail."

She handed the envelope over and he took it, struggling to stand for a moment against the strain of his back. He landed back down in his seat and eyed the letter.

It was a nondescript envelope with his name and address printed smartly dead center.

No return address.

Tyler scrunched up his face in confusion, looking up to thank the mail lady. She'd already gone. Tyler put the letter down and picked his beer back up. He finished it, then opened the little minifridge he kept next to his chair on the porch. Always stocked with beer. It was a man's dream, he thought, cracking his second. Doing nothing at all.

Lord knew he'd done enough in his life. He wasn't so sure for the better, either.

A darkness clouded his face in that instance. He thought of signing up for the United States Army. The smart uniform he wore. The buddies he made in his airborne division. The hell of training. The girls at the army bar winking at him. The good times.

But it was all smothered by a single thought.

Cuba.

"What a shitshow," Tyler muttered to himself, taking a deep swig of beer.

He'd been part of a vanguard paratrooper force during the Bay of Pigs invasion. The drop had gone wrong, the CIA was withholding information, and worst of all...

He dropped his beer. He hadn't realized his hands were shaking. He took a breath, then picked the spilt beer can up off the porch.

"Those damn civilians."

A man and a woman in a boat. Their spook shot them dead, citing collateral damage. It was a bullshit mission, and two innocent Cubans got killed for doing nothing at all. Just like he was doing now.

He sometimes thought about whether that couple had a family of their own back home. Children, whose parents weren't coming back. Just like his own son Brian.

Hell, Brian had been a good kid. Damn well the best of them. Moral compass straight as an arrow. Tyler knew one day it'd get his son in trouble. It had sent him into law. But somehow he'd ended up going military like his father. Didn't matter what Tyler said to convince him otherwise. Brian thought the best place to do good was in the worst places and with the worst people.

Damn it all.

They hadn't told him his son was dead. The bastards he worked for didn't acknowledge family. But Brian kept in touch discreetly. And then he'd stopped. Tyler knew. He didn't need some army boy knocking on his door to tell him.

He realized he was clenching the letter in his hand. He put down his beer and opened it up.

Dear Zeddy...

Tyler's eyebrows went up. No one had called him by his callsign in years. Hardly anyone knew his callsign. It wasn't as if he was a somebody in the Force. He blinked and read the words again, continuing on this time.

Dear Zeddy,

I killed the person who killed your son.

Where a signature would normally be, there was simply a long line, like something had been crossed out. No initials. No name. Nothing.

I killed the person who killed your son.

Tyler put down the letter and held his lips tight. His mind was blank. After a long moment staring off into the street, he managed to stand up with some creaking bones and a long groan.

He opened the screen door and shuffled inside. Past the TV room where he'd watched baseball earlier that afternoon, and every afternoon before. Through the kitchen where he had his lonely meals. Down the hall with the bare walls where photographs of family used to hang. He opened the door to the basement and struggled down the steps, tugging a pull-string light bulb once he'd hit the bottom.

He went over to a corner cabinet he used to stash a bunch of old memories. Photos and the like. He rifled through and found a picture of his old paratrooper team. Arms around each other, a day before the big jump in Cuba. He felt his gun at the back. He pulled it out and examined it as if it were the first time he'd seen it. It was a special issue Bay of Pigs Colt .45 Pistol. The government had given them to honor those involved in the invasion. He grunted to himself and tucked it back inside the drawer. He brushed past a few old papers and file folders and finally found what he was looking for.

It was a picture of Brian. One that he wasn't supposed to own. Brian was done up in some sort of sleek-looking tac gear that was beyond Tyler's time. Brian was grinning ear to ear, thumbs tucked into the chest plate of his body armor.

He always felt like his son's death had been his fault somehow. He knew that wasn't true. Just the grief talking. But damn it all, he felt like he could've done something different.

Tyler found a paper clip and tucked the letter behind the picture, clipping them together.

He shut the drawer, and felt the first wave of tears threatening to fall from his eyes. He blinked them away, turned out the light, and walked back through the lonely house and onto the porch.

The air had changed. Humid, but moist.

He sat back down in his chair again, pinching his fingers over his nose together as he wiped the tears that stung his eyes. He looked to the sky. Clouds forming there. Looked like a storm. Fitting, he thought.

He picked up his beer and his eyes fell on the sidewalk across the street. He thought he saw a man standing there through his blurry eyes, staring back at him.

A bus rolled by on the street. It didn't stop. But when the bus had passed the man was gone.

Tyler blinked. He'd probably imagined it. He was old.

A low rumble of thunder sounded from up above. Tyler looked up again, watching the clouds roll in.

He turned back to his beer, turned back to killing time, turned back to old forgotten memories. But something was different. Something felt better. Felt right. Felt...finished.

"*Gracias amigo,*" Tyler whispered softly as the first drops of rain fell on the street.

Acknowledgements

It takes a village. I do the writing thing myself, sure, but I've got a really great community of support helping me put things together to really shine. A lot of the time I just feel like some dude messing around with a keyboard. It's those around me that make me a writer.

I'd like to start by saying a warm thank you to everyone who picked up the book and gave it a read, to those posting reviews or ratings for me, and those folks who even reached out and sent an email! It's been really nice connecting with some of you, and the encouragement is so appreciated.

Thank you to Raciel Hernández for double checking my Spanish and making sure things were accurate and appropriate.

Thank you to Hampton Lamoureux at TS95 Studios who designed the kick-ass cover. He also designed my *Vaulter's Magic* cover and I love them both. I encourage you to check out his website: https://www.ts95studios.com/

Shout out to Ben Keffer who is not only a great friend, but also knows a bunch more about military protocols than I do, and endures all kinds of pestering from me. Thanks for helping sort out some things in the book such as CIA/FBI affairs and radio communications.

I'd like to thank Meg Young at Fishing for Success for checking my Newfoundland fishing details and making sure they were authentic. Also thank you for many great work sessions together where I wrote some of my favorite material. You have always been kind and supportive of my work.

Thank you to my wonderful beta readers Jen Enns, Dave McAdams and Brian O'Riordan who helped me with the final draft. Jen, your companionship and support throughout the years has made all the difference and I treasure our friendship. Dave, your feedback made a distinguishably better book, and you've always been a great neighbor. Brian, thank you for finding the time to read the draft and share some very kind words. You're all awesome--thank you!

My editor, Ross Mosher. Oh Ross. My dear, dear Ross. Thank you for making my words sound professional and crisp, knowing and researching things I know nothing about, and being patient and understanding. It has been a sincere pleasure working with you, and I'm so glad you were a part of this whole project.

A big thank you to my lovely mother who always checks in on me, knows when things are amiss, and continues to be the best mom a son could ask for, especially with difficult artistic projects. You're a big sweetheart and I love you.

And finally, my father, who is the reason these books exist. Thank you for believing in me. Thank you for pushing me. Thank you for giving your all, and emulating radical commitment. But most of all, thank you for choosing to share this special collection of stories with me. I can't believe we made it.

Dusk falls on this book, and the John Carpenter trilogy is finally brought to an end. I hope you had fun with all the gunfights, were intrigued by the spy games, and enjoyed your time in Latin America. I have more books to write, but it's nice knowing that John Carpenter finally gets to rest. Thank you.

About the Author

Collin Glavac is a Canadian-born writer from Southern Ontario, now living in beautiful St. John's Newfoundland. He has written, directed, and acted in two original stage plays: *In Real Life* and *LoveSpell*. He has four self-published books: *Ghosts of Guatemala, Operation Nicaragua, Cuban Conspiracy,* and *Vaulter's Magic*.

Collin completed his Dramatic and Liberal Arts B.A. and M.A. at Brock University. When Collin isn't writing he enjoys painting miniatures, performing improv, and drinking too much coffee. He loves hearing from readers, so please don't hesitate to contact him by email at: collinglavac@gmail.com

Please sign up for our newsletter, watch book trailers, see Instagram posts, and stay tuned for more at: www.collinglavac.com

Printed in Great Britain
by Amazon